*Recent Titles by Gloria Cook from
Severn House*

The Meryen Series

KEEPING ECHOES
OUT OF SHADOWS
ALL IN A DAY
HOLDING THE LIGHT
DREAM CHASERS

The Harvey Family Series

TOUCH THE SILENCE
MOMENTS OF TIME
FROM A DISTANCE
NEVER JUST A MEMORY
A STRANGER LIGHT
A WHISPER OF LIFE

The Pengarron Series

PENGARRON DYNASTY
PENGARRON RIVALRY

The Tresaile Saga

LEAVING SHADES
REFLECTIONS

REFLECTIONS

A Cornish saga from a much-loved author

Cornwall, 1920s. Beth Tresaile has been happil
reconciled with her estranged mother for over
year and is looking forward to her best frien
Kitty Copeland spending Christmas with them
But Kitty's request that her brother Stuart joi
them throws Beth in turmoil for Stuart and Bet
were once lovers, and she lives in fear of he
friend discovering her secret shame. But Stuart'
arrival sets in motion events that even Bet
could not have expected...

REFLECTIONS

Gloria Cook

Severn House Large Print
London & New York

This first large print edition published 2012
in Great Britain and the USA by
SEVERN HOUSE PUBLISHERS LTD of
9-15 High Street, Sutton, Surrey, SM1 1DF.
First world regular print edition published 2010 by
Severn House Publishers Ltd., London and New York.

British Library Cataloguing in Publication Data
Cook, Gloria.
  Reflections.
  1. Mothers and daughters--England--Cornwall (County)--
  Fiction. 2. Family secrets--Fiction. 3. Adultery--
  Fiction. 4. Cornwall (England : County)--Social
  conditions--20th century--Fiction. 5. Large type books.
  I. Title
  823.9'2-dc23

ISBN-13: 978-0-7278-9925-5

Severn House Publishers support The Forest Stewardship Council
[FSC], the leading international forest certification organisation. All
our titles that are printed on Greenpeace-approved FSC-certified paper
carry the FSC logo.

MIX
Paper from
responsible sources
FSC® C018575

Printed and bound in Great Britain by the
MPG Books Group, Bodmin, Cornwall.

One

It was a strange thought to occur to her, that since her return here over a year ago to her mother's house, this was the first time she had been alone in it. Why should that matter now? Beth Tresaile was eagerly awaiting the imminent arrival of her closest friend Kitty, so why think of something so unnecessary, and give it a second thought and even a third?

There was, of course, bad history for her here in the cliff-top Owles House, of the bitter quarrels between her parents, her mother's heavy drinking, the neglect and fear she had suffered during her early childhood. At just seven years old, Beth had been abandoned alone, locked outside in the bitterly cold dark winter. She had run terrified along the drive, out into the lane and had somehow found her way nearly all the way down to the fishing cove of Portcowl, where a kindly fishing family had taken her in. Beth's maternal grandmother, Marion Frobisher, from Wiltshire, who had raised her, had showered her with love and care, all the while stressing to Beth that her unstable, alcoholic mother Christina had been fully to blame for her past miseries.

Years later, following her grandmother's death, and feeling raw from a tragic miscarriage

5

and broken heart, Beth had been driven to confront and rail against Christina over her selfish, demented motherhood. Kitty Copeland, her friend from her peaceful childhood days, had travelled down with her. At the initial reunion, frosty and guarded on Beth's part, eager and apologetic on Christina's, emotional for them both, Beth had seen that Christina was rather frail in health and living a quiet, simple life.

While being put right by various locals about the unfortunate past, Beth had soon discovered that much of Christina's shameful behaviour had been cruelly provoked by her social-climbing, bullying husband Phil Tresaile, and to Beth's utter dismay, by Christina's own mother. Taking a Cornish holiday with a young impressionable Christina, Marion Frobisher had made it obvious she despised her daughter. Beguiled by the artful charmer Phil Tresaile, Marion had been observed carrying out an affair with him, before he had seduced and impregnated Christina. Furious and jealous, Marion had allowed the couple to marry, and Owles House had been bought with Christina's money.

Beth had learned that her father Phil Tresaile had constantly and unjustly accused Christina for being responsible for the almost immediate death of Beth's sickly twin brother, the son he had so wanted; a secret kept from Beth. Phil Tresaile had deserted his young family but had gone on to partly redeem himself by dying a hero's death in the Great War. Beth, encouraged by trusting, kind-hearted Kitty, had rightfully concluded that Marion and Phil's abuse of

Christina had pushed her towards alcoholism and her final mental breakdown and disappearance, resulting in her incarceration for many months in a mental institution. Beth had accepted everything about her past. She had no lingering issues, only sad reflections, mainly about the baby she had lost and the secret she was keeping from Kitty, a secret that would shatter her. The father of Beth's baby had been Kitty's adored older, married brother, Stuart. The pregnancy had brought the affair to an end, Stuart fearing that a scandal would ruin him and Beth had not wanted to hurt his young family. Ironically, months later Stuart's wife had left him and their two children for another man, and Stuart had tried, through Kitty, to wheedle his way back into Beth's life, asking if he could come down to Cornwall where Beth had decided to settle down. Beth had put off the suggestion firmly. Having found strength in her new life she had had no desire for a weak man and she wasn't going to be second best. She had reflected that it had been selfish and wrong of her to embark on an affair with a married man, and after her years of unjustifiable resentment towards her mother, to be careful in future of the judgements she made.

Beth had sold her property in Wiltshire and bought a cottage locally but she stayed at Owles House most of the time. She continued looking out of the sitting room window into the blustery grey October day for the taxicab ferrying Kitty from St Austell railway station. Beth already had her coat on. She would hurry outside and cry

7

excitedly, 'Welcome Kitty! I've been so looking forward to seeing you again and for you to be back once more to share in the magic of this place.'

Part of the magic Beth had found here was that the impressive, wisteria-clad mid-Georgian house, the mighty rambling cliffs sheltering the fishing cove below and the waters of the bay were not as her tormented childhood view of them, desolate, lonely and menacing. Instead everything including the tangy salt of the sea and the endless views were enchanting, trustworthy and soothing. Beth had everything she wanted here. She had a fond relationship with Ken Tresaile, landlord of the Sailor's Rest, the uncle she had been denied access to because her father had fallen out violently with his family. And there were two special people she had not known existed before: Joe Vyvyan, her younger half-brother by her mother's late second husband; and her older half-sister, abandoned by Phil Tresaile, adopted fisherman's daughter Evie Vage.

Presently, Christina was attending a social committee meeting at the vicarage and Joe was at school. The daily help, the cheerful Mrs Reseigh who lived down in the cove, had left an hour ago. Normally, Beth would have gone with Christina, they did almost everything together, but Beth was waiting for Kitty's arrival. Alone. And for some odd reason it unsettled her. Almost as if it was a portent that something bad was on its way.

'That's daft,' she said aloud. 'Don't be silly.'

Yet a shiver seared up her back and made her

8

glance over her shoulder. Had it suddenly gone cold in the spacious room where a log fire crackled and hearty flames soared towards the chimney, or was she simply imagining it? All was as usual in the room, the furnishings a careful blend of arts and crafts and gentle lines. The tall windows were allowing plenty of daylight in and there were no shadows. Carlton Ware vases were filled with russet, gold and cream chrysanthemums. A French brass carriage clock ticked softly on the mantelpiece.

Something wet pressed into her hand. 'Oh!' Her heart lurched and beat wildly.

She looked down ready to thrust something dreadful off her hand then she was laughing, feeling foolish. 'Oh, it's you Chaplin.' It was Joe's handsome German shepherd. She wasn't alone in the house after all. She crouched down to hug Chaplin's broad neck. 'I'm such a silly to have forgotten you were here, faithful old thing, such a silly to have taken fright of you, and really daft to get the chills over absolutely nothing at all. And if there were any ghosts here you'd have growled and seen them off, eh?'

Ghosts. Why on earth was she thinking about ghosts? She had lain to rest all the ghosts from her past. Her old loathing and resentment and need for revenge against her mother had been replaced forever with deep love and concern. After his initial distrust, Joe had accepted her. As a boy now approaching his fourteenth birthday he kept a natural distance from her but he showed her the odd touch of affection.

Chaplin suddenly scrabbled away from Beth

and barked excitedly with his front paws up on the window ledge, and Beth was nearly upended. 'Kitty!' She had missed her friend's approach, something she loved to see. Since returning home to Wiltshire Kitty had set up a small business, but she had twice come down for weekend stays and back in May she had managed a whole week. Now she was allowing herself a long stay that would wonderfully extend through to Christmas and the New Year. Kitty was leaving her personal assistant in charge of Copeland Crafts. It pleased Beth that Kitty, although she never complained about it, would be free for a while from having to shore up Stuart, who was finding life rather hard since Connie's desertion.

'Do you think I tipped the driver enough?' Kitty asked, surveying her mass of luggage, which the obliging taxicab driver had hauled up to the guest room. 'I've brought down heaps of clothes, of course, but I've also packed some things for Christmas presents, and some samples I'd like you all to see of a few of the wonderful crafts I've picked up for the business. And he was so good with Grace.' Grace was the young, long-haired collie-cross that she and Joe had rescued the previous summer as an abandoned starving puppy.

'Well, he went away with a big smile on his face.' Beth laughed, petting Grace and thinking that the gorgeous glossy-coated dog reflected the stunning looks of its Titian-haired, grey-green eyed owner. Every inch of Kitty's slender frame revealed her open friendliness, her avid curiosity and unshakeable optimism. She loved exploring new opportunities, acquiring knowledge, and anything that seemed to be the slightest mystery. 'You've brought enough stuff to last for months! I'll start on your unpacking while you change and freshen up.'

Chaplin, who was more or less allowed the run of the house, followed them up with Grace, to the twin-bedded, charmingly Regency-themed room, and Kitty fell to her knees to give him an affectionate hug. 'Us dogs and people are going to have a brilliant time, eh, boy? How's Charlie, eh? Are you and the lovely pure white cat still the best of friends?'

'They are.' Beth grinned wryly. 'Just as long as Chaplin allows Charlie to have the superior position, you know what cats are like.'

Kitty hefted a heavy suitcase up on to one half-tester bed. 'Would you start pulling this one out, Beth? Don't touch the tartan case. The presents are in it. I'll push it under the bed.' She went to the window, which was west facing and looked out over a neat lawn and sheltered flower beds at the side of the house. Just beyond the straight staunch hedgerow were the woods where Grace had been dumped. Kitty also got a glimpse of the sea. 'Oh, it's wonderful to be back and not to be leaving for several weeks. I can't wait to get out on the cliffs and down to the beaches and to spend lots of time down in the fishing village. How is everyone? I want to hear all about the Reseighs and the Praeds and young Richard, and your Uncle Ken and Evie, but first tell me about the new vicar. I want to know all about him

11

before Christina gets back from the vicarage. How have the locals taken to him? Does he match up to the curate who held the fort so admirably after the poor old Reverend Oakley had to retire? He's young and single, you said over the phone, so are any of the young ladies showing hopes for him? Is he handsome?'

'Sort of handsome, I suppose. Actually, he's a bit strange,' Beth replied, from where she was putting Kitty's clothes away into the large rosewood wardrobe. She immediately regretted her quick judgement. She had met the Reverend Jacob Benedict twice. The first time when she'd shaken his hand after his first morning service. The second time when he had called here at Owles House as part of his aim to meet everyone who lived in the parish. Beth hadn't given him much thought but Christina described him as pleasant and easy company. He had shown great interest in the people of Owles House and its animals, the house itself, the well-maintained gardens and the splendid views. He was not high-minded and had begun his round of visits at the terraced Quayside Cottages down in the cove, all inhabited by fisherfolk, including Beth's half-sister, Evie Vage. Iris, when pregnant with Evie had gratefully married a man much older than her, fisherman Davey Vage. Beth and Evie had bonded at their first meeting, but it was hard for them to meet owing to Davey's possessiveness and contempt for anyone named Tresaile.

Kitty whirled round from the window. 'Strange? How brilliant! I can't wait to meet

12

him. One of the best things about coming to Portcowl is there's always a sense of mystery here among the superstitious, spiritual Cornish.'

'Oh, Kitty,' Beth smiled. 'Portcowl is just a hard-working fishing village full of ordinary people living ordinary lives.'

Kitty's eyes sparkled and she gaily dragged Beth to gaze with her into the dressing table mirror. Kitty spoke to Beth's startled reflection. 'Now tell the truth, when we first came here did we not discover mystery after mystery and get involved with some outlandish characters? Gabby Magor, a woman who's more like a man.' Kitty added softly. 'Spinster Muriel Oakley's tragic dead baby, another child your father had sired. Ordinary, my foot.'

Beth was struck at the stark differences between her reflection and her buoyant, almost innocent friend. Beth was taller and not as good-looking as Kitty, her butterscotch-coloured hair was bobbed while Kitty's was shingled, but the outstanding disparity was Beth's tendency to be serious and more grounded. Right now Kitty's whole being was pulsing with possibilities of entertainment, while Beth wanted only to look forward to happy, quiet times.

Why had she termed the Reverend Benedict as strange? Beth mused. Why had her mind suddenly decided to believe that about him, when in fact he had come across as a congenial and polite individual suited to his position. Was Kitty right about the whole region being steeped in mysticism? Only a short while ago being alone in the house had made Beth feel unaccountably anxious and the house seem creepy. Was she picking up on something and if so, what for goodness sake?

She shivered. 'Tell you what, Kitty, despite the heating being on it's a bit chilly, don't you think? You carry on here and I'll pop downstairs and bring us up a hot drink. You're probably gasping for one anyway.'

Right, she told herself, doing something as ordinary as making two cups of steaming hot coffee will end this silly eerie rubbish for good.

But before she reached the foot of the stairs she was turning round to glance behind. It was as if something was trying to catch up with her.

Two

Joseph Vyvyan was brought home from his St Austell private school in a taxicab. Today the cab had taken a short detour beforehand to the vicarage and collected his and Beth's mother, Christina Vyvyan from the committee meeting.

In her energetic manner, Kitty beat Beth outside to greet them. She opened the back door of the taxi and helped Christina out safely on to the gravelled drive. Christina's former years of alcohol abuse and poor mental health had left her a little frail and since then she had developed an arthritic hip, and with her soft pale looks and

14

edge of uncertainty she drew the need in others to cherish and protect her. She used an ebony-handled stick to aid her walking.

Beth held back and waited while Kitty and Christina exchanged kisses and sincere, excited pleasantries. Christina beamed on as Kitty and Joe joined in a matey hug and lots of jollity. Beth felt a pang of envy. Joe had bonded with the outgoing, open-eyed, sporty and fun-loving Kitty from the outset, while he had remained wary and suspicious of Beth for some time, warning her at first never to upset Christina, whom he shielded vigorously against the slightest distress. Next Joe made a great fuss of Grace. He and Kitty had rescued the shiny-coated dog, then only a tiny whimpering rag-gedy handful, and they had that in common too. They believed the local misfit Gabby Magor had dumped puppy Grace in the woods at the side of the property.

Beth walked Christina up the steps and into the house. 'Did you have a good meeting, Mum? Kitty and I have got afternoon tea all ready and the fire is roaring nicely in the sitting room.' She studied her mother's perfectly made up, wanly elegant face for telltale hints of disquiet. Like Joe, Beth's chief concern was to ensure their mother never took on anything she wasn't up to. Christina's second husband, Francis Vyvyan, had been the one responsible for lifting Christina out of her despair, to cope with life without drink, and cope with losing Beth, her then seven-year-old daughter. After his untimely tragic death in a boating accident, Joe, despite being so

15

young, had admirably shouldered the task as Christina's mainstay. Christina had rarely gone out of the grounds, but on becoming reconciled with Beth she had taken on the confidence and zest to take part in village life again. Beth was pleased to see Christina was looking not at all tired but quite animated.

'Yes, darling, the meeting was very interesting. There were quite a number of people there. Tea will be lovely. Thank you, darling. Thank you, Kitty.'

The three women had started on the tea, lemon drizzle cake and sultana scones when Joe hurtled, as was his way, into the room with Chaplin. Joe had changed out of his school uniform and was wearing an open-necked shirt and patterned sleeveless pullover, and he was proud to be at the age to wear long trousers. He sat down near the tea table with all the aplomb of a great statesman and stretched out his long legs. He steepled his fingertips together and smiled at the women in a satisfied manner, as if he was pleased to see them all together and safe under his care. 'You ladies all look very elegant.'

'Thank you, Joe.' Beth smiled, as he jumped up right away to take the poker to the fire, pushing and prodding the logs to produce gentle nuzzling flames – taking responsibility for the ladies' comfort. It wasn't a common sight in Owles House for Beth, Christina and Kitty to be dressed up, but for Kitty's arrival they had all made the effort. They were in tubular, low-waist frocks, Christina's had a scalloped hem and the

16

younger women's had handkerchief points. All wore shimmery cardigans and Louis heels. Christina was usually in plainer and looser things for comfort and easier movement. Kitty preferred a sportier look and often wore loose trousers and walking shoes. Beth didn't often trouble herself to follow the dictates of fashion. Any new clothes she bought nowadays were of watered down fashions to fit in better with the local women's plainer mode.

Joe helped himself to a tea plate and covered the china with two buttered scones and a large wedge of cake. He smiled at Christina as she spooned gooseberry jam, his favourite, on top the scones. He also took a tumbler of milk. He drank pints of the stuff to build up his burgeoning muscular body. He had numerous capabilities beyond his years, his self-assurance made him look a young man already. All three women took pleasure and pride in watching his every move and Joe, unembarrassed by their scrutiny, accepted it as his rightful homage.

'We must all have lots of news to share. How are your family, Kitty?' Joe said from his armchair, a second large bite of scone and jam on the way to his mouth to be devoured.

'Stuart and young Louis and Martha are in pretty low spirits, but little Martha can be distracted and have some fun,' Kitty replied sadly. 'But both children are still taking it hard that they barely see their mother. It's so unlike the Connie I used to know, but there it is. Stuart sends his regards to everyone.'

'It's a good thing they have you in their lives,'

said Beth glossing over the facts and the worried intonation of Kitty's remarks. She felt guilty that if their affair had gone ahead, she would have been responsible for wantonly separating the two children from their father. And Christina did not need to be reminded she had once been a bad mother; she had more than made recompense for those terrible former days. Beth didn't want to hear anything at all about Stuart Copeland. She had some sympathy for him and wished him well but those feelings were all she had left for him.

'Joe,' Kitty said. 'How's the little gang, Richard and Lily? Does he still complain about you allowing her to tag along with you both and is she just as noisy and cheeky. Has she grown at all yet?'

'All is much the same as when you last saw them. If anything, Lily's even noisier. Richard still threatens to tie her up and gag off her chatter every time.'

'I'm proud of you for being so patient with a fisherman's little girl, Joe,' Christina said.

Joe merely shrugged his widening shoulders. Lily Praed who he and his mate Richard Opie had taken home after she'd been badly hurt in a fall which was partly their fault, amused him with her tomboy impish ways, and she was tough enough to keep up with whatever he and hotelier's son Richard did. Lily was the youngest and most precious child, the only surviving girl of one branch of the extended Praed family. Joe felt a measure of responsibility for her. While she was with him and Richard they could keep her safe. 'Now Mum, tell us what happened at the vicarage meeting today. I hope you haven't allowed yourself to be roped into anything that will be overtaxing.'

'There's to be a new event called the Grand Tea Party, darling. It will be held at the vicarage. You need have no worries over me. Mr Opie, Richard's father, was elected the chairman of the new social committee, and he and Mrs Opie are taking charge of the event. Mr Opie is a Methodist lay preacher, but the church and the chapel are eager to mould together for the good of the parish. I shall be in charge of the cake stall, and I'll be able to sit down as much as I want to. I'm sure Beth and Kitty will help me.' Christina received smiling nods of assent from her seconded two. 'Posters will be put up in the shops in the cove. The committee has unanimously decided that we want to reflect a cosy relaxing image, something all ages can enjoy. There will be a large bran tub so the children can have a little foretaste of Christmas. Ken Tresaile will help Mr Benedict to move the furniture about in the vicarage. His housekeeper and cook, and our own Mrs Reseigh, will be in charge of the refreshments.'

'Good luck with having Mrs Opie at the helm,' Joe snorted. 'Even Richard says his own mother is insufferably stuck up. His older brothers rarely come home for visits from university now. He says Mrs Opie is badgering Mr Opie to convert to Anglicanism, which she sees as a step up. As for his sister Claire, all she'll think about is finding a husband at this tea party. The Reverend

Benedict might find Claire all over him.'

'Don't be uncharitable, Joe,' Christina scolded, but mildly. It was a fact that the Opie women could be difficult, but Douglas Opie was a pleasing humble sort. Richard was an easy-going boy and Joe's lifelong pal. 'Mr Opie will be in charge, he's not henpecked, and Mrs Opie does, I admit, have an eye for suitable decor, so I'm confident the Grand Tea Party will be a success. People are hungry for something the whole community can join in with, something to look forward to. Claire, I'm sure, will make herself quite useful. She'll bring along her acquaintances, I should think, and that will boost the funds and that's our aim. We're hoping for a good amount to share between the Seamen's Mission and new equipment for the village school. 'Besides–' Christina lowered her eyes enigmatically as she took a sip of tea – 'Mr Benedict is spoken for.'

'What an old-fashioned phrase.' Beth eyed her mother. 'You mean he's engaged to be married.'

'I do mean that.'

'Tell all,' Kitty said eagerly. 'I wonder if his fiancée is strange too.'

'What's this talk about strange?' Joe demanded, although he was sure the turn of conversation was soon going to bore him. 'That's a really silly notion to connect with the vicar. He's just an ordinary young man of the cloth, isn't he?'

Kitty grinned. 'Please go on, Christina. Do you know the young lady's name?'

'Yes, she's a Miss Bettany Howard-Leigh, and she's the granddaughter of a baronet and the daughter of a bishop. She's to arrive at the vicarage with her maid very soon for a short stay. They are to be married early next year in her neck of the woods, Shropshire.'

Joe yawned. 'Before the talk turns to wedding dresses, I'm off, if you'll all excuse me. I'll take Chaplin and Grace for a long walk.'

'You do that, darling,' Christina said.

'Indeed, sir.' Beth said mischievously. Her younger brother was so adult like, with a touch of militarism about him.

'Beat you later at chess.' Kitty said with a grin. 'He's such a dear,' she added indulgently when he and the dogs had vacated the room.

'Mmm.' Christina smiled too. 'But I fear we'll be hearing fireworks when he learns he and Richard have been signed up to run about generally to fetch and carry for the tea party. Oh well, I dare say little eager Lily will enjoy tagging along with them too, and the boys will have to lump it. Mrs Reseigh and I are going to bake a lot of cakes, and other typical tea fare. So you two won't mind being sent out to buy lots of ingredients, will you?'

'Of course not,' Beth and Kitty agreed together.

'When shall we go over to Mor Penty, Beth? I'd love to see what you've done to the place since you bought it from Farmer Read. Seems ages and ages ago since we stayed in it as a holiday let when we first came down to Cornwall. Actually, I've got a huge favour to ask you concerning Mor Penty.'

'I'm sure it will be fine whatever you want,

21

Kitty,' Beth replied, pouring out another round of tea. 'Fire away.'

'Well, I hope you won't think this a terrible cheek, but Christina and I have arranged what will be a nice surprise. There's nothing as wonderful as a big family Christmas, don't you agree?'

'Of course,' Beth nodded enthusiastically. 'Has this anything to do with Evie?' Evie's father, fisherman Davey Vage only reluctantly tolerated Beth in Evie's life. Had her mother and Kitty somehow managed to persuade Davey Vage to allow Evie to spend part the Christmas festivities here? But what had that to do with Mor Penty, Beth's roof that she hardly spent any time under – that would change in due course when the day came that Joe took a wife.

'No, it's not Evie. Someone would like to come down to Portcowl for Christmas, and as you're bound to be staying here, I'm hoping–' Kitty faked a pleading face but her eyes were twinkling – 'that you'll agree to allow Stuart and Louis and Martha to stay at Mor Penty for a few days. As college principal, Stuart will be on holiday. You haven't seen him and the children for ages so it will be good to see you all reunited. Christina assures me she can cope with the extra company. I wouldn't dream of putting her to any extra work, of course. The children's nanny, Miss Marchant, will be joining them anyway. What do you say, Beth? Isn't it simply something marvellous to look forward to?'

Beth used both her hands to stop herself from dropping the fine china teapot with an awful

22

clatter. Stuart coming here to Portcowl and actually staying in her own home? Nothing could be worse. But it was all arranged. What on earth could she say?

Three

A vicious wind blew up that evening making the cold waters of the sea roar and charge and pound against Portcowl's outer harbour wall, and driving in the waves to smack against the quayside. It sounded like booming thunderclaps, and the cove dwellers' windows rattled as the wind whistled like banshees, threatening chimney pots, causing the whole community to worry about the fishing fleet, at sea miles up the coast in the bight of Rame Head hunting down pilchards.

Along with luggers from Mevagissey, Porthellis and other neighbouring fishing villages, the Portcowl men had already shot their nets, but all had caught nothing. Every skipper and seasoned crew member knew from instinct that they'd only haul back in empty nets tonight. There would be no countless silver flashes exploding through the dark depths showing a great solid phosphorescent mass of pilchards, or as more usual, smaller catches. Only empty fish boxes were expected, and now with the conditions heaving and growing ugly, and the

23

luggers rolling heavily, every skipper ordered their crews to run the nets in and stow the gear. The shore of Whitesand Bay once seen clearly had quickly disappeared in the glowering murk. There was nothing to be gained by confronting the elements, or God's will, of risking the loss of their means of livelihood. All the fleets would make a run to safety to their respective homes.

One Portcowl lugger, riding and lurching through the angry waves and sheets of towering spray was about to have more than 'a bad night of it'. The families of the fleet – a few boys were out on the thirty-to-forty feet luggers learning the trade – sighed in relief and thanked God as one by one, after midnight, the boats struggled into the protection of the inner harbour. The waves were slapping heavily and noisily against the quayside, spraying salt water almost up to the walls of the nearest cottages then splashing down on the stone-slab ground making it slippery and unsafe. Every fisherman's home had lanterns or candles lit in the windows, twinkling lights of hope, warmth and comfort to the men as the boats breached the outer harbour wall. The lights would stay on until the very last boat was safely home.

Evie Vage was among the women periodically staring out of their terraced-cottage windows and praying for their men's safe return. Evie's first-of-terrace home was on the quayside, and she was watching out for her father Davey, engineer on the lugger *Morenwyn*.

The boat was among the last to appear. 'Dad's home!' Evie called to her four slumbering cats,

24

then she whispered with a grim smile, 'Thank God.'

She set about making a pan of oxtail soup and laying the kitchen table, adding thick slices of home-made bread. There was no hurry. It would take a while for *Morenwyn*'s crew to batten down the lugger. It would be no surprise to Evie if equipment had been lost or there was some damage to the boat; the cost would be hard to bear; it happened and was accepted as a fisherman's lot.

After putting her father's slippers and some warmed socks beside his hearthside easy chair, Evie thought about her next-door neighbour, Alison Praed, who worked in a sail loft, waiting for her brother Rob on board the *Our Lily*. She looked out again then put her hands together prayer-like to see *Our Lily*'s prow nudging through the murk. Evie pictured Alison bustling about to make Rob a hot meal. Alison's fiancé and her married sister's husband were both safely home on *Sea Days*. All the quayside cottage kitchens stretched from the front to the back of the homes, and mostly, like the dwellings in the whole cove, now sheltered third and fourth generations.

Rob Praed, who worked on his uncle Lofty Praed's lugger with his four cousins, was at times a disagreeable individual. He had well-defined swarthy good looks but in the strong angles of his face were hints of his underlying hardness. Women were drawn to him, and Evie had been so herself for a few weeks last summer when he had shown an interest in her, after

25

rescuing her most adventurous cat, Smoky, who was trapped up a narrow drainpipe. Then Beth had publicly exposed him as the heartless libertine he was, after he'd flirted with Kitty Copeland and given her expectations, but had then gone on to throw her over at a Praed family gathering, deliberately humiliating her. It was a great pity the kindly and friendly Praed family had a nasty rogue within its ranks. Evie's father loathed Rob. Rob had obviously deeply offended Davey on some other matter, but Davey refused to discuss it.

Later today Evie, who was delighted to have been asked to be one of Alison's bridesmaids at her December wedding, was to go next door for a fitting of her dress. Evie hoped Rob, who tended to merely glare at her now, would not be there.

Finally Davey Vage entered the stable door round the back of number one Quayside Cottage, dripping wet in his high sea boots and oilskins. 'Hello, my handsome. Good of you to stay up for me.' His deep voice was thick with salt and fatigue.

'You know I never go to bed until I'm sure the fleet's all safely home.' Evie would have helped Davey out of his wet weather clothes, but like her mother before her, Davey wouldn't hear of her getting wet or made uncomfortable on his behalf.

'You're a good girl,' Davey replied, putting his oilskins up on a hook on the door. He placed the bucket Evie had there ready for the oilskins to drip into. He peeled off his sea boots and damp

26

thick woollen stockings, washed his hands and face at the sink, and then padded across the stone floor and mats to his chair. Evie passed him a towel and he dried himself off. Balding, small-framed and weather-trampled and appearing much older than his sixty-four years, and although quite stooped, he was still strong and healthy. Through clean living, he oft times said. 'You all right, Evie?'

It was touching to Evie the way he called her 'good girl', and often 'his little maid'. She had just turned twenty-seven and was heading towards being an old maid. She didn't mind that, it was inevitable there were many spinsters without hope of marriage after the horrors of the war had wiped out so many young men. She was devoted to caring for her father, but part of her would love to have children. When young women hereabouts were married, Davey never mentioned the same prospect for her, that he'd like to see her settled and give him grand-children. 'I'm fine, Dad. I'll have the soup on the table in a minute. I'm going to have some my-self. I had some supper but I'm feeling peckish again. Are all the boats in?'

Davey nodded. 'Well, we've all been spared in much worse than this, and on the other hand men and boats have been lost in a lot less. It's all in the Lord's hands. I b'lieve there's been a bit of trouble on *Our Lily*.'

'Oh? What about?'

'Don't know, but I caught a glimpse of Lofty Praed and I've never seen him so angry.' Davey turned the talk to his own lugger. 'Will have to take the engine apart, was sounding a bit watery.'

When they were tucking into the hearty soup, Evie said carefully, 'Miss Copeland is down again. She'll be staying a few weeks this time.'

Davey acknowledged this with just a nod.

Evie's stomach grew achy and she couldn't eat any more. Kitty Copeland was connected to Beth, and Beth, whom Evie had met for the first time last year and instantly connected with, was a moot subject to Davey. Although Davey did not stop Evie from seeing Beth and mixing with those at Owles House, he refused to be drawn into making any comment about them. It hurt Evie, he had no legitimate reason to stay set against Beth, apart from his never changing desire to keep Evie all to himself, which others frequently remarked on. This also irked Evie. Her company and constancy might be enough for her father, but it didn't seem to occur to him that she might wish for more. She should at least be able to see her relatives, Beth and their uncle Ken Tresaile, the landlord of the Sailor's Rest, without feeling she was doing something wrong.

The mean braggart Phil Tresaile was Evie's natural father, nothing could change that, but he was long dead and was no threat to Davey. Phil Tresaile had wanted nothing to do with Evie and her mother anyway, and that had never bothered Evie or Iris. Ken had faced Davey out on the quay and shamed him into allowing Evie and Beth to have a sisters' relationship, and after that Davey, who used to go occasionally to the

28

Sailor's Rest for a glass of lemonade and a game of euchre had shunned the pub.

'I'm going to tea at Owles House on Friday.' Moments later, Evie frowned, 'Say something Dad, *please.*'

Davey looked at her from piercing, sad eyes. 'You know how I feel, Evie, but you go and enjoy yourself.'

'It's hard to enjoy myself when I know how much you disapprove of me being with Beth, when I can't invite her here in return.' Evie forlornly circled her spoon in her soup.

'You think me selfish. I suppose I am.' Davey sighed wearily. 'Miss Tresaile hasn't tried to slock you off or tried to get you take on ways I'd hate to see in you, so I suppose it wouldn't hurt for her to come here, occasionally.'

'What?' Evie lifted her head cautiously and hopefully. 'You mean it, Dad?'

'You know I never say anything I don't mean, Evie. But you also know I'm a very private man and don't like to be disturbed under my own roof. Invite her here, by all means, but only when I'm not likely to be at home. Of course, you must go out and about when you like, you're a grown woman, although I'd give anything to go back in time and have you as my little girl again. Just be careful, eh? That's all I ask.'

Rushing to her father, Evie hugged him and kissed his whiskery cheek. 'Thanks Dad, you're wonderful.'

'I wish I was,' Davey said dourly. 'Go on, eat your soup.'

* * *

29

'You haven't really said much, Beth.'

'About what, Kitty? Gosh, it's a bit chilly in here. The downpour's eased off but the atmosphere is gloomy. I'll light a small fire and then make us some coffee. I've lots of butterscotch biscuits in the barrel.'

The friends were in the cosy sitting room of Mor Penty, having driven in Beth's car to the cottage, a little way down-coast just above a tiny beach. Beth had talked the previous owner, a local farmer, of Mor Penty, once the tumbledown home of a nineteenth-century crab and lobster fisherman, as a holiday let, into selling it to her, for a very good price for him. Beth and Kitty had stayed here last year, and while trudging across the sand Beth had recalled a happy childhood memory of Christina bringing her to the beach for a picnic. When Beth had decided to stay in Cornwall she had wanted this place more than any other as her own. She had further updated the cottage, replacing the nautical theme of her own sea-facing bedroom with warm feminine flair. It was anathema to Beth that her former lover who had so easily dumped her, was to actually stay here. Her home, her private domain would never be the same afterwards. But she could hardly have refused the petition. As far as Kitty knew, she and Stuart had always been good friends and Beth had doted on his children. Beth was worried how she would now relate to the motherless seven-year-old Louis and six-year-old Martha.

'You know what I'm talking about, Stuart and the children coming down. If something is wrong, Beth, please do say.' It had not occurred to Kitty that her brother might not be welcome, but after Beth's unenthusiastic reaction and her offhand attitude since then, Kitty was actually feeling a little guilty about her excitement over the prospect. Had her concerns for her beloved family made her thoughtless in asking Beth to rent out her home? Kitty was eager to see Stuart and the children smiling again and some healthy colour replacing the grim paleness of their faces. Understandably, Stuart had taken the sudden wanton desertion and the scandal of his wife Connie leaving him and the children very hard indeed. He was still in shock and he was unfairly blaming himself. It seemed he was always looking for something. If only he would open up and talk about his deepest feelings, but of course, it wasn't a man's way to do so. The poor children were equally as bewildered, and from two happy and bright little souls they were subdued and often anxious.

'No, nothing's wrong,' Beth replied quickly, syringing a smile into her fraught expression. 'I'm just a little worried that the children might be afraid when the sea is running high and the winds are blowing hard inshore.'

'Oh, they'll be fine.' Kitty laughed off Beth's disquiet, not realizing it was a hastily thought up excuse. 'You've had trees planted for extra shelter and the window shutters will block out the worst of the noise. The beach and the sea will be ideal for Louis and Martha to play about on mild days, and perfect for Stuart to find some peace and come to terms with his heartbreak. We

31

know, don't we, just how soothing and inspiring everything on the coast can be. It has an edifying effect on a person's soul. The children will greatly benefit from mixing with Joe, Richard and Lily. Down here where no one knows them they won't have to bear the shame about what their rotten mother has done to them,' Kitty ended vehemently.

'Oh Kitty.' Beth felt ashamed at not considering the full effects of the incomprehension and fears of young Louis and Martha. She knew herself what it was like as a young child to have to endure parents' bad behaviour. And once she had been willing to take Louis and Martha's father away from them. She had carried and lost their half-brother or half-sister. Shocking secrets were being kept from them. She owed these dear children more than she could possibly repay them. She must forget her horror at being faced with Stuart again and make some compensation to his children. She'd also not thought much about the upshot of it all on Kitty, other than seeing it as a tie for her. 'I'm so sorry. I've centred all my time on my happy reunion with my mother and thought too little about your family's terribly sad situation. I promise I'll do everything I can to help. I'll arrange for plenty of logs and coal to be delivered. You're fully welcome to make suggestions for their comfort, Kitty. I'll ask Joe and his gang to suggest suitable toys and games for Louis and Martha. We'll bring over a wireless and some adult reading material, and lots of stationery for Stuart. As I remember he liked to write.'

Beth flushed about that. She knew far too much about Stuart's preferences. He'd been interested in mountaineering, and in his university days he had gone on climbing holidays with his pals. He would like the Cornish cliffs and trekking for miles along them. An unexpected sharp twinge deep inside her hoped he wouldn't be tempted to climb high up the craggy granite, especially alone, she'd hate for him to get hurt and be hard to find. No, she scolded herself – she mustn't allow her old feelings for Stuart to be resurrected. She felt her stomach sinking more and more. How on earth was she to act when she next saw him and during all the time he was around?

'Thanks Beth,' Kitty sighed stridently, and Beth could see the intense relief in her gorgeous features. 'I knew I could rely on you. It will be fun planning for their arrival. I'll ring Stuart this evening and remind him to bring down lots of warm clothing, rubber boots and things, although I expect Miss Marchant will think of everything. Actually, Christina has said if the weather turns really terrible they'll all be welcome to stay at the house.' Hugging her body happily Kitty twirled about. 'I just know we are all going to have such a wonderful Christmas.'

With her coat collar turned up against the heavy rain, Evie dashed next door to the Praed's whitewashed cottage. Clutching a bag containing her best high-heeled shoes, which she was to wear with her bridesmaid dress, she knocked and let herself in through the back door. 'Hello! Alison!

33

I'm here.'

'So I can see,' replied a gruff male voice.

Evie froze. The Praed kitchen was empty of the female wedding party she was expecting to find gathered there, but Rob Praed was sitting under the low ceiling beams, at the long oilcloth-covered table, near the front window. A plate was pushed aside from which he had eaten a late cooked breakfast. The pleasant smells of bacon and toast filled the large room. Evie's spirit dropped like a stone to see he had a thick bandage wound halfway up his thickly muscled right arm. She was sorry he had been hurt, but this meant he was unlikely to go outside and attend to the boats like the other fishermen were.

'Oh,' she couldn't help squirming in her shoes. 'Alison is expecting me. She said to just come in if the weather was rough.'

'Yeh, so she said. She's just slipped out to get me the *West Briton,* and then she'll bring along old Mrs Coad. The old dear gets nervous on the wet ground, Alison said. Though she's only got to come from the other side of the house,' Rob pegged on scathingly.

'Judy's not here yet then? Or Lily?' Evie referred to Alison and Rob's sister, Judy Crewes and their nine-year-old cousin. Evie stayed rigid on the spot. She would rather be in the company of the dirty, smelly Gabby Magor, than this hard-hearted man.

'Can you see them?' Rob uttered with mounting scorn. 'Well, take your coat off and come in properly. I'm not going to eat you. Alison said to get yourself a cup of tea and sit down and wait.

You can pour me another.'

'Rude devil,' Evie muttered under her breath. She was feeling uncomfortable but she wasn't afraid of the high and mighty Rob Praed. Taking off her coat she hung it up with the others hanging on the coat rack on the wall. Putting her bag down on the old-fashioned wooden settle, she strode to the table and picked up Rob's giant-sized blue mug without glancing at him but she noticed his bandage was badly bloodstained and grubby. She would ask Alison and not him how he had come by his injury. She assumed it likely had something to do with the trouble that occurred on *Our Lily* that Davey had mentioned. She could smell surgical spirit and coal tar soap on Rob. He was badly in need of a shave. In another couple of days he'd have the start of a full black beard. His hair too needed a trim and was presently unruly. Grudgingly, she thought it would make him appear something like a handsome pirate.

She didn't want tea herself. The stuff in the dark green and cream teapot was well brewed and she liked only fresh and not very strong tea. She knew Rob took his tea as it came. He had told her so last summer when he had showed a liking for her. He had even sent her a letter from Newlyn, where the fleet had moored up each weekday early morning after offloading each night's first annual pilchard shoals, asking her if she would like to go to a tea room with him. She had thanked God she had been spared more of his deceit by Beth's timely intervention, but she had until then been flattered by his interest, and she had wanted to meet him as he'd asked.

She padded back to the table and plonked the full mug down beside him. He was gazing down as if brooding over something. That didn't surprise her. He used to be more easy-going but the mean streak in him was taking greater precedence. His thank you was a grunt. She glared at him, and he caught her narrowed eye. 'What? Do want a tip?'

'Some good manners wouldn't be amiss,' she returned frostily. She spun round and moved to the settle at the other end of the room and positioned herself on the long knitted cushion so she wouldn't have to look at him. What a pathetic, small-minded man you are, she thought, to turn against me so sourly after Beth showed you up for exactly what you are, a wicked wretch.

The staircase, as in her own kitchen, came down into the side of the room, and something long and large suddenly flew out of the dark confines underneath the stairs, where Rob's fishing gear was stowed. 'Oh!'

'Damn it!' Rob shot to his feet, spilling tea over the oilcloth. 'One of your bloody fleabags is in here again. It must have crept in when Alison went out. Keep it out of here or I'll kill the stupid thing.'

Evie was up on her feet too, recognizing her cat Smoky. 'You will not!' she flew at Rob. 'You had better not ever hurt one of my cats or I'll make you sorry.'

'Oh yes,' he advanced on her until he was just a breath away. 'And exactly what will you do to me, little Miss Quiet Homebody? Threaten me

36

with a knitting needle?' His dark eyes were blazing in anger and mockery.

Evie wasn't going to let him enjoy himself at her expense. She glared at him, not straight eye to eye for she was a good deal shorter than his towering bulk. 'It takes a very small and dismal man to threaten to hurt an innocent little animal. Why are you like this anyway? Last year you rescued Smoky when he got stuck in a drainpipe. You were really concerned for him. Why are you now taken so against him?'

'I hate stinking cats, always have. Scratchy, demanding things. They're only fit for catching rats. People must be mad keeping them indoors and making such a stupid fuss over them.' In any other circumstances, Rob thought, Evie would be scuttling away from him. Right now she wasn't budging an inch. 'You really aren't a little mouse at all, are you? Tell me, if your hoity half-sister hadn't put the kibosh on it, would you have gone to the tea shop with me? Were you at all interested in me, Evie, even a tiny bit? Are you not totally under Davey's thumb then, as everyone thinks?'

'What I do, and the way I am is none of your business,' Evie bit back. Abruptly leaving him she went to Smoky, gathered him up and after giving him a quick cuddle she let him outside. Pursing her lips she retook her seat on the settle and gazed down crossly at the linoleum on the floor. She'd wait this way until Alison and Mrs Coad, the elderly widow who lived on the side of the Praeds' cottage came in.

'Mmm, interesting, you've just answered my

37

question,' Rob drawled, and grinning in malicious amusement he sat himself down close beside Evie. She didn't shunt away from him but leaned her head to the side. With their hostile sparring ended he breathed in the soft fragrance of her. He found it captivating, found Evie captivating. At that moment he thought how he'd love to capture her completely. It would be innocence and sweetness at its best yet she had some fire in her.

He said, deliberately huskily, 'You know Evie, last year it came to my mind that you'd make the perfect fisherman's wife. I still think that. I had a way past Davey's objections, and I still have, even though he doesn't think so. He thought he'd got the better of me, but not long ago I realized his ruse. I didn't care that he'd tried to outwit me, but I do now. You know Evie I really would like to have you. If you fancy moving in here you only have to say, married of course. I know you're too strait-laced and honest to consider any other way. Why don't you think about it?'

Evie turned her head to him and now they actually were eye to eye, and Evie didn't flinch. She had never uttered a curse but for the first time in her life she wanted to tell someone to go to hell. 'What do you mean you had a way to get past my father's objections? What ruse are you talking about?'

'Now Evie,' he put his mouth up to her ear and she shuddered and edged away. 'If you want to know all that, you're going to have to get close to me. Very close.' He got up and returned to the table, sat down and drank the stewed tea in his mug.

'I'd rather die,' Evie hissed at him. 'And I don't care what you meant.' She did mind and she was troubled about it. She couldn't mention it to her father but she would to Beth. One of the best things about having a relationship with her sister was having someone to share her concerns with. 'You're a pathetic bully Rob Praed, not manly at all.'

'From a mouse to a cat,' Rob jeered. *What would you be like I wonder if I pushed you metaphorically up a drainpipe? Would you screech as much as your bloody cat did when I did it to him for real?*

'Uh!' Resolving to ignore him from now on, Evie pulled her shoes out of the bag.

He was smiling to himself when Alison ushered in Mrs Coad. The elderly widow, who sat outside the cottages on warm days with Evie, and with Judy Praed before her marriage, knitting fishermen's jerseys to augment the family income, had been invited to offer her wise advice on the dress fittings, and for her to gain some company. Evie rose. 'Shall I make us a fresh pot of tea, Alison?'

'Yes, please, Evie, I told Rob to ask you to do that and to pour yourself a cup while you're waiting. I've put the cups out.' Short and clear-featured, Alison helped the slightly bent-over, shuffling Mrs Coad out of her numerous warm wrappings and hung them up. 'Rob, come and get your newspaper. I can't believe you forgot to give my message to Evie. I'm glad she's some-

39

how managed to wring a smile out of you at last. You'd better go up to your room. I'm sure you won't want to stay with us women and Lily, when Judy arrives with her.'

Rob took the newspaper off Alison ungraciously then stood back as she led Mrs Coad, still wearing her black bonnet and a doubled-over crochet shawl, to the armchair near the hearth. 'I'm going out,' he muttered darkly.

'No you're not. You can't,' Alison said stridently. 'The district nurse is calling to look at your arm. It needs more attention than the bandage Uncle Lofty put on it. She'll probably chide you for refusing to let me put on a clean bandage. She'll probably send for the doctor to put some stitches in it. Good job we pay in the medical insurance every week. She might be here any minute. I'll send her up to you. On the other hand she might be hours so you'll just have to be patient and wait. Anyway, you can't go off gadding about, you might get an infection.'

The door opened and in came Judy Keane and the tomboy, chatterbox Lily Praed, youngest child of Lofty. Forgetting her wet coat and boots, Lily made a beeline for Rob. 'How's your arm? Dad said you were lucky it wasn't ripped off. There was blood everywhere on the deck, he said. He's some mad with you. Said you weren't paying attention and suddenly let go armfuls of net. Everyone went down and Linford was lucky he wasn't dragged over the side. He'd have drowned; the sea was so steep and breaking. Dad's said he don't want you back on the boat 'til your arm's better, or you'll be a li'bility.'

40

'Uncle Lofty said that about Rob?' Judy, who was a sparkier version of Alison, made disapproving noises. 'But—'

'I did nothing wrong! I've never lost concentration on the boat ever! It's not my fault my arm's in a mess.' Rob's face grew ever darker with wrath. 'If that's the way Uncle Lofty's thinking of me, I'll get my own boat. One thing's for sure I'll never fish on *Our Lily* again. No one treats me like this!' Storming off he thumped up the stairs and his bedroom door was heard being slammed shut.

'Well! Somebody's not telling the truth. Will need to be sorted out sharpish.' Mrs Coad said, clutching her well-rounded bosom, shocked by the fierceness raised in the man she had watched grow up from a 'dear little tacker'. 'That tea ready yet maid?'

'Yes, something's up somewhere,' Judy frowned, rubbing her brow while looking anxiously up the stairs. 'Rob's never been afraid to own up to his shortcomings.'

Evie glanced overhead where the ceiling board above told of Rob pacing angrily about his room and flinging things about. The news would soon spread all over the cove. When her father got home he would be full of indignation over Rob's apparent disgrace. Dangerous negligence among the fishermen brought a cloud over the community. Rob had protested his innocence over the incident, it was why he had been brooding, and once again he had been publicly humiliated, in front of women too. Alison, with her arms round a trembling Lily, was looking deflated. It

41

had taken the shine off what should be a happy event for her. If things weren't put right, and it must be left to the men, if Rob was not reconciled with his uncle and cousins then her wedding might end up being the first celebration the close-knit Praed family would undertake estranged, in a half-empty chapel.

Evie began pouring out the tea. She couldn't help feeling sorry for Rob.

Four

Singing brightly, Beth was in the hall getting ready to call on Evie. Evie had rung with the unexpected wonderful news that her father had relented and Beth was now able to enter under his roof. The sea was still choppy but the wind had blown itself out and the fleet would be preparing to recommence the pilchard hunt. The weather was what the locals called 'misty wet'. In all likelihood Davey Vage would be helping to make ready *Morenwyn*. Beth was feeding her bobbed hair in under her favourite cloche hat. The grey hat had a front brim, and a pink lace art deco style motif on the side made by Evie who was a gifted lace maker. Beth was already in her one-buttoned crossover coat and leather ankle boots. She heard the squeaky, gravel-crunching sounds outside that heralded the arrival of the postwoman on her bicycle. She ran down the steps to meet the jolly, middle-aged war widow.

'Good morning, Mrs Paull, how are you?'

'Right as a new ten bob note, thanks, Miss T.' Mrs Paull trilled. 'Nice of 'ee to come out in the wet, though there was no need. Got a whole lot of letters for the house today. Cheerio.'

Back inside Beth dealt out the large handful of post into piles on the hall table. Six were for Christina. Beth guessed the four that weren't official might be to do with the Grand Tea Party. Two for Kitty, one Beth recognized to be Louis and Martha's joint writing, and the other was from her personal assistant. There were two for her. One was from Louis and Martha and she felt touched they had written to her too, probably to thank her for the use of Mor Penty. She felt ashamed for having virtually ignored the polite, well-behaved children since moving to Cornwall, sending them only birthday cards and postal orders to spend. The light wording on the second letter she recognized vaguely; from some former school friend or neighbour perhaps. Once certain people heard an acquaintance had moved to a popular holiday area they fished for somewhere to stay for a hopefully cut-price holiday.

Opening the children's letter she had the urge to cry over the crayon pictures Louis and Martha had made for her. Both pictures were roughly the same, indicating that Martha had likely copied Louis's, depicting a small beach with a few people and two dogs, probably Grace and Chaplin, dotted about the bright yellow sand. On the blue and green sea was a sailing ship and high in the sky was a huge yellow sun, with streaming beams. Perhaps the children believed hot summer weather could always be found at the seaside. At the bottom of each piece of paper were the words thank you and each child's name. Beth laid the pictures out on the hall table for the rest of the household to delight in. She pushed the other letter into her wide coat pocket to read under her umbrella on the walk down to the cove.

The telephone near Beth suddenly rang and she made a face. Could she creep out on her way and avoid answering it? No, she had not said goodbye to Christina yet, who was in the kitchen with Mrs Reseigh. She reluctantly picked up the receiver, for since Kitty had arrived Stuart had rung often and so far Beth had avoided speaking to him. Crossing her fingers, she hoped she was about to speak to anyone but Stuart.

She gave the house number.

'Just putting you through caller,' she heard the telephonist advising the person on the other end of the line.

'Beth, hello! It – it's lovely to hear your voice again, um after ... all this time. Um, are you um, are you well?'

Beth's every emotion was shot to pieces and she felt her shoulders sag. The voice she had hoped to never hear again sounded like that of an insecure boy's, not strong and confident as it once was. From knowing Stuart intimately, she could see him clearly as he probably was right now, one hand in his trouser pocket and jiggling on his feet, red-necked and blinking in discomfiture. He had always had a little boyish shyness

44

about him, something that had once endeared him to her. He would be humiliated too, for he had come begging in a way to her. She couldn't see there was any reason for him to want to come down to Cornwall other than he was finding it hard to manage without Kitty with him. He must be feeling totally lost.

'Beth, a–are you still there?'

She had to clear her throat. 'Yes, I'm here, Stuart. I'm afraid you've not long missed Kitty. She's out with my brother, walking the dogs along the cliff. Perhaps if you try again in an hour or so she'll be back by then.'

'Well, if it's all right, may I tell you what I wanted to say? I ... I don't want to be a nuisance to ... you in particular.'

Beth could imagine him tugging on his collar; his voice was so small, hesitant and choked. His plight was tugging at her. She felt torn in every direction. She had loved him, adored him once. Despite their hurtful parting she could never despise him or wish him ill. 'Of course, go ahead, Stuart.'

'Thank you, Beth, thank you so much.'

His mighty sigh of relief was blown down the long distance into her ear, making her flinch.

'The thing is, Beth, things haven't been too good with Louis. He's not well. He mopes and gets into the most terrible moods. I think he blames me for ... for his mother walking out on us. Martha seems to be coping better, but Louis just can't seem to come to terms with it. The thing is I've taken compassionate leave for the next three months and the children's schools

45

have agreed that I can teach them at home. It was my suggestion that Kitty spend a lot more time than usual with you, and Louis is furious with me. He relies rather too much on Kitty, I'm afraid. I've told him he can ring his Aunt Kitty at any time but he just shouts, "What's the point." Then he clams up and refuses to speak for hours. He barely eats. He's so insecure. I don't want to put an extra burden on you, Beth, but I'm so worried about Louis. I was wondering, if it doesn't put you out too much ... I was wondering, if ... if ... oh dear, this is going to seem a terrible cheek.'

'If you can come down to Cornwall early, is that what you're trying to say?' Beth wasn't pleased at the idea but she couldn't help feeling compelled to help Stuart out. And Louis didn't deserve to suffer over what his mother had done, or his father's failings. 'That will be fine. Could you give Kitty and I a couple of days to get my cottage ready for you all?'

'Yes, oh yes! Oh, thank you so much, Beth. We won't be any bother, I promise, I swear. Louis will buck up a bit, I'm sure, as soon as I tell him he'll shortly be seeing his Aunt Kitty again. He and Martha love hearing her tell how wonderful the beach and cliffs are down there.'

'I dare say you could do with spending some time alone,' Beth said blandly, pleased with herself for the good idea. 'The children must spend lots of time here with Kitty. My mother will be pleased to have them here at any time, there's plenty of room in the house and grounds.'

'Thank you so much, Beth. Um, I'm really

pleased that everything has worked out so well for you concerning your mother. I remember how upset you were in the past.'

Stuart's tone sounded ingratiating, to Beth's mind. 'Thank you, but please don't mention it again. I really have to go. Goodbye, Stuart.'

Rather than getting their boat ready for the night's fishing, the crew of *Our Lily* were gathered at Lofty (Linford senior) Praed's home. Wildflower Cottage was a perfect description for the homely large place standing alone in its own long strip of ground, near the bottom of the long winding Portcowl Hill that led down into the fishing cove. Normally when members of the extended family got together, a regular occurrence for meals, birthdays, Easter and Christmas, it was a very happy occasion. Today, Lofty and his sons, Linford junior, Douglas, and the twins Barry and Andy, and his nephew Rob, were sat solemnly round the table that dominated the cosy cavernous kitchen. Cigarette smoke filled the air, masking the pleasanter lingering smells of cooked breakfasts.

Mugs of tea, the vast teapot replenished and on a huge tin tray, with a large jug of milk and glass bowl of sugar, and numerous spoons, had been placed in the middle of the table by Posy Praed. Then the matriarch of the family had retreated with two-and-a-half-year-old Rowella Reseigh, her precious granddaughter by her late daughter, to the next room. A serious meeting like the one about to get under way was the men's business. Posy, a motherly, lumpy shape in a full print apron, her short greying hair pinned under a hairnet, was deeply worried. As in every family there had been squabbles and arguments, but until now they had always been quickly forgotten. The incident, in which Posy had nearly lost her eldest, married son, had been blamed firmly on Rob but he had furiously denied it. Now there was a simmering atmosphere of great hurt and anger that had never been known before. Was the family about to be ripped asunder for the first time after generations of Praeds fishing from Portcowl? And so soon after the elation of last month's announcement that Linford's wife of six months was expecting a baby? Grandma Praed had died last Christmas. At least she was spared this, she would have despaired that the incident had come this far.

The younger men waited for Lofty to utter the first word. The brothers had their heads down and were fidgeting, those who were smoking nervously tapping ash off their cigarettes, for Rob was chain-smoking and he was fuming. Barry and Andy, either side of him, had intimated to each other by wrinkling their noses, their wish to move away from Rob because his bandaged arm smelled horridly overripe. They wouldn't dare do that, Rob would be offended and he wasn't in any sort of forgiving mood.

'We all know why we're here,' Lofty began gravely. 'Linford is lucky to be alive. If he was dragged into the water by the nets he'd have been mangled and drowned. Rob denies letting go suddenly while heaving in, upsetting the balance, and says the first he knew something was wrong was when his arm was raked over by the falling nets and he was brought down on deck. I bawled him out over it, but,' Lofty slowly tapped his middle finger on the table and homed in hawklike on his three younger sons, 'I was in the wheelhouse and didn't see what happened. So, was I unfair to Rob over another's guilt? Linford couldn't be responsible because of where he was. In Rob's defence, I've never known him to lie about anything important. It's not as if he's afraid of anyone. So, therefore,' he stared in turn at Douglas, Barry and Andy. 'Has anyone got something that needs saying?'

Rob bore his eyes at Douglas and the twins, his hardy features sharp and hostile.

Lofty was praying one of his younger sons would do the right thing and own up. He didn't believe that Rob was responsible for the grossly negligent act that had injured him and could have cost Linford so dear, and he was remorseful that he had blamed Rob in the heat of the moment. Rob was scrupulous about safety on the boat. If Rob were forced to continue to shoulder the blame he would do as he had threatened to, go to the bank and borrow the funds to buy his own lugger and start up his own crew. Rob had mastered every job on the boat while many fishermen only excelled at one or two. He was quick-minded and had a sense for shoals of fish that evaded many of his peers. He would make a natural skipper, most young fisherman's dream, and earn more, but until now he had been content to work alongside his family. Rob would never forgive the family if he were permanently made out to be a wanton liar.

An acute silence reigned round the table and the tension grew to suffocating levels. Knowing Rob was about to explode in fury, Lofty spoke quickly. 'Linford, you say you don't know what happened exactly?'

'No, Dad,' Linford shook his head, emitting an overwrought sigh, darting an uneasy look at Rob, for he shared his father's belief. 'It was dark and I was concentrating on counting in the nets as I hauled away. Then I felt everything lurch away and was pitched forward. Instinct told me to let go the nets and throw myself sideways and grab the gunwale, and then I heard Rob yelling in pain.'

'Do you believe I did it?' Rob's eyes glittered at him in challenge.

Linford knew everyone's eyes were on him. He shook his head again. 'To be honest I don't. I could never believe that you'd lie about something like this, Rob.'

'Thank God one of you can see sense,' Rob barked, aiming his angry sight from Douglas and then either side of him at Barry and Andy. 'Well, is the guilty party still willing to keep my head on the block?'

The twins gulped at each other then the mouths in their fresh open faces gaped open. It seemed to Rob they had swapped looks of horrified innocence. Douglas had been nearest to Rob on the boat at the time. It was Douglas who Rob believed was the despicable culprit, lying by keeping his shallow mouth shut about his flagrant carelessness.

Eyeing Douglas harsh enough to freeze him to the bone, Rob muttered dangerously, but also speaking to the twins – he believed they were sure of the truth. 'This is your last chance. If I walk out of the house I'll never step inside it again. I don't want to shun the innocent in my family, but I couldn't mix with a Praed who is a–' Rob checked himself to forestall a profane swear word – 'filthy lying bastard.'

Lofty sighed in dismay as silence again spat out the culprit's cowardice and increased the flesh-tightening pressure. He was ashamed of his guilty son, whoever it happened to be. He was wilfully heading the rest of them to live with suspicion and causing even deeper bad feelings to eat away and defile his once happy family.

Snatching up his cigarette packet and matches, Rob pushed back his chair with a horrible accusing scrape of its legs. 'That's it then.' He felt light-headed and sick.

'It was me!' Douglas squealed, hiding his face in his hands.

'About bleddy time!' Rob raged. A wave of nausea washed over him. This rotten affair had affected him more than he could have imagined.

Douglas began to sob, his shoulders shaking. 'I'm sorry...'

'Lift your head up and face your cousin like a man!' Lofty snapped, banging his fist on the table. He got up and leaned towards his wretched son. 'Apologize to him face to face. I'm ashamed of you, Douglas Praed. You've shamed, disgraced and hurt Rob in one of the worst manners a man could do to another, and you've made the rest of us look bloody stupid fools all round the cove. You deserve a bloody good thrashing. Apologize to Rob, and then to your poor mother, and then get out of the house! Don't come back until the rest of us are out at sea. You'll have to work damned hard for all of us to forgive you over this. If Rob doesn't want you back on *Our Lily* then you'll have forfeited your place on it and it'll serve you right.'

Lofty turned to Rob with both hands stretched out, and tears of shame stinging his pale eyes. 'I can only offer you my sincere apologies, Rob. You've been ill served and by your own flesh and blood, and I'm mortified by it. I'll never be able to hold up my head again after these last three days. Will you shake my hand?'

Rob's head was spinning. He felt as if his strength was seeping out of him. Mutely, he accepted his uncle's rough brawny hand, then Linford's, and then the twins'. He glared at Douglas, now up and quivering and wiping his tears away with the back of a trembling hand. Douglas's lips opened. 'Save it,' Rob growled. 'I need some fresh air.' He had never needed to get out of a house more than he did now. Grabbing his coat and woollen hat he half-stumbled out of the room. He had to move hand over hand down the passage wall before pitching himself outside.

On her way down to Evie, Beth frowned in disgust to see, several yards ahead of her, Rob Praed staggering drunkenly out through his uncle's gateway. He was so inebriated he needed to grab at the wet wild hedgerow to keep his feet.

Lofty Praed was a sober upright man and doubt-less had ordered his self-seeking nephew on his way. Rob Praed should be ashamed of himself to be so drunk this early in the day. Not wanting to be near a man whose present condition might make him capable of improper behaviour, she slowed her steps, watching as he lurched on, leaving Wildflower Cottage a little behind.

She was appalled as he reeled and lunged face down into a ditch. Well, he could stay there, and if he got soaked in the cold muddy water it served him right. His place was in a ditch. He treated women as playthings. He was whining that he was innocent of his inexcusable disregard of his own family crewmen's safety. She looked away as he lifted his head and started to retch and was violently ill. Could this man make a worst spectacle of himself? It was a pity Evie had to live next door to such a common individual. Evie was misled to feel sympathy for him. Rob had bewildered Evie by some rubbish story that, last year, he'd had a ploy to get round her father's opposition to him forming a romance with her, and that recently Rob had seen through a ruse of Davey's to prevent such a happening.

Her gloved hand across her face, Beth speeded up and strode past him. She stopped. She could-n't leave Rob where he was; the water in the ditch was deep enough to drown in. He was a danger to himself. She must alert his family in the cottage – poor things. Actually, it was poor Mrs Praed and herself. The men, of course, would be tending their boat, so it would mean she and Mrs Praed having to drag the drunk out

53

of the ditch to safety. Wretched man! She had the urge to kick him.

He was trying to lift his head. Beth was sure he sensed someone was close by and she hoped he wouldn't find the strength to reach out and grab her. 'H–help me,' he gasped.

Beth bit her lip. It wasn't the usual response of a drunken man – invariably they were past realizing any danger. She edged up to him. As well as his disgrace there was the dreadful stench of something rotting. She saw blood and stuff seeping down from his right arm and over his hand. It had to be from his wound. It was badly infected and he was very ill. 'Oh my God.'

Heaving and puffing she managed to drag him out of the ditch, he yelling in pain. She placed him on his side then pushed her scarf under his head. 'Stay still, Rob, don't try to move. I'll get help.'

Five

Kitty was holding her little niece's hand and her other arm was round her nephew's shoulders. 'Well, didn't I promise you it was a lovely beach? Few people come here so you've practically got it as your own private playground. There are so many things you can do. Daddy and I can trust you to be careful, can't we?'

'You bet,' curly-haired Martha chirruped her

54

latest favourite saying. Slightly chubby, cutely round-faced, her curious nature was reflected in her probing eyes.

'Miss Marchant's preparing lunch and as soon as you've eaten you can change, put on your boots and I'll take you to explore.' With Kitty's brother Stuart, they were standing at the side of Mor Penty cottage, gazing down over the garden to the little driftwood-strewn beach. The air was fresh but there was shelter from the gentle rise of the cliffs.

'What do you think, Louis?' Stuart asked, sadly aware of the disinterested scowl on his son's pale, rather sickly face. Louis had refused to speak much on the journey down, sulking each time they'd had to change trains, barely touching but complaining about the refreshments Stuart had bought, and whining about the engine smoke smutting his face and making his eyes itch. All the way here from St Austell railway station he had wailed in the car that he was feeling sick. Kitty had stopped the car and Stuart had climbed into the back with Martha, who had cuddled into him, believing this to be an adventure, allowing Louis to sit in the front beside Kitty. They had driven on with the front windows wound down, leaving Stuart to feel the dreadful draught. Louis appeared to feel better in the front of the car and had chatted to Kitty, ignoring Stuart when he added a few remarks.

'It's all right, I suppose, not a patch on the beaches we've been to in France and Spain,' Louis muttered. Tall, lean and fair like Stuart he shuffled stones with the toe of his shoe.

55

'I'm sure you'll love it, and the fishing cove, which is only just round the headland there.' Kitty pointed up the coast. 'And later we'll all be going to Owles House for tea. You'll be seeing Miss Beth again, and meeting her brother Joe, and Grace will be there. And Chaplin and Charlie the cat, they're quite a pair of characters. Joe's got a tree house. With his friends Richard and Lily, you and Martha will have lots of fun.'

Louis shrugged his shoulders over the promised treats. 'I don't want to wander on this silly beach. I don't want anything to eat. I'll go up to my room and stay there.'

Steamed up with increasing frustration and anger with his son, Stuart growled, 'You will not, you'll—'

Kitty interrupted, giving Stuart a leave-this-to-me glance. 'Yes, you take a rest, Louis, as you're not feeling too bright. Miss Marchant can bring you up a tray, and I'll take Martha to explore the beach.'

Louis stomped away inside.

'Martha, darling, you pop along and take a look at the room you're sharing with Louis. Daddy and I will be in soon.'

'I don't think I can take much of this, Kitty.' Stuart virtually crumpled when the children had gone in the cottage by a little side door. He ran his hand over his face dragging down his tired, wan features. 'Louis hates me and I don't know what to do about it. I should have been a better husband to Connie and she wouldn't have left me.'

Kitty looped her arm through his and headed

56

him towards the extended and modernized cottage, kept in line with its origins. 'It's not your fault she met someone else,' she said vehemently. 'She's the one who's done wrong. She should have walked away before starting the affair and remembered her wedding vows. She certainly shouldn't have left her children. She's hardly made the effort to see them since and that's inexcusable. She was the one who swanned off abroad, but it wouldn't take long for her to jump on a plane to see them, to have them with her in a hotel for a weekend. It's no wonder Louis is so unhappy. He's confused, the poor soul, because he's been rejected and feels unloved. You're doing a wonderful job with the children, Stuart. You spend every spare minute with them. You don't mope about feeling sorry for yourself. You mustn't berate yourself. If you were doing anything wrong then Martha would be acting up too.'

'But I am responsible for Louis's unhappiness. Whatever you say Kitty, I didn't make enough effort during our second honeymoon.' Stuart sighed, propping himself up against the cold damp wall of the cottage and cupping his hands to light a cigarette. Connie had accused him of being somewhere else in his mind. He had been, with Beth. He had missed her so much from the moment they had said goodbye. He had hated himself for his shallowness at leaving her to cope alone while carrying his child. Kitty had been with Beth during her sudden onset of 'illness'. If Kitty had known the truth she would have been devastated, as Beth must have been

57

over the miscarriage. He had guessed the truth about her emergency hospital treatment. She had spoken so much about how she would devote herself to children of her own after having such a miserable earlier childhood herself. He had wanted to go to Beth, but he had felt sure she would have hated seeing him, so he had made some excuse, and Connie had gone on her own to visit Beth during her recuperation. Connie had believed the lie that Beth had suffered 'women's trouble' and it had never been mentioned again. Stuart could not think of a reason to contact Beth on his own, it would have seemed odd to Connie and Kitty, but he must have come across as cold and calculating. It had been no surprise when Beth had refused his request last year that he and the children come down for a break, saying that she wanted to concentrate on her new relationship with her mother. What a creep he was. He was terribly nervous about seeing Beth later today.

Kitty took his cigarette case and lighter and lit up for herself. 'But the rot had already set in,' she protested. 'Connie had already been seeing this man. You must have sensed something was wrong, that's why the second honeymoon didn't work out.'

'Oh, Kitty,' Stuart said, like a desperate lament, shaking his head. Her innocence about his broken marriage made him feel more of a heel.

Kitty sensed his ruefulness and his pain. She knew he was referring to things she didn't know about, and she had been unsuccessful at getting him to open up his thoughts, to share his despair.

58

Stuart had stuff on his mind that was tormenting him. This overdue break away from routine might help, the earthy beauty of the region and the peace, sometimes spiritual peace to be found here, hopefully would help him to come to terms with his heartbreak and feelings of loss, and the children too. Kitty was hoping Beth would provide a vital lift for Stuart. They had got on very well in the past. They had seemed to have a lot in common in their quiet, pensive ways. Kitty would ensure that the pair of them would get some time alone together, during which, Kitty prayed, Stuart might perhaps reveal things to Beth and be set on the road to recovery.

Two people were walking from opposite directions towards the entrance of Owles House. The Reverend Jacob Benedict and Miss Claire Opie were out of sight of each other at the moment. The vicar, a former town dweller, who enjoyed a good stretch of his legs, was ambling smartly along, head up, peering all about him and taking in all the sights, glorious sights to him, despite everything being rather murky under an overcast sky.

To Jacob, the trees and bushes although naked of leaves, leaving stringy skeletal branches and drooping slivers, were fascinating shapes. The muddy ground passing under his walking boots (his patterned socks were up over his flannels like plus fours) had scrubby grass growing along the middle where horse and cart, motor car, van and the twice-a-week boneshaker bus wheels didn't reach, but it was a pleasing natural sight to

Jacob. He could glean all manner of shapes and designs down below him, as he did in the few wind-blown clouds scudding across the heavens. The hedgerows either side of him, in the narrowest parts the lane seemed only a crow's wingspan apart, had sagging dead foliage that reached out to wet his legs and dark blue overcoat, but Jacob took delight in the raindrops dropping off the ends.

'God's jewels,' he said aloud, in the strong voice some of his parishioners had described as fine and noble.

In places where the hedgerow was much lower, beaten down by generations of children, and perhaps courting couples, scrabbling over to play or to be alone in the fields, he saw fabulous glimpses of the bay. To him it was a display of God's mightiness, part of His glorious creativity.

He halted every now and again to consult his notebook to remind him of the names and addresses where he was going to today. He was 'scatty', as the locals kindly called him, until all things unfamiliar were finally rooted in his mind. First today it was Owles House. Then down to the cove to call on a fisherman, a Robert Praed, seriously injured in an unfortunate accident out at sea. Apparently Praed could be something of a difficult character, and sadly the accident had caused serious strife in his family, something unknown among the Praeds until the incident. Jacob wasn't going to plough in and preach about forgiveness to Rob Praed, who wasn't a church or chapel attendee anyway. He was hoping to get to know Praed and see if he wanted to unburden himself about anything. Family hurts ran deep, and Praed was likely to be suffering more than physical hurt.

Jacob caused a mild stir when he was out and about in cold weather because he usually shunned a hat and only casually threw a thin scarf round his neck. The local women, apt to be concerned about any young unattached man, although confident he was well served by his housekeeper, cook, kitchen maid and a parlour maid, were anxious his carelessness wouldn't end with him catching a chill. It was a relief to all that he did not flap and rear about in all his ecclesiastical robes as the last vicar had done, disturbingly so. The old and increasingly senile Reverend Oakley, apart from apparently giving stirring sermons, had long been unable to offer any pastoral care, and he and his put upon spinster daughter, had allowed the vicarage to fall into desperate disrepair. It had taken the church considerable time and expense during the interregnum, when a curate had efficiently been locum soul curer, to bring the early nineteenth-century vicarage up to a dwelling suitable for its station. Even so, it had still been leaky and draughty, and Jacob had spent his own money, part of his sizeable inheritance from his colonial farming parents, to ensure the comfort of his bride-to-be Miss Bettany Howard-Leigh. Jacob had received a lot of useful advice from the pushy (not that he really minded) Mrs Opie. And also some, quietly given, when he had asked the opinion of the charming, unassuming Mrs Vyvyan, who was considered to be the 'lady of

61

the manor' in the parish. Mrs Opie had hinted that Mrs Vyvyan had 'an unfortunate past' but Jacob had refused to listen to the full story. Gossip tainted lives and even destroyed them. He certainly was not going to allow bitterness and trauma to circulate in his parish if he could prevent it. He might come across as lenient and a bit eccentric, and he was eager for all his flock to trust and respect him, but he was no pushover.

The neglected vicarage grounds had been replanned and replanted by the local gardener, Mark Reseigh, the widowed son of Mrs Vyvyan's delightful, 'mumsy' daily help. Jacob's mother had been obsessed with her Kenyan social life, and he had been educated in England from the age of nine, so he had not known what it was like to be mothered. It was the ordinary women in his former parish, as a curate, and now this parish who filled in those missing pleasures and securities for him. The work in the vicarage grounds had given Mark Reseigh many hours of extra work, a great benefit to the able young man to earn enough to tide him over the winter months, when a lot of his regular work dried up, but which gave him more time with his beloved infant daughter. Jacob was still giving Mark work. Last week he'd had Mark paint the inside of the new summer house. Mark also took care of the plants in the new conservatory, which was Jacob's pride.

The new central heating was a great addition in the vicarage, installed just in time for when Bettany, his sweetly dippy Bettany, arrived next week. Jacob preferred to keep blazing log fires, a delight and an indulgence to him after spending so many years in burning hot Kenya. He was anticipating romantic evenings with Bettany, the flames riding up the huge chimney in the drawing room, dusky shadows shimmering on the walls, glasses of wine in hand, and soft music on the gramophone. His dear Bettany in his arms. He couldn't wait. A new parish and soon a new wife, heaven on earth.

'Ah, Mrs Vyvyan, she does a splendid Victorian sandwich sponge, and Mrs Reseigh of the legendary sultana scones.' Jacob smiled to himself with relish as he closed in on Owles House. He had a very healthy appetite and he enjoyed eating his way round the parish, and nearly always he was given some of the particular delicacy of the lady of each house to take home, which he hid in his study and scoffed late at night, after his jealous cook, Mrs Morcombe had retired.

On hearing slow careful taps, cautious footsteps, he looked straight ahead. A well-dressed young lady in unsuitable high heels was picking her way along the lane, presumably heading for the same destination as him. There was to be a meeting of the Social Committee. The young lady was Miss Claire Opie. The Opies had intimated that on the occasions they were tied up at their hotel they would be represented by their daughter. The Grand Sea View Hotel was quite small and the Opies did not live in, but one or both of them called in there every day.

'Good morning to you, Miss Opie!'

Claire Opie was staring down at the muddy

63

ground. Wishing she had worn more sensible shoes and hoping she would not slip over and foul her clothing and make a fool of herself by arriving at Owles House with ripped stockings and covered in mud. That would be a disaster. Few people took her seriously and she would be thought stupid. She could imagine whispers of glee. 'Serves the snooty so-and-so right. Who does she think she is? Her mother carries on like she's mayoress of Portcowl.' Her schoolboy brother, Richard, many years younger than her, a pest, who swaggered about like some old time hero, took every opportunity to snipe at her. 'Uh, look at you done up like a dog's dinner. Going up to the hotel again to see if you can catch the eye of a rich young gent? Or an old one? Anyone would do as long you can turn him into a husband. Or are you going to haunt the cove today in the hope some dashing holidaymaker will sweep you off your feet? Pathetic.'

Horrid, beastly, despicable child. Claire hated him. Why did her mother have to turn out the brat eleven years after her own birth? Why couldn't he be just fun like her two older brothers who had doted on her? Claire had never been overlooked or denied anything, but her brother, growing up noisy and acting out his childhood fantasies all over the house and garden, had utterly ruined the peace and gentility of the house, which Claire and her mother prized above all else. Good thing Richard was at school or he would very likely be at Owles House with Joseph Vyvyan and planning some humiliating barb for her. Claire knew that her mother was

64

secretly relieved Richard spent so much time at Owles House because she 'didn't quite know what to do with him'.

It's not my fault there are so few suitable young men about, Claire screamed inside herself. *What's wrong with wanting a good life for myself? And why should I lower my expectations?* Which was one of Richard's jibes at her. She didn't want a fisherman or someone of the like. She wanted her own house, a better house than her parents had and in a better area, with servants. She wanted to be noteworthy. Her mother flaunted her position, for what it was, but Claire had hopes of something higher, like Mrs Vyvyan's. Sadly Mrs Vyvyan did not mix in esteemed company. The only man regularly at her fine house was Mark Reseigh, the local gardener. He was a hauntingly attractive man, having tragically lost his wife soon after childbirth, but even if Claire lowered her sights and considered him rather than ending up an old maid, as she feared, Mark Reseigh existed only for his infant daughter and memories of his late wife. Now Portcowl had a new vicar, a brilliant replacement for the last batty old incumbent, but almost at once Claire's hopes for him were dashed when he told the Social Committee he was engaged to be married. To be a vicar's wife, the mistress of the updated grand vicarage would have been a dream come true for Claire. Especially as Mr Jacob Benedict was a commanding, jolly-hearted individual, and good for Portcowl, breaking up the boredom of the place.

At least today she would get the chance of

taking morning coffee in refined surroundings with Mrs Vyvyan and her classy daughter. Claire set aside the fact Beth Tresaile was the offspring of a lowly common publican's son, a womanizing brute, for he had married well and died as a hero in the Great War. Claire desired to become a close acquaintance, perhaps even a friend of Beth Tresaile. Claire had never had a friend before. While attending the village school, the other girls, mainly from families in the fishing trade, thought her a 'toffee-nosed mare', because she had refused to join in their energetic games, and during the holidays to scramble about playing hide and seek, to pick primroses or blackberries, or to go 'nutting' or play conkers with the boys. Claire was something of an outcast, self-made she admitted, and she knew if she did not soon appear less haughty she was heading for loneliness in later life.

Suddenly being hailed startled Claire, her steps faltered and she careered sideways into the hedge. 'Ohh!' She spied Jacob Benedict hurrying towards her and used all her might to throw herself upright. She hastily straightened her new hat and brushed down her wetted coat sleeve.

'No harm done,' she replied, putting an amused catch in her tone to the vicar's effusive apology and inquiry if she was hurt. 'Partly my fault really for not wearing more suitable shoes.' She was pleased with her response. It deflected her embarrassment. He was genuinely sorry, as he should be, he had made her feel foolish, but he didn't treat women like they were fragile and feeble, and after the concern had left his frank eyes she detected nonchalance in them. He had mentioned his first area of work had been in the tough underprivileged East End of London, and before that in view of the suffering he had seen as a very young officer in the Somme in the war, he found much of various experiences, were 'not the end of the world'. Claire found herself actually thinking her falling against the hedge was not the end of the world. She led a rather privileged life, she did not have to work, she lived in good circumstances and she was about to enter and socialize in the local big house.

On the walk up the long drive Claire strode rather than picking her way along. Jacob sauntered at her side with his hands behind his back. 'Splendid gardens here,' he said. 'And a magnificent panorama of the whole bay. It's a pity one can't catch a glimpse of the sea from the vicarage; too far back along the lane.'

'Yes, indeed, it is very lovely here in every way. We're also blessed at home with fine sea views. It's rather enchanting to watch the fishing boats going out to sea and returning safely. May I ask you Mr Benedict when your fiancée is due to arrive? I am looking forward to meeting her.'

'You may ask of me anything you wish, Miss Opie.' He gave her a sideways smile. 'I shall have the pleasure of Bettany's company in a few days time. She will stay for a while to look over her new home and will be here for the Grand Tea Party. Ah, look, it's Mark Reseigh. Good morning to you, Mark!'

Claire blinked at his sudden hearty address and frowned over his use of an underling's first

67

name, both inappropriate – but *not the end of the world*. Claire felt herself slightly rebuked. It didn't really matter, did it, how one person related to another, as long they were polite? She halted, in line with the vicar, while Mark Reseigh approached them from where he had been among some trees, skirting a lawn to avoid his boots churning up the grass. He had a sack hanging from one weathered hand. He lifted his cap. Good, thought Claire, he knows his place, his betters. She was uncomfortable to feel her conscience prick her. She got an unwelcome remark in her ears that Mr Benedict might chide her with, 'We're all equal in the eyes of God.' Life had never seemed like that to her before – perhaps it should have though. She couldn't recall her father preaching such a thing in one of his long, dreary sermons in the Methodist pulpit. Her mother would prefer to attend the Anglican church; she had confided to Claire that she felt embarrassed to admit to guests at the hotel, if any asked her advice where they could worship on a Sunday, that she and her husband were not Anglicans. Mrs Opie had received, so she said, many a disapproving turn of head. 'It puts us among the tradespeople, Claire. I hate it. I have to get your father to change camps. He could easily become the church warden and have standing in a higher place.' Claire had shared her mother's opinions. Now she thought the only way that the church of the Cornish St Irwyn was higher than the Methodist chapel was merely in relation to its greater height in regard to sea level.

Gosh, she mused, a little stunned, Mr Benedict's character is rubbing off on me. And she was pleased, she felt released from her normal beliefs and assumptions. She would reflect on all this when she got home.

'How are you, Mark?' Jacob asked the gardener when he was near. Jacob was aware that the young lady at his side, instead of being the intense, flustered soul he knew her to be from his calls at her home, was growing relaxed and patient.

'Yes, and how is your lovely little girl?' Claire added. 'I must say she is such a credit to you.' Where had that come from? Claire asked herself. She had noticed the dark-haired, strikingly pretty, chirpy two-and-a-half-year-old was bright and well behaved, but otherwise she had not given her another thought. She had not cared about the local children and wasn't – hadn't – been at all interested in this Grand Tea Party raising funds in part for the village school where she had known much misery.

'Rowella is very well, thank you, Miss Opie,' Mark replied, with evident pride and devotion.

'Currently with her other grandma, Mrs Praed, I suppose, being doted on,' Claire added. She was pleased she had gained the confidence to lead the conversation, a first for her. Usually she just followed her mother's ideas, after listening to her with only half an ear.

Mark concurred she had supposed right, then after explaining he was at Owles House to attend the greenhouse and the conservatory, and to pick up blown about debris in the grounds, he excused himself and returned to his work.

'A good man,' Jacob said. 'Had many such chaps under my command during the war. Mark was about to enlist when the Armistice was called. Thank God his youth saved him.'

'Yes, indeed,' Claire replied in the hearty manner he might have used. She saw the proceedings ahead in a different light. She even realized she had an idea or two she might put forward, to be helpful rather than to impress. Only really important things were important to her now. She hoped Mr Benedict would not mention her mishap in the lane inside Owles House, and he did not.

Six

I don't know how I'm going to get through this. Beth was in the dining room, waiting for Kitty to bring Stuart and his children, and Miss Marchant, to join her, Christina and Joe for the teatime meal. At this early hour they were to eat a hearty beef stew, followed by apple and cinnamon pie and custard, to nourish and warm the visitors, and enable the children to return to Mor Penty for their usual bedtime.

Beth had laid the cutlery perfectly but she was fiddling with the arrangements. 'I hope this isn't going to be too much for the children. They've done a lot of travelling. They must be quite worn

70

out, poor things. Perhaps it would have been better if this had been put back until tomorrow.'

'You may be right about that, darling,' Christina replied, doubt also etched on her soft, naturally pale features. 'But it was what Kitty thought would be best. It will mean the children won't be going to bed tonight possibly nervous about meeting Joe and I tomorrow, and Mr Copeland will be glad to be in adult company, I should think.'

Beth gave a careless shrug, but her nerves and emotions were in havoc. In normal circumstances the coming visit would be a delight and she'd be eager to do all she could to help the Copelands, but how was she to meet her former lover. Damn Stuart for wanting to come down here. How selfish could he get? He must know how unsettling this would be for her. Or was he so insensible that he believed she had moved on so far in her new life she now only saw him as a friendly acquaintance from the past? The pictures and words sent to her from Louis and Martha tugged at her heart – it was always the children who suffered in these situations – but had Stuart contrived for them to send their sweet polite thanks to her?

Something else came into her mind. She had received another letter that day, but watching Rob Praed falling into the ditch outside Wildflower Cottage had pushed the second letter out of her mind. The cause of Rob Praed's injury, the terrible infection that had caused his collapse, and the tale behind it, had caused a maelstrom of shock and high feelings among the fishing

71

community and the rest of the cove. With his innocence established, practically every family in Portcowl had beat a path to Praed's door with good wishes, gifts of foods and other stuffs and the proceeds of a monetary collection, so he and his sister Alison would not suffer financially while Rob was laid up and not earning.

Beth had run straight into Wildflower Cottage, bewildered to find Lofty Praed and all his sons there, one of them was sobbing with his head on his arms at the kitchen table, and the rest standing about shamefaced. 'Come quickly, Mr Praed!' Beth had cried; she had realized the cause of the strange scene later. 'Rob is down in the ditch out in the lane and he's very ill.'

'Oh my God, no,' Lofty Praed had wailed. 'What now?'

All except the weeping Douglas Praed, had lifted Rob, now near unconscious and moaning, his muddied body drenched in sweat and jerking, and carried him inside and laid him down on the lumpy settee in the front room. Rob's predicament was obvious. Mrs Praed had handed Rowella to Beth and hurried off to the kitchen; the medicine box and lots of boiled water was called for. Linford Praed had raced down to the cove to fetch the doctor.

Linford had returned with Rob's two sisters. 'Doctor won't be long. I told him the trouble. He's just getting some surgical stuff together. Said it sounds like the wound needs urgent lancing. We're to lay Rob on the kitchen table, scrubbed down first, and put clean linen on it, and for us to strip him to the waist and carefully

72

wash off any dirt. We need to get all the animals out of the house.'

'We'll help Aunty Posy do that,' Alison and Judy had declared. Linford had told the sisters about Douglas's disgrace. 'Can someone make sure that lying swine isn't in there? We might kill him! He'd better pray that Rob will be all right.'

Beth had kept Rowella out of the way, in another small downstairs room at the front of cottage, where the furniture was made up of odds and ends and there was an ancient harmonium. It was a cosy room, warm from the other fires lit in the home. It was where young Lily often played, so there were some toys to amuse Rowella with. The beautiful raven-haired little girl was perfectly happy with Beth, as Beth was with her. They were wholly familiar with each other from the times Mark or Mrs Reseigh brought her to Owles House. Many times Beth had wondered if her lost baby would have been anything like clever little Rowella.

Doctor William Powell, of wrestler stature, rolling voice, full gingery beard and a waxed edged moustache, and high, brown, laced boots and tobacco-smelling Norfolk jacket, had announced he'd been alerted to the patient's side in the nick of time. 'As I thought, no time to get this chap to hospital, but I saw a lot worse in field dressing stations at the Front.' First fitting up a drip into Rob's arm, the men holding a delirious Rob still, Dr Powell had lanced the deep wound and cut out the infected flesh. The arm was then stitched, dressed and put in a sling.

'You should have seen his fingers working,' Posy had told Beth, after the doctor, fortified with a cup of her strong sweetened tea and two thick slices of yeast cake had left. 'As swift and neat as could be, as expert at lace making as Evie, I'd say. Now we got to carry Rob upstairs. Rob would probably prefer to go home, but doctor's forbid it for now. He's to go in the twins' room. He won't want to go in Douglas's. Doctor'll call back this evening, he said. We got to get some liquid into Rob when he comes round, lots of sips, as much as he can take.'

'Rob's coming home as soon as possible,' Alison said, almost in tears. 'He didn't deserve this. Rob would never do anything remotely dangerous on the boat and he'd never lie about it! An accident's an accident and everyone understands that so Douglas needn't have lied about it. It just shows how low he has sunk. If Rob loses his arm, I'll never forgive him.'

'And we insist that we'll pay for the doctor,' Judy had added, forcefully. 'Uncle Lofty offered, but Rob wouldn't want that.'

Rob's recovery was going to be a drawn-out affair.

The letter writer must think I'm very impolite or uncaring, Beth thought. She didn't have time to fetch the letter now, still inside the pocket of the coat she'd worn that day. The dogs were barking, and Joe called out that Kitty and the others had arrived. Beth swallowed hard and dredged up a smile on her face. As far as everyone else knew she and Stuart were friends from way back

74

and she had no reason not to give him a warm welcome.

Taking a deep steadying breath, Beth walked with Christina out to the porch. The telephone rang. 'I'll get it,' Beth blurted out, glad of the interruption as a face-saver for a while. 'I'll dash to the study so the call doesn't encroach on the arrival.'

'Hello, Owles House.' Beth stood in front of Christina's desk with her back to the door.

'I'm so glad it's you who has picked up the phone, Beth,' replied a familiar and totally unexpected voice.

'Connie?' Stunned in surprise Beth was forced to unscramble a rush of confusion. 'Is that you?'

'Indeed it is, Stuart's wife, one and the very same. Has he and my children arrived in Cornwall yet?'

There was harshness in Connie's tone, and Beth believed her to be shaking, not with nervousness or contrition, as she should be, but anger. There was a fighting spirit to Connie, something unusual in the Connie that Beth had known before, and Beth sensed trouble brewing. She blew out between pursed lips, damning Stuart again for bringing himself and his family back into her life. Beth didn't want these Copelands upsetting the peace for Christina and Joe and herself. 'They got here safely today. In fact they've just arrived here at my mother's house for a meal. Do you want to speak to him or the children? I know the children have missed you terribly.'

'I do want to speak to the children very much

of course I do, but not yet. I miss my children more than you could ever know, Beth Tresaile. So you saw fit to ignore my letter?' Beth's mouth fell open, now she knew why the mystery letter's writing had been recognizable to her. Connie's voice was pitched icy and bitter. Beth could interrupt her and explain why she had not yet read her letter but she decided to listen to her.

'I asked you to meet me where I've been staying for the last few days, at the Grand Sea View Hotel. Did you think I'd just go away? I'll repeat what I wrote to you. I made a terrible mistake but I'm alone now and glad if it, and I want my marriage and children back. I want you to help me, Beth. I knew all about your affair with Stuart almost from the beginning. Stuart was useless at hiding the facts. I didn't mind because I'd fallen in love with someone else too, but that's come to a sorry end. I want to revive our marriage; we both owe that to the children. I know poor Louis is having a rough time of it. The problem is I can't stand knowing that Stuart still hankers after you, Beth. I want you to show him he hasn't got a chance in hell of getting you back. Another try at our marriage would be empty and dry if he can't get you out of his mind. You owe me, Beth. I didn't reveal your affair with Stuart, and I'm pretty sure you lost a baby to him, didn't you? I'm not a vindictive woman. I don't want to spoil your friendship with Kitty. But now I feel no consideration for you whatsoever after you chose to ignore my written plea.'

'Listen to me, Connie,' Beth said urgently.

76

'I'm sorry about the letter. I would have read it the day I received it but I came across a local fisherman who'd had a terrible accident and he had collapsed and was in danger. I'm sorry but I forgot all about your letter, I swear. I can assure you the last thing I want is to have Stuart back.'

'Good! You can help *me* win Stuart back. I want you to do only what you can do. I want you out of his head. It's as simple as that. If you don't help me exactly as I want, then I'll spill the whole truth about you and my husband to Kitty. I'll make out you were a marriage wrecker. Kitty will hate you for it.'

'There's no need for that.' Beth couldn't keep a little acrimony out of her reply. 'I didn't want any of this. Believe me, I don't want Stuart back. I wish to God he hadn't asked to come down here. I only agreed to allow him to stay in my cottage for the children's and Kitty's sakes. I've moved on from him, Connie.' Then she found herself saying, 'Actually, I'm seeing a local man and I've never been happier. Look, we really need to talk in person.'

'We certainly do. Come here tomorrow for morning coffee. Ask for Mrs Smithson. It's the least you can do for me.'

'I won't be a minute late. I really ought to go, Connie, or the others will think it odd.'

'Well, you can start working for me straight-away, can't you? Have a good evening, Beth. Make sure you do the right thing.' Connie's clipped tones faltered. 'G–give the children a secret kiss from me.'

This last emotional request eased some of

Beth's growing horror. 'I will.'

Aware of the artificially jolly voices coming from the hall, as often happens during introductions, Beth replaced the receiver and put a hand to her agitated stomach. She did not have time to go through all her chaotic feelings. She patted her face to smooth out any giveaway signs that she had just been shocked, challenged and put in the tightest spot of her life. She turned sharply on her heels while splashing on a big smile, hoping it would appear natural and sincere, that she would seem relaxed and not to be feeling out of the ordinary. She went to the hall, keeping her gaze low so she would first focus on the dear, rather tragic Copeland children.

It worked Beth's way. Pulling off her second red and white woollen glove, Martha Copeland came rushing to her, and Beth bent and scooped the lovely chubby little girl up into her arms. She hugged and kissed Martha and laughed when Martha did so to her. Beth realized then how much she had missed the children who had been brought up to look on her as an aunt.

'Oh, Auntie Beth.' Martha squeezed her neck. 'It's ages and ages and ages since we saw you. I like your house by the sea. Will you be spending lots of time with us, like Auntie Kitty?'

'Of course, every minute I can,' Beth promised. 'Auntie Kitty and I will take you and Louis all over the local area. It will give your daddy a chance to have lots of time to himself.' *Heed the point, Mr Copeland. I don't want to spend time with you.* Beth then sought Louis and holding Martha's weight with one arm she put her hand out to the petulant-looking boy. 'Hello, Louis, won't you come and say hello? You probably think you're far too grown up for hugs. We can just shake hands, if you like.'

Much like Stuart in looks, Louis also had a sprinkling of freckles over a neat nose and full lips like Connie. Beth was moved by how break-able he looked under his sullenness. She could tell he'd just about had enough of change and upset and was on the verge of tears, and it wrenched at her heart to see how he was trying to hold his tears back. Here was a boy of seven years whose father wasn't coping and who needed his mother. Beth carried Martha to him and Louis went tenuously to meet her. Beth placed Martha down and kept her arm round the little girl, and with her other arm she gently pull-ed Louis to her. 'It's all right, darling,' she whis-pered in his ear. 'Don't worry. You like dogs, I remember. You can have lots of fun with Grace and Chaplin, and there's so much else you can do here. Will you be OK? Auntie Kitty and I will show you lots of exciting places. We'll go ex-ploring.' Then she raised her voice. 'It will give Daddy lots of time by himself to relax.'

Louis nodded, clung to her for a moment then shuffled. Feeling his tension Beth let him go.

'Louis wants a puppy. We both want a puppy,' Martha piped up in the hard-done-by manner of a child trying to manipulate getting her own way. 'But Daddy won't let us have one. He said he couldn't cope with a puppy as well as us. Auntie Kitty found a puppy down here. Will you take us to the place she found Grace so we can see if we can find a puppy? Daddy can't refuse us having an abandoned puppy, can he, not really.'

Finally Beth looked up to Stuart. It was a shock to see the difference in him. From a confident professional of manly physique he was thin and a bit bony, with dark shadows circling his eyes that were dull and lacking their blueness. His stance was uncertain where he stood with his hands locked behind his back. His good looks remained but in a soulful sort of way. 'Hello, Stuart, welcome to Portcowl, and welcome too, Miss Marchant.' She greeted the good-natured, attentive nanny, who was devoted to the children, and who wore her mid-blue uniform with pride. She was rounded and rosy all over. 'I hope you and the children find Mor Penty comfortable. Do say if you need anything.' She said it all cheerfully, caringly, and told herself it was for the children's sake. She was no longer attracted to Stuart in the least. He had let her down following an affair they should never have embarked on, so she owed him nothing, but she did these dear children. If their father had left them to start a life with her then she would have been responsible for tearing apart their happy secure lives. The fact that Connie had done that to the children instead did not exonerate Beth.

'I can't thank you enough for the loan of your home, Beth,' Stuart replied, his discomfiture obvious and growing. 'It's very kind of Mrs Vyvyan inviting us for a meal.'

Both Beth and Christina were aware that Joe was bored with the event, but he didn't disappoint them and played the perfect host. 'The food's all ready. Let's eat. I'll settle the dogs in front of the sitting room fire.'

'Yes, I must say I'm feeling ravenous and the stew smells delicious,' Kitty said, taking Stuart's arm and then following Christina into the dining room.

'Come along Master Louis and Miss Martha.' Miss Marchant ushered them along in her mindful dutifulness.

While Christina got the guests seated, Beth fetched the stew. Kitty had said not to bother with a starter. Throughout the meal Beth made a fuss of the children. Joe offered to show Louis his tree house and collection of model aeroplanes. 'There's a girl who hangs round with me and my pal Richard. She's called Lily and she's looking forward to meeting you, Martha,' Joe said.

Good old Joe, Beth thought. But Louis only shrugged. Every few seconds, she felt Stuart's eyes on her. *He doesn't know how to take me.* Good. He must understand he needs to keep his distance from me. Beth had been searching her heart. It was with relief and gladness she knew she really had lost all her old love and desire for him, but she did feel sorry for him, and the close connection they had once shared made her want to help him, to be his friend, but she could not allow any complications to form. Stuart was obviously desperate and achingly lonely. He would want nothing more than to fill the void in his life, to fill his moments, to rely on someone else. At all costs she must not allow him to think, if he was holding out any hopes for her, he had the slightest hope of regaining her affections. She had to talk to him, be friendly, otherwise it would seem strange and rude to Kitty. 'Did you bring your hiking boots, Stuart? There are some lovely long walks along the cliffs, taken with care at this time of the year of course.'

'Yes, Beth, I did,' he answered with a polite smile. 'It's one thing I'm looking forward to.'

'Stuart would like to look over one of the fishing boats. I'm sure Lofty Praed will be happy to allow him on *Our Lily,*' Kitty said.

'Absolutely,' Beth said.

'I've got the message clearly, Beth. I can see all my hopes are gone.' Stuart had managed to separate her from the children while coffee was being drunk in the sitting room. They were on their feet before a tall cabinet, apparently admiring Christina's collection of arts and crafts glassware. 'It was very wrong of me to even hope to fall back on you. I promise I won't bother you. It's good to see you again though, Beth. You look so well. You've changed so much and attained the peace you badly wanted for so long. Mrs Vyvyan is a fine lady.'

Beth smiled sheepishly. 'I did make rather too much of ignoring you, Stuart. I'm sorry about that.'

'You don't hate me, do you?'

'Goodness no! I did resent you for wanting to come down here. I suppose I was confused. If I admit the truth, I was a little afraid I might still have feelings for you, but I don't Stuart, not in

82

that way any more. My life here has overtaken everything I felt in the past. But...' and she gazed thoughtfully, meeting his eyes directly for the first time in about two years.

'Yes?' he asked hopefully, shyly, boyishly, which Beth found endearing. In his university days Stuart had been sports mad and full of fun, messing about like a juvenile, then as a family man with a responsible position, he had brimmed with assertiveness, still sports loving and always he'd been humorous. All those things and much more had made Beth fall in love with him. Stuart had promised her all sorts during their passionate love affair, but his panic over her pregnancy had proved to Beth that, although he had genuinely cared for her, he had been seeking excitement outside the commitment of his marriage.

'We could return to our friendship as in the old days, couldn't we? I do so want to do all I can for Louis and Martha. I feel I owe them that but I genuinely love them. It wasn't until I saw them again that I realized how much I missed them, and I feel so for Louis.' Her eyes travelled to the front windows, and Stuart's did too, where Joe was pointing out to Louis the location of his tree house, through the darkness outside. Louis was uninterested and inching away from Joe.

'Can't say how much that helps to hear you say all that.'

Beth saw Stuart's shoulders drop and she sensed his whole inner self had fallen with relief now he knew he wasn't staying in Beth's home under her sufferance, and that he had regained her friendship. Beth was calmed and pleased also, now Kitty would glean nothing unnatural about her responses to Stuart. Kitty had been showering all her attention on the children, so she wouldn't have noticed Beth's earlier reticence with Stuart.

'Would you like more coffee, Mr Copeland? And you, Beth?' Christina asked, from her fireside chair.

Both said they would. Beth seated herself beside Kitty, who had Martha cuddled into her. Kitty, who was encouraging Martha to drink a glass of milk, smiled happily at Beth. Beth smiled back. Kitty was obviously optimistic that all might now work out well for her family. Beth sought Louis. He was lined up on the carpet between Chaplin and Grace, lying on his side hugging Grace with his face buried against her long coat.

Beth glanced up at Joe. Joe shrugged. He had got nowhere with Louis. Louis was traumatized by his mother's desertion, and his father didn't know how to cope with him. Perhaps his mother coming back into the family's life would bring Louis back to the playful trusting little boy he had once been. Beth prayed this would be the case in due course. She hated having to hold back her secret that she was to meet Connie Copeland tomorrow.

Seven

The wound on Rob's arm was extremely painful but it wasn't really bothering him. Not a lot was bothering him although he knew there should be, and would be, when he stopped feeling numb. He was just allowing his mind to drift. Unless he was sleeping or reading, he was thinking, thinking all the time about his life, his future, *possible* futures, and how he had come to be laid up at home, weak and barely capable of standing on his own.

This was the third day he had left his bedroom. As on the previous two mornings, he felt light-headed, and as always, horribly hot. Judy had joined Alison, and between them they had washed, shaved and dressed him and put on the new slippers they had bought for him. On his first day downstairs, Alison had said in his ear, making him shiver and rouse, 'Are you sure you should go downstairs?' She was gently brushing his hair. The day before, she had helped the district nurse to wash his lank sweaty hair over an enamelled bowl and Rob had passed out. When he'd come to, she had told him how strange it was, he being so weak and not in control.

'Fed up stuck up here,' he'd murmured. 'Not fixed to drip any more. I'll shuffle downstairs

85

on bottom.'

'Rob, my handsome,' Judy had said. 'You're still a bit breathless. You're not even managing full sentences. You barely open your eyes. Why not see how you feel tomorrow, eh?'

Rob had summoned up some strength. He had quite a lot in reserve but just wasn't bothering to draw on it. He'd opened his eyes wide. 'Sorry girls, you don't need to worry about me. I need a change of scene. Once I'm downstairs it won't matter if you can't get me up here again. Settee is comfy enough to sleep on. You've already taken down the commode lent us. Neighbours have been so kind.'

Here he was again, stretched out on the long horsehair settee, which the girls had pulled up in front of the fireside, a sheet underneath him, pillows under his head, the blanket the girls had tucked around him pushed down past his knees for he was so hot and sweaty. Rob insisted the fire was kept small because he couldn't stand the heat, and that a window was opened a little. To offset draughts, Alison kept the curtains partially drawn so the room was darkened. Sometimes he dozed, or snatched moments to read bits of the daily newspaper. Alison popped in to him every now and again with the foul-tasting medicine or with small meals or to remind him to drink. He had to drink lots of water to help flush out the infection. When Alison needed to pop out Judy, or his aunt Posy, or a neighbour stayed in the house in case he needed anything.

Today Alison, with Judy and Posy, had taken the weekly coach to town to shop for gloves and

86

other stuff for the wedding. He didn't know who was presently keeping watch over him – he must have been asleep when they came in. His throat was parched and he finished off half a glass of water. He was still thirsty, but rather than call for some more he waited, his sitter would soon be in to check on him. He was well looked after. The flow of concern from the neighbours had been immediate and unending once word got round that he'd not been responsible for the incident on his uncle's boat. It was heartening for Rob to know few had believed he'd be so slack and then lie about it. Even Davey Vage, the one person who loathed him, had called in, Alison said, with a box of vegetables from his allotment. The kindness was typical of the tight-knit community, where the fishermen pitted their wits and often risked their lives and limbs against the might and sometimes savagery of the sea.

Rob had been spared on the boat. The nets could have dragged him over the side and trapped him to drown in the freezing rough waters. His life had been saved by the swift skills of Doctor Powell, and perhaps by Beth Tresaile. If no one had been travelling along the quiet lane he might have lain in the ditch long enough for the infection, or pneumonia to kill him, or to drown in the muddy water in the ditch. He was lucky to have kept his arm too. He could have joined the five limbless fishermen in the cove; two had lost limbs in fishing accidents and three from fighting in the Great War. When he had regained his strength he would decide what his future would be.

Evie was in the Praed kitchen making Rob a mug of strong sweet tea. On the tray she also put a jug of fresh water and a large wedge of her own cherry cake. She had called in every day to ask about him, hoping to speak to him personally and wish him a fast recovery. She was pleased Alison had asked her to wait on Rob today. Evie was almost excited by it. She had never believed Douglas Praed's wicked lie and she wanted Rob to know this. She told herself it was just concern for a wronged, ill man.

She picked up the teak tray to carry into the front room. Something caught her eye. 'No, Smoky!' she hissed. Her disrespectful cat was padding down the stairs. Before she had the chance to put the tray down Smoky had slipped past the front room door, left ajar in case Rob called out for something.

Evie rushed to the door, her hand up to her mouth in horror, praying Rob was asleep and she could extract her cat from the room and the cottage and Rob would never know he'd been there. Smoky liked jumping up on people, if he leapt on to Rob's wounded arm...

Spying movement by the door, Rob watched as Smoky slunk into the room. He didn't have the energy or will to bother to shout the cat out. His trauma had seen off many of his old prejudices and irritations and he couldn't help smiling wryly. 'So you've come to torment me again, have you, cheeky damned bugger, aren't you?'

Rob's weak voice came to Evie as a mumble. What was happening? She shot into the room. 'I'm so sorry. I'll get him out right away.'

'Evie.' Rob was pleased to see it was her who was sitting for him. The girls had told him how concerned she had been about him, bringing in her own baking and offering to help any way she could. He sat up straight against the pillows. She looked so pretty, pink-cheeked, wide-eyed and anxious, and much younger than her twenty-seven years, in fact barely out of girlhood. 'Don't worry about the cat.'

'You mean you're not cross?' She glanced from Rob, whose voice had been low and husky, to Smoky, now stretched out on the woven hearthrug and rolling on his back. 'He has got an awful cheek. I'll put him outside.'

'Leave him, Evie. I'm getting used to him. Yesterday he was in here for ages, sitting along the arm of the settee by my feet, like king of the castle. He kept staring at me, all superior, as if daring me to order him out.'

'Did he?' Evie raised her brows and bent to stroke Smoky. 'You're incorrigible, aren't you, Smoky?' She was delighted Rob had changed his stance on Smoky. Rob's drawn features, once either flirtatious or hard, were still darkly handsome, and beguilingly mysterious in the low flickering flames of the log fire. 'I'm glad you don't mind him any more. How are you feeling today, Rob?'

'Still wiped out, I keep hoping every day I'll wake up and feel strong enough to go outside. I'm missing the fresh air, everything. But I'm still as weak as bilge water. I can't even stomach a fag at the moment. Never thought I could feel this way. I'm used to being in charge of things.'

He smiled weakly at her. 'Sorry if I smell sweaty and if this arm stinks with the infection, it's all I can smell on myself.'

'It's just cosy and warm in here,' Evie reassured him. He was a little sweaty but it wasn't offensive, it was an evocative manly smell. There was also a strong surgical whiff. 'Are you ready for a cup of tea and something to eat?'

'You women are never happy unless you're stuffing food and drink into someone. I've sipped enough broths to float a holed lugger.' He grinned, and sunk back down as he grew slightly breathless. 'But thanks, that would be nice. Have you brought in something tasty to eat with you?'

'Some cherry cake, would you like some?'

'Please, and Evie, I'd like it if you joined me, and Smoky.'

'You make the best cherry cake, Evie,' Rob munched. His best pleasure at the moment was to have regained his sense of taste, but on reflection, it was having Evie sitting on a padded stool, up close to him. Gazing at her, she was lovely. She was watching him keenly for signs he needed help in any way. It was so good the way a man, when helpless, brought out the caring side in women. He hated being lain up but he was enjoying being cosseted. 'You make the best cherry cake I've eaten. Bet the vicar likes your cake. He's called on me twice, and he stuffed his face with Allie's sausage rolls each time. Seems a nice enough bloke, nothing holier than thou about him.'

Evie was alert in case Rob became uncomfortable or choked on a crumb. He had found swallowing difficult at the beginning of his recovery. Alison had got a terrible fright one time and been forced to pound on his back. Ever since then, every time he took a bite he followed it with a mouthful of tea. 'Mr Benedict called on us when my father was at home and they had a deep conversation about creation and the afterlife. Dad's impressed the cove has a vicar who embraces us Methodists. Everyone's looking forward to his Grand Tea Party and meeting his fiancée.'

'Not as much as he is, he talked a lot about Miss Bettany Howard-something. One of those hearty types, all horsey teeth, I reckon. Don't know if I believe in God and all that stuff, but I admit I've prayed at times when the sea and the wind seemed hell bent on breaching the boat. Now I've been through all this it's made me realize I've got to live my life more than ever.' He studied her for a moment. 'Wasn't expecting you to be here today. Bet Davey's not happy about it. He detests me. Does he know you're here?'

'Of course, Alison asked me in front of him last night, if I'd call in. Dad doesn't mind me doing a neighbour a kindness. And you detest Dad too.'

'He's a difficult man.'

'So are you. You were more easy-going back along. As bad as one another.'

'But I didn't stop Judy getting married, or Allie planning hers. Davey's selfish for wanting to deny you a husband and family. Don't you want children, Evie? Surely you do. You'd make a wonderful mother. If you were to fall in love, would you go against Davey's wishes?' Rob leaned towards her as far as he was able to. Evie had no idea how calculated and vindictive Davey could be.

Rob had known as a boy, about Davey and his war-dead lover, Cyrus, after witnessing them together. 'You can trust me to make Evie a good husband,' he had told Davey last year, when broaching him on his intention to court Evie. 'Your private life is your own business. I said nothing back then and I never will, if you don't stand in my way.' Davey's reaction had been anger, and soon afterwards, while the fleet was moored up at Newlyn, he had arranged for a seductive young prostitute to climb aboard *Our Lily,* while Rob was alone. Rob had gone with the girl and paid her. Davey had then gloated she was under age. Rob had discovered quite recently Davey had duped him and the girl was in her twenties and just looked very young. Rob had done nothing unlawful, as Davey had done with Cyrus. He wanted to keep Evie as his exclusive comforter and companion. Any man who tried to separate them would find himself in deep water.

'Dad wouldn't stand in my way if I was in love with someone he approved of,' Evie said stoutly in defence of her father, but she wasn't sure about it. After her mother, Iris's untimely death from pneumonia, Davey had always seemed determined to keep Evie to himself. He had offered Iris marriage as a kindly gesture, as a solution to her predicament of being left a pregnant outcast by Phil Tresaile. Davey and Iris had not had a conventional marriage. Iris had shared the largest bedroom with Evie. Grateful to Davey, and having a good secure life for herself and her daughter, whom Davey doted on, Iris had made Evie promise she would always put Mr Vage, as Iris had called Davey, first. Evie had been happy to go along with that, although part of her wanted what every other girl dreamed of. 'And of course I'd like to have children one day. There's still plenty of time. What will happen will happen. I'm happy with my life.' Before this, Evie would never probe into someone's life, but strangely she was finding Rob easy to talk to. 'What will you do now, if I may ask? I know Mr Praed is anxious for you to go back on *Our Lily*.'

Relinquishing his mug and plate, Rob lay back on the pillows but turned his face to Evie. He sighed. 'I've got to wait and see how strong this arm is going to be, but the doctor don't think it'll be too bad, in time. I've been thinking things through, how I'd feel to be back on the boat. Skipper of the *Sea Days* says I'm welcome there. Good of him, but it would mean working with my two brothers-in-law, Judy's husband and Bernie Crewes. Don't want that. Alfie's moving in here after the wedding, don't want us getting fed up with each other. He and Allie say they're in no hurry to get a place of their own. Allie doesn't want to leave me without a woman to look after me. I'd cope, of course, but I'm used to always having someone around. Family is everything, so that brings me back to working again with Uncle Lofty and my cousins. Be great to skipper my own boat. Been thinking a lot about that.' He sighed again. 'But do I want all the worry that goes with it? Raising the money, going into debt for it, getting a strong experienced crew together. I could sell the cottage but I wouldn't take the roof away from Allie.'

Evie felt a sense of warm satisfaction that he was sharing his deepest concerns with her. 'I understand all that. How would you feel about fishing with Douglas again?'

'Wouldn't be easy.' Darkness passed over Rob's taut eyes. 'I still want to throw him against a wall and beat the ruddy daylights out of him. He's been here twice begging me to forgive him.'

'What did you say to him?'

'Told him to go to hell, with plenty of choice words.'

'Forgiveness is a great release, Rob. It's a healing.'

'You would say that; sermon stuff.' He smiled to convey he wasn't mocking her.

'It's partly that, but my sister Beth could tell you all about forgiveness and giving up the idea for revenge. She's so happy to be reconciled with her mother. Turned out Mrs Vyvyan was a very nice woman; she's very nice to me. Douglas gave into weakness. It was wicked of him but he's not evil. Don't you believe he's truly sorry? He's been well and truly punished, Rob. The whole cove is against him. Even young Lily refuses to speak to him. If you don't accept him back into your life then Mr Praed's made it known Douglas won't be allowed back on *Our Lily*. All he does is mope about on his own every

94

day, apparently. Can't help feeling sorry for him really.'

'Can I have some water please?' Rob feigned a cough. He didn't want to feel sorry for Douglas, to let go of his anger and grudge, but he also didn't want Evie to see it in him and think less of him. He was enjoying having her here, to be talking personally this way with her. Before this she wouldn't have been remotely interested in anything he thought or had to say.

Evie filled his glass and passed it to him and replaced it on the little table after he'd taken a couple of sips. 'If Douglas is exiled for the rest of his life he might hurt himself. How would you feel then? I'm sorry.' She reddened and looked down. 'I went too far.'

'That's all right,' Rob said quickly, afraid she'd slip away. 'Say what you like. I don't mind, Evie. We're friends, aren't we?' When she kept quiet, pondering, he said, 'I know I've behaved very wrongly towards you in the past, but I'd like us to be friends. Can we?'

Evie bit her lower lip. She would like to be friends with him but she did not want him to ask her personal things, and she wasn't sure if she trusted him.

'You have my word I'll never do anything to compromise you. I won't set out to embarrass you again, I promise. Please Evie, say something please, your silence is killing me.'

'You promise?' she eyed him cautiously.

He closed his eyes and nodded, suddenly breathless. He was sweating and had his hand to his forehead.

All her concern for him returned to her in force. Alison kept a bowl of cold water and a flannel on the sideboard near the window. Evie wrung out the flannel, then sitting on the edge of the settee she gently brought Rob's hand down to his side and dabbed the wet flannel over his feverish face and neck then laid it over his brow. Throughout he kept his eyes on her and Evie was struck at how young and vulnerable he looked. 'You need to rest, Rob. And yes, we can be friends.'

Eight

'I didn't sleep a wink last night.'

'Nor did I. I didn't know how on earth to face you. You'd thought I was a friend to you, but I betrayed you by having an affair with your husband.'

'I should hate you, Beth, but I don't. Finding out Stuart was being unfaithful to me with you surprisingly didn't bother me all that much. He had turned into a dull husband, you know, a good husband, but so very dull. I suppose he presented himself differently to you. He thought he'd covered his tracks, but I knew what the extra sparkle in him meant when you were around. I was glad Stuart was having an affair. It gave me the perfect excuse to embark on one myself. When George Beaumont joined the tennis club and swept me off my feet I willingly succumbed to his charms. Sounds silly and infantile now. One doesn't realize how deadly and heartbreaking these things are, that there's no charm or beauty in secret affairs. You found out that too, didn't you? I did try to give George up. Both Stuart and I tried on that second honeymoon but it was hopeless. He was grieving his loss of you, and I couldn't get George out of my mind. George promised that as soon as we were settled I'd ask for joint custody of the children, but he was happy to live in hotels and flit from place to place. Then it dawned on me that he would eventually move on from me. I missed the children so much but he didn't even want to talk about them. I'd made a terrible mistake. George didn't turn a hair when I said I wanted to return to Wiltshire alone. I want my old life back, more than anything I want my children. You must believe me that I know I got exactly what I deserve. You must believe that too. Your mother deserted you, and you must believe I'm the worst mother in the world. I didn't have a cruel husband and mental reasons for abandoning my children.'

'I don't judge you at all, Connie,' Beth said, relaxing a little now the meeting with Stuart's wife was under way, and apparently, going ahead without recriminations and not too much awkwardness. They were in the lounge of the Edwardian, Grand Sea View Hotel, sitting beside the balcony windows, facing the perfect view of the headland reaching out defiantly into the sea and half forming the cove. In the old-fashioned plush environs Beth was struck by

97

how much Connie, once of dazzling beauty queen looks had aged since her failed adventure. She was faded, tired, wore little make-up, and was dressed matronly. A sackcloth and ashes look, Beth thought, and she was sad for the woman. 'I certainly can't take a superior position. If Stuart had left you for me then I would have been responsible for taking him away from his children. I feel terribly remorseful about that.'

'So we're on a level playing field.' Connie gave a brittle smile, and Beth tuned into the desperation which lay behind it. 'People say we can't help who we fall in love with, but perhaps we should. It didn't bring you or I any happiness. I'll never forgive myself for leaving Louis and Martha. You saw them last night. How are they? I hear Louis is not coping. Is he dreadfully unhappy, do you think?'

'He is unhappy, but hopefully the change of scene will help to distract him.' Beth sipped her coffee, now gone cold in the delicate cup. 'Connie, how do you think I can help you? I can assure you there is nothing left between Stuart and I. I told him so last night, and he accepted it. So your way is clear to approach him. You have my word I won't do anything to get in your way. It's entirely up to you and Stuart what you do. I hope all works out for you both and the children.' Beth had many doubts that, considering all their differences, Connie and Stuart would be able to make another go of their marriage. She hoped it wouldn't be too long before the whole family left Portcowl. If Kitty ever found out about the past she would be devastated and she would never forgive Beth's betrayal.

Opening her diamanté clasp clutch bag, Connie took out a handkerchief and dabbed at the moisture in her eyes. 'Thank you for all you've said, Beth. It's strange for us to be allies, sort of. My worry now is Kitty. She was so furious with me, she shouted at me that I was a bad mother and a ... a slut. She's always been so close to Stuart. She's overprotective of him and the children. There were times in my own home when I felt an outsider. Please Beth, I need you to keep Kitty out of the way. She's called me some horrid names over the past fifteen months. She'll probably try to keep Stuart and I apart. She was always very bossy with him. There were many times when she was there I felt ignored and left out in my own home. Stuart always listened to her rather than to me. I need the chance to explain everything to Stuart and tell him how sorry I am.'

'Yes, I see.' Beth believed Connie deserved every possibility to rebuild her marriage. She seemed utterly lost and remorseful, slumped and acutely lonely. 'He is rather weak.'

'He is and he isn't. He does hide behind his charm – the charm we both fell for. I believe if my marriage is ever to get back on the right track, then Stuart and I need to make decisions for ourselves, by ourselves. I admit if he'll take me back I'll agree to any terms. I still love him, perhaps we could rekindle our first passion, and I miss the children more than I thought possible. When do you think the best time will be for me to approach Stuart? Miss Marchant will be there, but we always got along very well, and I'm sure she'll think it's better for Louis and Martha if their parents were reconciled.'

'Whatever the outcome turns out to be I think you and Stuart certainly need to talk. I agree that your decisions about the future should be made jointly. As it happens, Stuart will be alone at the cottage this afternoon. Kitty is to fetch the children and Miss Marchant, to spend some time with her in the cove, and then afterwards for tea at Owles House with my brother Joe, and two of his friends. My sister Evie and I are to meet up with them in the cove. Stuart is planning a long walk across the cliffs. I'll give you the directions to Mor Penty. If you were to arrive there just after one o'clock you should catch him before he sets off.'

'That would be very helpful, thank you so much, Beth.' Connie brightened visibly and sat up straighter. 'If he allows, we could walk together. It's sometimes easier to talk seriously when outside and moving. I'll wear trousers and flats.'

'Be sure you wrap up very warmly,' Beth advised kindly. 'The winds can be particularly biting on the coast. You'll need something better than ordinary shoes. You'll find my walking boots in the cottage kitchen. I wish you good luck, Connie.' She ended with a smile.'

'Thank you, Beth, I can't thank you enough.' Connie returned the smile. 'You've heartened me. I'm going to fight with everything I've got to get my husband back. We've let our coffee get cold. Would you like some more, and something to eat? I'd like to hear all about the fishing cove. I've watched the boats come and go.'

Over fresh coffee and wafer-thin macaroons, Beth chatted to Connie like she would anyone else new to the area.

'It's easy to tell you love your new life here,' Connie said. 'So you have a new man in your life. What does he do? A local businessman?'

Regretting she had mentioned anything of the kind, Beth said the first thing that came into her mind. 'A small businessman, he's a freelance gardener.'

'That sounds rather romantic. Tell me about him? What's his name?'

Beth wasn't sure if Connie was being conversational or fishing for reassurance that she really had moved on from Stuart. This was getting tricky. 'His name is Mark, he's a widower, with a darling little girl. He's very, very quiet.'

'Good looking?'

'Yes.' Beth put on a dreamy gaze to show she was besotted with her beau. 'It's all very understated between us. Mark prefers it that way.'

'If all goes well I might get to meet him.'

I hope not, Beth thought, almost in panic. The only person Mark had room in his life for was Rowella. He'd be horrified she was talking about him like this. If he ever found out how on earth would she explain it? The reason she was even saying such a thing went back to her affair with Stuart. If Kitty found out about all this, she would lose her best friend forever. Her old deceit was new deceit.

Nine

Two hours ago Stuart Copeland had stared at his wife as if seeing a mirage.

Now he was staring up at the ceiling of his rented bedroom in Mor Penty wondering if he had just made the worst mistake of his life.

Connie was nestled against him, with her head on his bare shoulder and her naked limbs were wrapped around his. Both were flushed and panting after the burst of frantic love making.

How did he get from being desperately lonely, life-was-hardly-worth-living to this? Because he had some honour left, by falling into bed with Connie he had recommitted himself to her and their marriage. Would it be the right thing in the end? If he and Connie could not forgive each other's indiscretions, and accusations flew about: he was the first one to stray; she had actually deserted him and worse still the children – they could end up hating each other, and the children would be more unhappy and confused than before.

'Do you mind if I have a cigarette?' he asked politely. He badly needed the nicotine to soothe his mangled nerves.

'I'd like one too, please.' Connie sat up against the wooden headboard, pulling the eiderdown in under her armpits. Thankfully it was cool in the sea-facing room, a single guest room, for she was perspiring from the exertion and from fear. During the love making she had given Stuart her all, which was a lot more than he'd been used to getting from her, and she was scared he was sickened by the new tricks obviously taught to her by George Beaumont. It was one thing to admit equal blame where extramarital affairs were concerned, but something entirely different to bring flagrant practices into your former ordinary intimate life. Stuart might be thinking she was a tart, and not fit to resume being the mother to his children. Stuart was reaching for his cigarette case and lighter and she feared he was moving away from her in more ways than a physical one.

Sitting up beside her and sharing the eider-down, Stuart lit both cigarettes and passed one to Connie.

'Thank you,' she said very softly, hoping he noticed the humbleness in her tone.

Before taking a puff, Stuart stretched out his arm and grabbed his shirt flung down on the messed up covers. 'Here, put this round you, don't want you getting cold.'

The cigarette wobbling in her fingers, Connie burst into tears of wretchedness.

'Darling, what is it?' The endearment tripped easily of his tongue. He dropped the shirt round her shaking shoulders, swung both cigarettes over to the ashtray, and gently pulled Connie into his arms. 'There's no need to cry, what is it? Tell me, Connie.'

'It's you being caring,' she sniffed, burying her face against his bare neck, the place where she'd love to be in the old days. 'I don't deserve it. I did an unforgivable thing. You ended it with Beth, you didn't go ahead and leave me and Louis and Martha, but I took things further. I've disgraced you. Some people must pity you and you must hate that. People who don't like you must have taken the opportunity to crow over you, and that must have been humiliating. You must despise me and think me a whore, and now my affair has come to an end, you, you...'

'There you are then, Connie.' He lifted her face so they could see into each other's eyes. 'You can't say what I'm thinking because you don't know. Actually, I think you are a noble woman. You didn't speak out about Beth and I. You could have done so, tearing apart her friendship with Kitty and tarnishing her reputation. I don't despise you, Connie. I despise myself, for seeking love outside of us, for not making any real effort on our second honeymoon. I had an inkling you were seeing George, that you preferred him to me, and I thoroughly understood about you looking elsewhere after I'd strayed. That must have hurt you so much. I'm so sorry, Connie, for everything.'

'I'm so sorry for everything too, Stuart. I was so angry with Beth, of course, but I didn't want to hurt her. I understood about falling in love with someone you shouldn't. It's all so strange – Beth was very helpful to me today. I've asked her and she's agreed, to keep Kitty at bay so we get plenty of time to talk things through. Kitty finds me despicable and I'm sure she'll have a lot to say to me. But you and I need to talk everything through and decide what we do next. We've just made love, but don't let that hold you to anything, Stuart. We must be honest, totally honest with each other, for Louis and Martha's sakes, and our own. Don't you agree?'

'Let's get dressed, go downstairs for a brandy and talk beside the fire. Or would you prefer tea and sandwiches? Miss Marchant's left some ready prepared. I'll slip down first.'

Connie plumped for tea and sandwiches. Stuart smiled as he put the kettle on the hob of the range then carried the sandwiches into the sitting room. He knew he had smiled because Connie had been thoughtful. He had always said he was hungry after love making, and, thank God, it had only happened after he had been with Connie, so it made it unique to them. His body was still tingling where she had touched and kissed him. They had made love for the first time without inhibitions. That meant a lot to him. He had given a lot more loving to Beth, and obviously Connie had been more open with Beaumont, and when he and Connie had dragged each other upstairs and tore off each other's clothes in their terrible need there had been nothing inside them to hold back. So he had not made a mistake going too far with Connie, had he?

He had waved off the children, Kitty and Miss Marchant for their visit to the fishing village. His winter clothing and walking boots were on and the walking stick that he'd taken on many long and arduous treks round Britain and abroad was in his hand. 'You should have a dog with you,' Louis had whined. 'No one should go walking without a faithful dog at his side. I want a puppy. I can't see why you won't let Martha and I have one. I've promised I'll look after it and it won't be a bother to anyone, so you're mean to keep on saying no.'

'I'll think about it,' Stuart had sighed.

'You often say that and the answer is always no! It's not fair. Other kids have a dog. Joe Vyvyan's had one for years. Why not me?'

'Get in the car, Louis.' Stuart had raised his voice in exasperation. 'I said, I'll think about it.'

'I really think you ought to allow him to, Daddy.' Martha had tugged on Stuart's coat.

A photograph of Kitty and Grace, with Joe Vyvyan and Chaplin up on the rustic mantelpiece caught Stuart's eye. He had promised Louis often he would think about allowing him and Martha to have a puppy but Stuart had never done so. He just couldn't be bothered with a puppy and helping with its training, the inevitable puddles, and ripped-up slippers. He had not kept his promises and the thought hit him in the gut like a terrific gust of wind and he let out a groan. He had not kept his promise to his son ... or Connie, that he'd remain a faithful husband. He had loved his family but he'd soon put them in the background to his work and all else. He had promised all manner of romantic things to Beth for a happy future together, but the moment she became pregnant he'd taken fright, and Beth had seen through all his weaknesses and had cut him completely out of her life. He was as selfish as hell. How cheap it had been of him to actually ask, hiding behind Kitty, if he could stay in Beth's home! It was outrageous of him. He had placed Beth in a dreadful situation, and now because of his selfishness she was caught up in keeping another secret from Kitty, in this current meeting with Connie. What a heel, what a louse he was.

When he saw Connie coming hesitantly towards him, having stayed concealed behind some bushes until the car had disappeared down the road, he had hurried towards her, his heart in pieces. She had deliberately missed seeing the children so she must be here on some serious matter, perhaps to ask for a divorce. Then he had noticed how drawn and shy she was and his hopes to have all his crushing loneliness taken away had leapt into life. He had so missed Connie running his home and being mother to the children. He had missed her too, the Connie he had known at first, just lovely and good-natured, her hair and clothes fashionable but not painstakingly so, until she had tried to turn herself into a perfect, chic hostess, the sort of wife a man of high position should have. Their home had become a place where a cushion mustn't be out of place or a speck of dust to be seen. Pets were out of the question. They made a noise and a mess. He had gone along with everything Connie had wanted, not wanting to be bothered with anything domestic or how the children should be brought up. In time he had given Connie, Louis and Martha no particular thoughts. Everything

107

had become routine and predictable, and boring and unfulfilling. If he had not had an affair with Beth, the intriguing best friend of his sister, then he certainly would have done with someone else. He was a bastard and a complete shit.

Connie had turned up begging to be listened to, as penitent as a saint, hoping for a full reconciliation and return to family life, promising she would do anything he wanted, just to be given a second chance. His relief, the promise of release from some of his most pressing responsibilities had overwhelmed him. He was being offered more than Connie would get from him. He wanted things to be as they were before. Anything was better than this soul-sapping loneliness. Just how more bloody selfish could he get, he asked himself now. Connie had wept, and he had touched her to tell her she need not cry, and that touch had turned to them clutching each other for reassurance and had ended in lust. Connie had been vulnerable and wholly regretful, and he had exploited her body. At that moment he could not hate himself more.

He fell to his knees and cried and sobbed.

Connie reached him. 'It's all right, Stuart darling.' She hugged him in her arms. 'Everything will be all right, I promise.'

'I don't deserve you and I certainly don't deserve your promises, Connie darling. I'll be the one to put everything right. And that's one promise I swear I will keep.'

'What a grossly ugly woman, is it a woman?' The unremarkable-looking Miss Marchant, who was conscientiously dressed to combat the bracing coldness, as she had seen to it her two charges were, had quietly addressed Evie. With the rest of the party, they were on the quayside, watching the luggers preparing for the night's work. Evie had pointed out her father, hard at his task servicing the engines on *Morenwyn*. Davey had not acknowledged them; it wasn't his way. The sea had filled the little harbour, the water deep and green and a little choppy.

'That's Gabby Magor,' Evie replied in confidential tones about the person lumbering down towards them in hobnail boots, from a steep alley between the cottages. 'She's a bit of an outcast, I'm afraid, but it's her own fault really. She can be aggressive and sometimes rolls about drunk. The little dog with her is called Tickle. Strangely she dotes on him, before that she was always cruel to the different kinds of animals she's kept. Miss Copeland and Master Joe believe it was she who abandoned Grace in the woods. Since then Master Joe and his friends have furtively kept an eye on her place, up out of the cove in a lonely place.'

Miss Marchant pursed her lips. 'There should be a law against a woman dressing so obviously like a man. She seems quite filthy too. Does she not know how to wipe her nose?' The nanny frowned, going off down a different track. 'Doesn't she feel the cold? Do you think she can't afford a coat?'

'I've only ever known her to wear a woolly hat and scarf in winter,' Evie said. 'Her nose is bright red all year round. I suppose she's warm

109

enough.'

Beth and Kitty had also seen Gabby Magor approaching and had turned the children's heads to look out to sea. Gabby was rather a gruesome sight, and they didn't want the children to be scared, plus Gabby swore a lot, and if she was in a bad mood she might try to pick a quarrel. She had never forgiven Kitty and Joe for confronting her about abandoning Grace, and for trying to take Tickle away from her.

''Lo, Evie Vage, how are 'ee this chilly af'noon then?' Gabby blurted out from several huge granite slabs away on the quay.

'I'm very well, thank you, Miss Magor,' Evie answered nicely. 'And how are you, and Tickle?'

'Can see for yourself, can't 'ee?' Gabby searched out a dirty rag from her pair of rough, ancient man's trousers and blew her nose vociferously and not cleanly, making Evie and Miss Marchant inwardly cringe. 'Tickle's in fine fettle. I love him and he loves me, and *no one*,' she stabbed an angry look at Kitty, 'can part us, 'less they want their bleddy heads bashed in. How's your neighbour, Rob Praed? Going on all right, is he?'

Beth looked closely at Evie for her response. After Evie's loathing of Rob's undesirable ways, Beth had the uncomfortable feeling that, since his injury, Evie was warming to him. Beth hoped she was wrong, a situation like that could lead to all sorts of problems for Evie.

'He's making a good recovery. Everyone in the cove is pleased about that.' Evie's reply was bland. She was trying to be careful about everything concerning Rob, especially her growing attraction to him. She enjoyed being with him. She was able to talk to him as easily as she did to Alison, Judy and Beth.

''S'e going back on *Our Lily*? Even after what his bleddy rotten cousin did to him?' Gabby asked charily, as if she wanted to make a fight of it on Rob's behalf.

'I don't know anything about that, Miss Magor,' Evie said then looked down, hoping Gabby would take the hint and move on. It wasn't a wise thing to ask her to excuse you. She would probably see it as a dismissal and take offence. Actually Evie knew from Rob that he had decided his best course for the future was to return to fish again off *Our Lily*. He was going to allow Douglas to work on the boat too, but Rob would be wary of him for safety's sake, and keep his distance in every other way. Evie admired Rob for his decisions.

'Who's she with you then? And who's them kids with those two stuck-up mares?' Gabby demanded.

'The children are the nephew and niece of Miss Copeland, and this is Miss Marchant, the children's nanny.'

'Oh yes, her brother's staying at Mor Penty. Nice looking little maid, though that boy's a bit sickly. Don't you b'lieve in feeding him up, missus? Be charged with cruelty next. People like to 'cuse innocent people of cruelty round here.'

All four women were hoping Gabby Magor would push off.

111

Tickle made the decision to leave by scampering off back up the narrow cobbled alley. Gabby grunted as way of a goodbye, and with her hands stuffed in her pockets plodded after him.

'Ghastly soul.' Miss Marchant faced the sea to expel Gabby Magor's mouldering stench out of her nose.

Everyone shuffled about. 'I'm getting really cold, Aunt Kitty,' Martha moaned.

'It's time for us to go to the tea shop for hot drinks and fancies and to get warm,' Kitty said gaily.

The party moved off towards the Sailor's Rest, the tea shop was located past the pub by a short climb into the little square. Suddenly Miss Marchant cried, 'Where's Master Louis? I can't see him anywhere!'

'He was beside me a moment ago. How could he have slipped away so quickly?' Kitty exclaimed.

'Oh, dear Lord, he might have gone back to the edge of the quay and slipped into the water,' Miss Marchant wailed in fear and horror.

The four women stepped off several yards in different directions, Martha clinging to Kitty's hand, all shouting shrilly for Louis.

They were about to make a wider search for him when, after long agonizing seconds, he came running past the pub towards them. 'Sorry about that, I got lost for a minute,' he apologized heartily.

Only Martha could tell that he wasn't at all sorry and that for once her sneaky brother did not have something to grumble about.

Ten

Joe and Richard Opie were whizzing along the lanes on their bicycles to the vicarage. Lily Praed was perched on Joe's crossbar and enjoying the speed and slight risk. If Joe wobbled she might be pitched off and hurt, but the scrap of a nine-year-old was almost fearless, and she totally trusted Joe's sharp mind and abilities. On the front of each bicycle was a basket packed high with a bag of small items, ready wrapped, for the bran tub, for the vicar's Grand Tea Party.

'What a way to spend a Saturday afternoon,' Richard had grumbled, after arriving with Joe at Owles House following a meeting of their school athletic club. Lily had been there, having helped Mrs Vyvyan wrap the last of the little parcels. Once they had been plied with sandwiches and hot chocolate, the trio had been sent off on the delivery. 'Be glad when this stupid tea party's over and done with. It's all my mother and sister talk about. One good thing has come out of it, though. Claire has stopped swooning about. She's even dropped her horrid friends, and she doesn't go on about her hair, nails and clothes all the time. The staff at the hotel like her now, it was embarrassing the way they used to whisper about her.'

113

'Don't you want to see inside the vicarage, specially now it's all been done up?' Lily had said, in a chirruping voice that was designed, and never failed to annoy stocky, ginger-haired Richard. 'And meet Miss Howard-Leigh? She's a real lady, so don't forget we got to bow and curtsey.'

'Huh! Don't be stupid, and I don't bow to anyone,' Richard scoffed, the redness of his face highlighting his freckles. ''Cept the King and Queen, of course, and I'm not likely to meet them. She's only minor gentry. My mother says she's not pretty or elegant, despite having a personal maid and the latest clothes. She's all teeth and far-flung smiles, and has to be told everything twice. Mother can't see what the vicar sees in her.'

'Ah-ah, see, you like passing on gossip so you will be interested in the vicarage, and its new lady.' Lily proudly fingered the glass bead necklace, taken from the bran tub prizes, that Mrs Vyvyan had given to her for helping, then tagged on piously, 'That was an unkind thing your mother said, even if it's true. I shall see for myself what Miss Howard-Leigh looks like.'

'Shut your trap,' Richard snarled at her. 'Or I'll dump you in a bloody hedge.'

As always, during these frequent spats, Joe endured it patiently, unless he felt Richard went too far.

It wasn't far to the vicarage, which was set back from the church, and on the quick journey much was flashing through Joe's mind. Mainly Kitty's shock and hostile reaction to her brother suddenly turning up at Owles House with his wife, and her subsequent cold behaviour; so out of character for Kitty. Despite Mrs Copeland's sheepishness and apologies, and her emotional delight of her children running to her and clinging to her, Kitty had shrieked, 'Stuart! How could you? You must be mad.' Then she had stormed out of the sitting room.

Louis and Martha had not cared one bit about their aunt's negative response, they had been too happy to see their parents happily together again, to have their misery lifted and security returned. Louis had changed as if touched by magic. His posture had become straight, healthy colour flooded his face and all traces of anxiety and scowl had vanished. Beth had been pleased about the situation. She had even kissed Mrs Copeland's cheeks, and told her, 'I'm so glad for you all.' Mr Copeland had gone to Kitty, who had rushed to the kitchen, and tried to explain that the reconciliation was what he wanted more than anything, but he'd come back saying Kitty could not be reasoned with.

'Oh well, we all need time to adjust,' Mr Copeland had said, ruefully glancing towards the kitchen. 'I hope everyone will understand that Connie and I and the children need time to be just a family again. We'd like to stay on in the cottage for a while, if that's agreeable to you, Beth, neutral ground and all that. We shan't go out much, will keep ourselves to ourselves.'

'Of course,' Beth replied. To Joe's mind, Beth had seemed mightily relieved, as Joe was, not to be lumbered with two needy children, one an irritating whinger.

'We'd be glad to see you all any time at Mor Penty, of course,' Mr Copeland had said. 'Tell Kitty for us please. She will have to understand, however, that no matter what she feels about it, I have to put my family first.'

'I'll speak to her. I'm sure everything will be all right,' Beth had said, but she was biting her bottom lip.

'Right children,' Miss Marchant said, 'We'll gather our coats and woollens.' The nanny had appeared delighted with the occurrence. She and Mrs Copeland had shaken hands before going out to the hall.

Before the leave takers had gone, Louis had achieved the promise from both parents that he and Martha could have a dog. 'As soon as we get home in Wiltshire,' Mr Copeland had yielded gaily. 'You can each have a puppy, pedigrees.'

In the time between then and now, Kitty had resolutely refused to go to Mor Penty. Joe was disappointed at her obstinacy. It was unkind of her, and hinted of jealousy over her brother not needing her support any more.

'It doesn't make sense,' Joe had mentioned to Beth. 'It's understandable Kitty might have reservations, but I'd have thought she would have been pleased. Mrs Copeland came across as sincerely sorry. Marriage and family life are important. Mr Copeland doesn't seem full of recriminations and he and the children are happy. I'd have thought that should be enough for Kitty, her nephew and niece having both their parents together. I wish my father hadn't died. It

116

would be heaven to have both my parents.'

'I agree with you, Joe but it's best not to say anything to Kitty.' Beth had smiled but Joe had seen doubt in the smile. 'Hopefully she'll come round in time.'

'We're there!' Lily cheeped merrily, bringing Joe out of his reverie.

The boys cycled past the new conservatory and went round to the back of the vicarage and stopped at the French windows, outside the room next to the dining room, where they had been asked to go. The parlour maid, Winifred, trim in a straight black dress, starched white apron and frilled cap, opened the windows and beckoned them inside. 'The Reverend Benedict is busy in his study, but I'm to take you through to Miss Howard-Leigh.'

The children followed Winifred through the room out into a long passage towards the dining room. Impressed by the modern, light decorating, the latest in geometric pictures and square lines of furniture, Lily glanced up at Richard to show her awed expression. He shrugged his shoulders. Lily's short legs left her behind but Richard reached back and dragged her into line. Despite his frequent protests about having too much of the 'little pest's irritating company' Lily was one of the gang. His protectiveness of Lily made Joe smile wryly.

'Master Joseph Vyvyan and friends, madam,' Winifred announced.

'Thank you,' Bettany Howard-Leigh replied, her voice clear and top-drawer. 'I think this jolly trio of helpers would appreciate some warm

117

milk and biscuits in a few minutes, in the kitchen.'

'Yes, madam.'

'It's splendid of you all to bring the items for the bran tub. Well, Master Joseph, you must introduce me to your friends, and then you all must tell me what you think about the arrangements made so far for the tea party. Early this morning Mr Benedict was helped by Mr Tresaile from the public house and the gardener Reseigh to place the tables and chairs in position. Over there in the corner is the tub, decorated and ready for the bran and little parcels to go in.' Bettany Howard-Leigh was thin in body and seemed unbending, but her rounded face and large blue, slightly slanting eyes made her look quite fetching. She wasn't fussy in dress and wore a simple long cardigan and a plain over-blouse and matching pleated skirt. A short row of blue beads was round her elegant neck. Pinned on her blouse was a brooch of a man and woman in evening dress, dancing. Her brown hair was lightly waved and flat over her scalp. Joe felt she wasn't as at ease as expected for a lady of means, leisure and excellent expectations.

'So you're Mr and Mrs Opie's son?' she addressed Richard. Bettany was ill at ease. She knew little about children and was never comfortable with them. The three before her were obviously bright-minded and capable, and she found them a little intimidating. It was silly, and she was cross with herself for feeling this way. She was the adult and superior here. 'You bear resemblance to your father, but you're not at all like your sister Claire.' Then to Lily, whose natural untidiness, although dressed in a good coat and clean boots, and new knitted pixie-style hat, scarf and gloves, made her seem rather like a little savage; she would undoubtedly be impertinent and nosy. 'And you're Lily Praed, and the sweetheart of the village, by all accounts.'

Lily responded to Bettany's extensive smile by curtseying. 'Yes, my lady. My father's a fisherman. Us Praeds are one of the oldest families in Portcowl.'

'Really? How fascinating.' Bettany was praying Winifred would soon return to take this lot to the kitchen. Why on earth had she offered these children hospitality? She should have thanked them and sent them on their way. Jacob should be here, but he had been called away to the telephone to speak to the archdeacon. Bettany only felt poised when with her own set and unassuming people like Christina Vyvyan and Claire Opie. If she had known that her first time here would coincide with one of Jacob's events, she would have postponed. He had taken it for granted she would be happy to pitch in, but she had not even got the bearings of the vicarage yet let alone the parish – this lowly parish.

'Everything looks fine,' Joe said, running his eyes over the white damask tablecloths. There was nothing else to say, there was nothing else to see.

Richard sighed. He was bored. If Miss Howard-Leigh had actually *offered* the warm drinks and biscuits, he would have declined. The

119

trouble with her sort of people was that they just assumed, and he was offended about being sent to the kitchen. He wasn't a beggar.

Lily piped up, 'You look lovely, my lady. I like your brooch.'

'Really, dear?' Bettany's eyelids fluttered wildly and she stared at the girl. 'You shouldn't address me as my lady, but as Miss Howard-Leigh. Well? I'll ring for you to be shown to the kitchens.'

The boys pushed their bikes out through the vicarage gates, with Lily trotting after them like a dutiful puppy. 'It was lovely, the cook putting honey in the hot milk. Her biscuits are made with real butter too, did you hear her say so?'

The boys ignored her.

'This wretched party is going to be horribly twee. It's for grown-ups and little kids.' Richard scowled, with disgust.

'You won't be as glad as Miss H-L, from what I saw of her,' Joe said.

Bettany retreated to her bedroom and took out her journal. *When I agreed to marry Jacob I knew I would have to become involved with some of his parishioners, but I did not allow for dealing with parishioners' children. I thought, as his wife, I would dine with the local ladies, but there are few ladies here. Fund raising is a must, of course, but I did not expect to have to get involved beyond committee level.*

Her pen dashed across the pages with more negative comments concerning her bridal future.

Eleven

Running her fingers down the folds of her satiny sea-blue bridesmaid dress, Evie turned from side to side and stood up on tiptoe to try to gain a full view of herself. She had just sewed the lace she had made over the bodice, and was trying on the dress. Tomorrow the dress would hang in Alison's bedroom until her wedding day, where all the wedding party would get ready. Her father was out at sea, but she wouldn't have shown him the dress anyway. He wasn't interested in Alison's wedding and did not intend to go, even to the chapel. For a moment Evie wondered what it would be like to be a bride herself, making all the preparations, and looking forward to lying in the arms of a new husband and making love. With the right man the supreme intimacy would be wonderful, she was sure.

She heard someone come in the back door. 'Hello, Evie! You in the front room?'

It was Rob. She couldn't be more pleased. Thrilled was a better word, for delicious feathery sensations were slinking up and down her back. 'No, I'm up here, trying on my bridesmaid dress. Give me a moment to change.'

'Don't do that,' Rob called, at the foot of the stairs. 'Let me see you in it.'

'Oh, I don't know if I should.'

'It's not bad luck for the bride's brother to see anything before the big day. Don't be shy.'

I'm not shy with you, Rob, Evie thought, ecstatic at her confidence. More than anything she wanted Rob to see her dressed in something beautiful. 'Be just a mo.'

Kicking off her flat shoes she put on her high heels and made a quick tidy up to her hair. With her palm over her rapidly beating heart, she made herself walk slowly to the top of the stairs, and halted there and looked down on Rob, and smiled.

'Wow.' His eyes glowed large in his strong face in distinct male appreciation. He stretched up his hand. 'Come to me.'

Evie floated down the stairs, putting her hand into Rob's hand and he supported her down the last three steps. He held on to her hand, firmly.

'You look stunning, Evie, you're beautiful, like something out of sea myths. I'm going to dance nearly every dance with you at the reception and I don't care what anyone thinks, especially Davey.'

His mood was so buoyant and sparkling, Evie laughed. 'And you'll look handsome in your suit.' Then common sense prevailed. 'Rob, this is the first time you've been out. You'd better sit down. Is everything all right?'

'I'm stronger now, will soon be my old self. In fact this is the second time I've been out today. I walked with Alison along the quay and had a few words with all the crews. Davey ignored me, of course. I'll go mad stuck in the house.

122

Alison's gone to Alfie's for supper. She's left me something to eat, but what I really need is company. You don't mind, do you, Evie?'

'Not at all.'

'And I wanted to give you this.' Rob picked up something he had dropped on the table, a large box of chocolates, with a picture of a country rose-covered cottage on the lid. 'To thank you for all you've done for me. My recovery would have been a lot more miserable without you popping in.'

'You didn't have to do that, Rob,' Evie whispered, staggered by the gift. She had never thought to receive such a grand gesture, an expensive and meaningful one too. 'But thank you very much.'

'I wanted to see that lovely amazed expression you take on at times, just like now. You'll have to keep the box a secret from Davey.'

'I'll keep it in my room. Dad never goes in it. I really ought to get out of this dress.'

'Does that mean you want me to go?'

'Not in the least, stay and chat. You get settled. Just give me a few moments and I'll be straight back down.'

'Fine,' Rob smiled with genuine warmth. 'I enjoy talking with you, being with you, and Evie, you really do look gorgeous.'

Slipping up to her room, Evie's heart was thudding like heavy waves while she undid every tiny satin button of the dress and laid it carefully over the foot stead of her bed. Hastily, she pulled on the clothes she had worn before, but she kept on the high heels, they made her legs look longer and shapelier. She wanted Rob to see her at her best. If she had any make-up she would have dashed on a little, but her reflection in the looking glass literally shone back at her. Taking a deep breath, darting her fists about in frenzied glee, she took the stairs down quite sedately.

Rob's eyes were on her, from were he was sitting in the middle of the couch.

'Would you like some—?'

'I only want you to come and sit beside me.' Rob patted the spot.

Evie did so, turned to face him.

'There's no need for us to dance all round the quay, is there, Evie?' There was a low huskiness in his tone. 'I'm not mistaken in saying that we've grown very close, am I.'

'You're not mistaken at all, Rob.' Her whole being was on fire at his words, words she had wanted to hear more than anything. She should be floating up to the clouds but there was an immovable obstacle to them going on from here. 'But...'

'No buts, darling, I know it's Davey you're thinking about. Right now I want to kiss you and I know you want it too, and we mustn't deny ourselves.'

Evie's arms went to him at the same moment he drew her tightly into his arms, their eyes closing. Their lips touched in the sweetest intense sensation. 'I love you, Evie,' he murmured, taking her lips again. 'You're mine, mine.'

Evie kissed him and held on to his powerful body, giving to him, being melted into him. It was so right. She shivered in rapture as he kissed her behind her ears, and she shuddered when he caressed her back, arms and throat with the backs of his fingers. 'I love you too, Rob. I never thought I would. It's happened. I couldn't help it.'

They let the kissing and loving go on and on. Then, with Evie resting her head in the hollow of his neck, they tightly held hands. 'We must be together, Evie, darling. We deserve to be. We can't allow our love to be for nothing. You have the right to find happiness, to get married and raise a family. It would be rotten and selfish of Davey to refuse you this, even though the man you love happens to be me. The accident has changed me. I know what's really important now, but I know I'll never be able to convince Davey it's true. But Davey wouldn't want you marrying anyone ever. I don't want to hide my feelings for you, to skulk about behind Davey's back. Will you be brave and confront him, Evie? You're old enough to do whatever you want. I know your mother made you promise to always take care of Davey but she would also have wanted your happiness too, I'm sure. If we marry, Davey will have to accept it. You're not afraid of your love for me, are you?'

'Of course not, never Rob,' she replied emphatically, gently touching his face. 'Don't ever believe that.'

'Or afraid of your father's reaction?'

'It won't be easy, but that's all, darling.'

'You mustn't let him talk you round, Evie. You might spend the rest of your life in misery if you don't follow your heart. What would be the point in that? And we'd find it unbearable seeing each other nearly every day knowing we can't be together.'

'I'll speak to Father as soon as he's home and rested. The only way to get through what lies ahead is to speak up and get it out in the open. You'd better not come round here tomorrow, Rob. I'll join you and let you know what he says.'

'I thought there was something different about you the moment I came through the door,' Davey muttered grimly. After a poor night's fishing, he had breakfasted, and warm in his fireside chair with a lit pipe, he had listened without interrupting Evie's 'something serious to tell you'.

'Are you angry with me, Dad?' Evie asked sitting opposite him, leaning forward, pulling at her skirt with taut fingers, her cheeks flushed red with anxiety. 'I haven't done anything underhand.'

'I know *you* wouldn't.' Clipped tones. Sigh like a cold blast of air. A long stony silence.

Evie waited for him, her insides in pieces. It had been surprisingly easy to spill out the speech she had rehearsed all through the sleepless night.

Davey dropped his pipe down in the fender. 'Will you go ahead whatever I say?'

'I'd hate to do anything without your blessing, you know that, Dad. I'll always be devoted to you, but I really want to marry Rob. I love him, and I know he loves me too, totally.' Evie begged with pleading hands. 'I trust him, Dad. I know he'll be good to me.'

'Everyone must be good to you or they'll have me to deal with,' he said gruffly, his weathered features set like granite. He entered another forbidding silence, his eyes staring at the floor, and it seemed to Evie the minutes of eternity were dragging by.

Although she was beside the warm range, Evie felt cold. She kept a small crochet shawl over the back of her chair and she put it round her shoulders and huddled up, feeling young and small and lost. Soon her eyes would spill bleak tears. Her father was thinking of ways to crush her dream.

At last Davey lifted his head. To Evie it was as if a cold bleak winter had passed and she was about to face another that would last all her life. 'Dad?'

'I understand you wanting to marry and have a family, Evie.'

'But?' She could barely speak from the disappointment at his coming objections. It would take the shine off her life if her marriage meant she and her father would end up estranged.

'It's a mystery and a trouble to me that you've chosen Rob Praed. There's many fine men hereabouts, sea and wind above him in morals. But if you must have him, as you said, you'll only be next door. I'll be able to keep a weather eye on you, and if that man as much as raises his voice to you, he can expect hell and high water from me.'

'You mean you're willing to accept Rob and I

getting married?'

'Evie, I hope you don't believe I've been, or ever would be cruel to you. I've held out against you leaving home for whatever reason because I wanted you to be absolutely sure it's what you wanted. I promised Iris that very thing. Both of us had witnessed too many heartbreaks and we didn't want that for you.'

Evie was up on her feet and hugging his neck. 'Oh Dad, I can't believe it. Thank you so much. I'll pop in every day to see to your meals and you can come round to us. I can't wait to tell Rob, and then Beth. She'll be as shocked as much as she was when Miss Copeland's brother was suddenly reunited with his wife.'

Davey hugged Evie then held her away from him. 'Will you allow an old man to make plans for you? I'd like you to wear my mother's engagement ring, as your mother did the day she accepted my proposal of marriage. Iris would have wanted you to have a nice wedding, fine dresses, flowers and everything. I'll be proud to walk you on my arm down the chapel aisle. I'd like a spring wedding. Give us time to plan it properly.'

'So I have your blessing, Dad?'

'You do. Now, after all this your father's throat is parched as sand. Put the kettle on, my handsome.'

Evie hummed happily as she set about making fresh tea.

Davey relit his pipe. He had spoken the truth about wanting her to be sure she knew what she really wanted out of life. Evie could make her plans but she would never become wife to Rob Praed, not him. Davey was unconvinced Praed was a changed man, and the braggart knew about Davey and his lover Cyrus. Once Evie became Praed's wife he might feel it right to tell her, and Davey couldn't bear the thought that Evie might look at him in horror and disgust. This wedding was not going to happen.

Twelve

'We're on our way to lunch. Can't you two cheer up a bit?' Christina addressed Beth and Kitty. Beth was driving them to Mor Penty. Kitty was in the back of the car with the dogs.

Receiving nothing more than glum expressions, Christina rebuked them. 'I don't understand why either of you are against the happy news you've received. Kitty, your brother has his wife back with him, and he and his children seem so happy. And you, Beth, have a sister who has just delightedly announced her engagement. I understand that you both have reservations in each case, but that shouldn't stop either of you supporting your respective brother and sister's wishes. You certainly shouldn't be so openly opposed to their new-found happiness.'

'I don't trust Rob Praed, Mum,' Beth said, carefully watching the bending roads as she drove but skidding a little towards a ditch. She

129

sighed irritably. 'He's not good enough for Evie. He'll break her heart. Evie's had her head turned by a handsome face and false promises. All she will have ahead of her is being torn between him and her miserable father. I can't see Davey letting go of the stranglehold he has on her. I'd be thrilled if Evie was marrying anyone else, someone kinder, without stubborn pride, and with her living further away from her grasping father.'

'And I don't trust Connie one bit.' Kitty's cheeks burned with resentment. 'Her lover ran out on her and she's come running back to Stuart. She's using Stuart because she's feeling rejected and lonely. The moment things don't suit her she'll be off again, and Stuart and the children will be left even more upset than before. You advised me to give her every chance, Beth. Well, now you understand how I feel.'

Beth saw in the rear view mirror Kitty dart her a thorny look. 'I thought she seemed sincere, that it was worth giving her the benefit of the doubt,' Beth said defending herself. 'It's different where Stuart is concerned. He was already married and was struggling with two young children. We all saw how ecstatic Louis and Martha were when they saw Connie. There seemed to be no strain at all between Stuart and Connie. From what we can tell, everything seems to be working out well.'

'The point is—'

'That Mr Copeland and Evie are adults and should be allowed to make their own decisions and their own mistakes, as we all are. It's really no one else's business,' Christina said firmly. 'If the pair of you go on showing your disapproval you'll drive a very unwelcome wedge between yourselves and those you're worried about. Your duty is to support them, and if things do go wrong to be there for them to help pick up the pieces. Now, Kitty, Stuart and Connie have extended an eager invitation to all of us to spend the day with them, but to you in particular. I'm sure they will have gone to a lot of trouble to make everything perfect. They're probably very nervous. The least you can do is make an effort to seem pleased for them, don't you think? To put them at ease.'

'I suppose so,' Kitty muttered, not brought to feel guilty, as was Christina's intention.

'And you, Beth, shouldn't be scathing about Evie's engagement. Evie is a sensible girl, and her love and happiness shone out of her. She trusts Rob and she should be allowed to happily plan her future like any other bride-to-be. No more moping about it. Do you want to bring her down?'

'Of course not, Mum.' Beth did feel bad about her lukewarm response when Evie had excitedly brought her the news. 'I'll see her tomorrow. I'll take her shopping and buy her something for her bottom drawer. But I'd like a private word with Rob. I'll do all I can to make things special for Evie, but I'll be watching Rob very keenly, and if I get the chance I'll warn him not to hurt her.'

'Fair enough,' Christina replied, relaxing in the strongly upholstered seat. 'Now let's enjoy the day. The weather's calm and the sun's warm, it's a great occasion for lots of fun with the children and the dogs.'

Stuart and Connie met the car hand in hand, and wearing big smiles and layers of casual clothes. Louis and Martha were also bright, and giggly and excited, their coats, hats, scarves and rubber boots on, and ready with buckets, spades and beach balls.

'Auntie Kitty!' Martha squealed. 'Come and see our sandcastle. It's huge, bigger and better than any other in the whole world.'

'So I can see from here.' Kitty laughed, as she and the dogs spilled out of the car.

'We've got a camp.' Louis jumped up and down. 'Come and see. Daddy helped us build it, back where the tide can't reach it. Mummy's given us heaps of stuff to make it like a real camp. Come and see it. Mummy said she'll bring out drinks and eats to us.'

'Did she?' Kitty turned her eyes on Connie, and saw with satisfaction how her sister-in-law shrunk back a little from her. *Good, madam, that you're not completely sure of yourself. Make sure you try hard for Stuart's sake.* 'I'll come with you right away.'

Beth and Connie carried the wicker picnic hamper to the campers. 'Everything is obviously going well,' Beth said, with pleasure.

'Couldn't be better. It's funny, that you and I should be on the same side. I'll be eternally grateful to you, Beth. Stuart and I have a proper partnership again. The break up was horribly painful but that's now in the past. Hopefully, Kitty will come round in time. She was rather spoiled by her parents and by Stuart. She must have felt I came between her and her doting big brother. I think she resented me from the start. Her sunny nature never really extended to me. It was one thing Stuart and I used to quarrel about, but never mind. Louis is back to his old self. Kitty should be glad about that.' Connie gave Beth a sideways glance. 'You and I had better not seem too friendly or Kitty will get jealous. I don't know why she doesn't look for a husband.'

'Kitty is happy to go along with fate,' Beth said. 'It would be good for her to fall in love.'

'It would make her see things differently, that husbands and wives have trials along the way. So what about your love life, Beth? Are things progressing with your romance with the fine-looking Mark Reseigh? I saw him in the cove the other day, with his daughter. Stuart and I introduced ourselves. He was very polite, but as you said, he was very quiet. He's so proud of Rowella. She's a lovely child. I can see why you would fall in love with her. You and Mark come from different backgrounds. Do you really mean anything to each other? If I may say so, you don't seem very enthusiastic about getting married and settling down. Did Stuart hurt you so very badly at the end of your affair? I've heard Mark Reseigh has never come to terms with losing his wife. Have you both got some sort of understanding that will go nowhere to avoid seeking anything deep and lasting?'

Beth didn't know what to say. She had noticed Mark a lot more since her lies about him to Connie. She had not spoken to him much in the past, respecting his introvert nature, but she had taken to drawing out conversations with him.

'Mornin', ladies. Nice bit of weather, eh?'

Startled, Beth and Connie nearly dropped the hamper. 'Gabby Magor,' Beth blurted crossly. 'What are you doing here?'

'Free country, ain't it?' Gabby bristled, screwing up her ugly, dirty face. She had a gone-out, rolled-up cigarette dangling on her bottom lip. She spat it out. Tickle was in the distance running towards the ebbing tide, and loud barking announced Chaplin and Grace were running to join him. 'This beach isn't private, never has been. I don't go on your land Miss High 'n' Mighty, so don't be so bleddy rude. Weren't you brung up to show respect to your elders? Well? Speak up, don't stand there with your gob open wide's a bleddy drawbridge.'

'Good morning, Miss Magor. How are you?' Beth said tightly and insincerely.

'Seen better days, some worse. This your friend's sister-in-law then. Mornin' missus. Heard you was staying at the Grand Sea View under the name Mrs Smithson. Very fishy, I thought. So he took you back then?'

'It's none of your business,' Beth belted out. 'We can't stop you being here but I'd like you to move away and stop bothering us.'

Gabby gave the most chilling leer, pulling back her lips and showing the blackened stumps of her teeth. 'Don't want your bleddy company anyway, toffee-nosed bitches.' Performing a lewd gesture, she slouched over the sand for the shore.

Peeping out from the canvas flap of his camp, Louis's tummy hit his feet to see the lumbering spectacle of Gabby Magor assailing his mother and 'Auntie' Beth. Was the smelly misfit telling his mother about the brief request he had made to her in the cove when he'd run off? Apparently not, as a minute or two later nothing was said when his mother arrived with the food and drink.

Gabby leered to herself all the way to Tickle and hung about throwing sticks for him, and Chaplin and Grace to chase. She had followed Beth and Connie for some time before revealing her presence to them only after she had over-heard all they had said.

Later in the day, Louis was the last to leave the camp, the others having drifted indoors a good while ago. He was on his hands and knees about to crawl out on the sand but shrieked when an unsightly face pushed into the canvas flap opening.

'Hello, my 'andsome. Don't be 'fraid, it's only me. Got good news for you about that puppy you asked me for. Be one ready to leave its mother on Sunday. Bit like your aunt's dog, it is, a little male. Sweet as honey, it is. I'll bring it to the beach in the morning and leave it to run about, and you can find it and your parents' will have to let you have it. Now, just tell me where you're going to leave that thirty bob.'

'B–but I don't need a stray puppy now, M–Miss Magor. My parents are getting my sister and I one each, when we go home.' Louis crawl-ed backwards further into the camp to get away from the woman's beastly smells and because he was afraid of her. Tickle squirmed inside past her heaving bulk and flew at his face, licking him madly. He tried to grab the excited little furry body but Tickle was too wriggly and suddenly Louis was flat on his back with the dog on his chest, licking him all over face.

Gabby pulled Tickle back with one giant-sized filthy hand. 'Don't want it! That's no bleddy good to me. I've paid for it, ten bob. I still want that, and a quid for my trouble, brat like you can afford it.'

'I–I'll still give you the money. I swear!'

'When?' Gabby bawled. 'Don't you dare try to pull one over on me, not 'less you want me to come here all quiet-like and push your mother and father off the cliffs and make you an orphan.'

'There's no need for that,' Louis pleaded. 'Look, take my penknife for now. I'll say I lost it. I'll have the money at the tea party thing. I could give it to you then.' The last thing he wanted was for this old witch to turn up here again, when she might carry out her threat.

'Mmmm, lemme think. Wasn't planning on going to that ... but it might be fun. You have a deal Master Louis. You can slip me the money then. Don't try no silly tricks. Be seeing you.'

Gabby shunted herself out of the camp and away, leaving Louis to cough and choke on her putrid smells and fretting over her menace.

Thirteen

Mark Reseigh was the first to arrive at the vicarage on the day of the Grand Tea Party. As previously arranged, he put up staves and ropes either side along the drive to prevent people wandering off in the grounds. He stationed brightly painted arty posters at the points outside, ordered fussily by Mrs Opie, and the same inside the house. The Opies arrived, and Mrs Opie oversaw Winifred placing the small tubular white china vases of dried flowers, prepared by Mrs Opie the day before, on the tea tables. Miss Howard-Leigh offered to help but was in fact just twittering about, giggling nervously and apologizing. Mark tipped the sack of bran, a bit at a time, into the tub, an old beer barrel, while Claire dropped in the wrapped prizes to be covered up.

She had gazed down at the bran, taking on a childlike wonder. 'It looked so ordinary before but now it's taking on that sense of magic and anticipation one gets when a gift is wrapped, don't you agree, Mr Reseigh?'

Thinking how like Rowella she was when his daughter was about to receive a treat, Mark nodded. 'The kids will line up to take a lucky dip before you can say nine pence.'

'Your dear little girl too, no doubt.' Claire glanced down at the polished floor.

Mark knew his reticence to openly socialize made Claire shy about making personal remarks to him. His mother regularly urged him to make an effort to seek a new romance, her knitting needles swiftly clacking away. ''Tis no harm to speak to someone, Mark,' she'd say. 'You're too inward-looking. It doesn't do you any good. Juliet wouldn't want you to hide yourself away all the time. One thing you mustn't do is to rely totally on Rowella to fill the empty spaces in your life. Don't want to see you turning out like Davey Vage, jealous of all Evie's friends and even her own sister. Miss Beth is a wonderful young lady. He's got no right to object to her. He may be showing acceptance about Evie's engagement, but I don't believe for a minute he's not going to try to put strife in the way of the wedding, try to get her to call it off. He's artful, that one. I've never liked him. Although he done right by Iris, and took on Evie as his own, he's cold-hearted. By the look of it Rob's learned his lesson and given up his wilder ways. I think he and Evie could have a good life together, if left alone. But they won't be, mark my words. There'll be heartbreak ahead for dear Evie. She's such a nice maid too, doesn't deserve it.'

'I'd never be like Davey Vage, Mother,' Mark defended himself. Invariably, when relaxing at home, with Rowella tucked up upstairs in her cot, he would dip his head in a book, a Western or detective thriller. 'I adore Rowella but my love for her is unselfish. I'd protect her with my life though.'

'So you should, every good parent should. But back to the point I was making. You want to start thinking about making a life for yourself. Juliet wouldn't want you to spend the rest of your life pining for her. There's some nice young women about. Claire Opie for one. Now she's stopped copying her hoity mother and dressing like she's going to a fashion show she comes across as a pleasant soul, a little shy and kind-hearted. She tries her best to speak to you, but as usual you barely notice her and you make her feel awkward. Shame on you, Mark.'

'You'll have that cardigan finished tonight,' Mark said, mocking her furious knitting. 'Be a new record for you.'

'You can't make me change the subject.' There were times when his mother's doggedness with him outmatched Davey Vage's subtle controlling ways with Evie. 'Have you noticed Claire is a pretty young woman?'

'Yes Mother, I have. I don't go round with my eyes shut.' Once again he put his bookmark between the pages of *The Lone Frontiersman*. Then he'd snickered. 'You're not seriously suggesting I think about having the dreaded Marjorie Opie as a new mother-in-law, are you? God help me.'

'Well, there is that, and it's a shame.'

'Now can I get back to my book? I've read the last sentence a hundred times.'

Mark picked up the sentence, but then his mother had made a remark that had astounded him. 'There is something I've noticed lately that

139

you haven't. Miss Beth is always looking you over. She finds excuses to take out your mug of tea and ask about the plants. How do you feel about that then, my son?'

Mark had scoffed. Then retired to bed before his mother threw the name of every other single woman in Portcowl at him.

But the very next day, during one of his regular times at Owles House, Beth had been there, in the doorway of the garden shed where he was collecting together some tools. 'Good morning, Mark. I'm on my way to the kitchen garden. I thought I'd look in and say good morning. How's little Rowella?'

Mark had not known how to take her sudden appearance. Was Miss Beth being more than polite? Could she be taking an interest in him? No, his mother was having daft notions. He and Miss Beth merely took each for granted. She didn't gaze straight into his eyes or search his face, not really. 'Morning, Miss Beth. Rowella is well, thanks,' he'd replied, in his usual manner, civil and brief.

'Well, I'll be on my way. I'll bring out your tea in an hour.'

She'd walked off, and for the first time he had watched her, while leaning across the work-bench, through the small smeary window. She had a good stride on her long legs, today in loose trousers. She was attractive and womanly from her back view, and Mark was surprised to acknowledge, she was sensual. He had not seen women as sexual beings since Juliet's death. 'Blast!' He'd hurled himself round and leaned against the workbench. He didn't want women back in his life in any way. He could cope with being left on earth without his adored Juliet as long as he had his precious daughter, and his mother. He felt safe, sane. If his daughter had died with Juliet he would have killed himself. Three times he had gone up on the cliffs with the intention of leaping into the rocky depths, a certain death, and only his baby's tiny beautiful face had kept him alive. He took pleasure from rearing his clever, gorgeous little girl. There had been times he had even felt content. He'd thumped his fist into the planked wall of the shed, relishing the pain and blood he drew. He cursed everything under the sun. He had put his life into a sort of bearable slumber and he did not, would not, be awakened from it. Since then he had made a point of giving Miss Beth only fleeting eye contact since and no more.

'Stop it, Mother,' he had crossly told her when next she had badgered him about looking for a new woman in his life. 'I don't want to hear another word on this matter. I'm happy as I am. Accept it, or I'll take Rowella and move out.'

Now he was here with Claire Opie and he was sorry for making her feel ill at ease. She was unassuming and ingenuous, and he did not want her to think he found her a nuisance or as someone only to be overlooked. It came to him that his whole attitude was rather ignorant, and unkind to undeserving people like Claire. 'It should be a good village event this afternoon, Miss Opie,' he said, adding a light smile. 'You have worked as hard as anyone to make it a success. Oh, look your mother is beckoning us. She's got our next jobs earmarked, no doubt.'

'Oh yes, we mustn't dally.' Claire returned his smile. Her spirits rose. At last someone had given her some credit for her contribution and her right to be present here.

'Rowella will love all the colourful sights and hustle and bustle.' Mark went on to form a conversation. 'She loves being with people and receiving lots of attention, like she gets from the Praed family.'

Claire was lost for a moment at how to reply to his unexpected addition. 'She is the brightest little soul. I can quite imagine her delight at dipping into the bran tub.'

Marjorie Opie was tapping impatiently on her notepad of tasks to be done. Then she gleaned that her daughter was on slightly familiar terms with the reclusive gardener. Her initial surge of indignation was exchanged by a sweep of approval. Claire had not managed to attract a husband of wealth and status and there was even less possibility she would now she had decided, despite Marjorie's reproofs, to dress down. The steady, self-employed Mark Reseigh would be better for Claire than no husband at all. 'Come along, you two,' Marjorie called gaily. 'We've so much to do and no time to lose. Miss Howard-Leigh wants a barrier put across the bottom of the stairs to stop people taking the liberty of slipping away upstairs. I've left a length of red cord on the newel. Apparently there are two narrow heavy china plant stands in the conservatory that will do for posts. Then return to

142

me quickly.'

Mark thought to protest that he could do the task easily by himself but Mrs Opie was already turning away and issuing fresh orders to the parlour maid. Claire was stunned her mother had ordered she go with Mark. Was her mother's mind so busy she had not realized she'd doubled her and Mark up unnecessarily. Claire shrugged. It was better to go along with her mother's demands and not reason why.

At the foot of the stairs, Claire picked up the red cord, while Mark went off to fetch the plant stands. In a few hours' time a steady trail of humble feet would tramp along the rush matting put down to protect the tiled floor. There would be eager faces, young and old, all curious to see inside the renovated vicarage, and excited about the event, one of a few that brightened their ordinary, often dull and hard lives.

From further up the long passage, Jacob emerged from his study, rubbing his hands together in readiness for what he fully assumed would be a memorable day for the parish. He smiled to himself at the gentle sight of Claire standing still and evidently waiting for something. 'Miss Opie,' he boomed heartily. Good morning to you, and thank you for coming so early to be part of the troops. I trust you are well? May I ask what the cord is for?'

Claire explained. 'Mr Reseigh is fetching the stands.'

'And Mrs Opie says that Miss Howard-Leigh requested this?' Jacob asked ponderously.

'I did, Jacob, for the sake of privacy and

security,' Bettany answered, starting to descend the stairs. 'Good morning, Miss Opie,' she said after she had alighted at the bottom, on Jacob's hand.

'But I hardly think it's necessary, my dear. I can't really see our guests taking the liberty of going upstairs. It would strike some as un-friendly. I can't ably care for the parish if it looks as if I don't think they can be trusted.'

Mark returned with the china stands. Hearing the resolve in the vicar's voice he did not speak but came to stand still beside Claire.

'Well, I do think it is necessary, Jacob.' Bettany was insistent, although the sleepless nights she had spent over today's event showed in her fraught nerves. Every bit of input Bettany had suggested for the Tea Party the damned Opie woman had overridden. The Opie woman had no respect for Bettany's position, and to Bettany's bewilderment and anger, Jacob had agreed with all the woman's outrageous interference. 'Leave it all to Mrs Opie this time, darling. She knows the local people.' He had said it in a soothing tone Bettany had come to hate.

'I've got some valuable items in my room and I hate the very thought of some stranger going through my things. The innocent wouldn't see a barrier as a slight; why should they? The mothers will be pleased; it will help keep their children under control.' Bettany felt near to tears. How dare Jacob put the feelings of his parishioners before hers? He could be romantic and he made her promises for a wonderful life together, but he was able to turn that side of him

144

off in an instant, and from what Bettany had seen, she came a low second to his calling. It would be understandable if they had been married many years, but his indifference to her feelings and comfort was getting dangerously close to an insult.

'Darling, I really think—'

'Well, if my opinions don't matter to you, Jacob!' Bettany's voice rose sharply with each word and she trembled with outrage. 'Mrs Opie didn't put any objections against my wish, and it's her opinion that counts, isn't it?'

Silence. The whole house fell silent. Staff who had been moving about in all quarters had heard their new mistress's furious cry. Mrs Opie came hesitantly out of the dining room, Winifred peeping worriedly over her shoulder. Claire and Mark glanced at each other in acute discomfort, instinctively drawing back. Claire's cheeks had reddened in embarrassment. She sympathized with Miss Howard-Leigh, she had heard her mother cast aside all the lady's attempts to have a say in today's effort. But her mother could be oversensitive as well as insensitive, if she felt offended she would march out and demand that Claire go with her. *Please God, don't let her do that,* Claire prayed. She had found a purpose for her life. She was at last content with her lot, not to be putting herself first, a shallow, determined husband hunter, as she was before her encounter with Mr Benedict in the wet lane. His easy-going attitude had helped her to change. But she did not agree with his public opposition to Miss Howard-Leigh's simple request, one that had

145

every justification in view of locals like the light-fingered Gabby Magor. He had humiliated his fiancée; it was cruel of him. Mark must have similar thoughts to Claire; she noticed him glaring at Mr Benedict.

In one overwhelming second Jacob was rocked to his soul at realizing how callously thoughtless he had been. He had belittled the woman he loved, treated her as if she was a petulant nuisance. He had embarrassed his best and most willing helpers, the two in front of him quiet, amenable people.

'Bettany, forgive me.' For the first time he fumbled over his words. 'I'm so very sorry. I've been – forgive me. Of course there must be a barrier across the stairs. It's what everyone does when opening up a big house to the public. People are used it. I – I don't know what I was thinking. You have my humblest apologies, darling.' His eyelids fluttered, his jaw twitched, and the whole of his face and neck was suffused with the darkest crimson as he appealed to her. 'I beg your pardon too, Miss Opie, and Mark, oh, a – and Mrs Opie. I – I'll disappear. You'll get on far better without me. Excuse me ... excuse me.' Moving many faltering steps backwards, Jacob whirled round and fled back the way he had come.

Claire glanced at her mother. She was gazing down dejectedly at her notebook. Claire thought, *Good, she realizes she went too far wanting to rule the roost where she had no right to.*

'I too owe you my apologies, Miss Howard-Leigh. I've overreached myself. I can see how it's upset you,' Marjorie said humbly.

'Thank you,' Bettany replied imperiously, pleased to have at last gained the upper hand. 'I shall arrange the flower displays for the hall. Do excuse me all of you.' Head up, she walked sedately off down the passage.

'Well,' sighed Mark, giving Claire a winsome look. 'Let's get this barrier up then. Miss Howard-Leigh hasn't realized she'll have to move it to one side each time she needs access or to use the servants' stairs.

Mrs Opie joined them. 'One thing is certain,' she said, quite maliciously. 'The romance between the vicar and the young lady is very one-sided.'

'Oh, Mother, really,' Claire protested, and Mark was glad to hear it.

'Blackmail or trouble? What do you think would make me the best fun at this daft tea party then, Tickle?' Gabby grinned maliciously, where she sat at her filthy kitchen table in her ramshackle home, Claze Wyn. Her elbows were on the space she had cleared of dirty mouldy dishes, and she was gobbling down splits slavered with fresh farm butter and golden syrup, her favourite food. Tickle was up on the table, his usual station on the few occasions his mistress sat here to eat. More often she took her meals into the front room, which doubled up as her bedroom. Up on his little hind legs, Tickle was licking off the sticky sweetness stuck to Gabby's chin. She took a swig from her tin mug of hot strong tea and kissed Tickle's tiny rounded head, allowing him

147

to continue with his fierce pleasure of cleaning her wobbly sun-damaged cheeks, chin and neck.

'I'm sure that Tresaile bitch and her friend's brother 'n' wife would pay me a pretty penny to keep me mouth shut at what I heard them women say. Love affairs and lies. Huh! Just so-called posh people who can't keep their knickers up and trousers on! Then they got the bleddy cheek to turn their fancy noses up at me. I haven't ever gone behind another woman's back and bedded her man. Me and my cousin Barbara might like a cuddle with each other and that'd be considered worse!' Gabby was getting angry now, seeped in the hurt and offence she believed was hers suffered over a great many years. 'But that's cus we were never considered pretty enough to take a man's eye. Not our bleddy fault!' Gabby thumped her fist down on the table, sending her oddments of crockery and cutlery to clatter off on to the grime-lagged floor, to join other pieces she had sent there during previous bouts of ill temper. Tickle leapt back in fright, but returned straight to Gabby and smothered her face in wet-lick kisses. Unlike other pets she had kept only briefly, Gabby had never hurt the little mongrel and she would never dream of abandoning him. She had taken to Tickle for some reason and had even grown to love him, her constant companion. Downing the last of her tea, including the tea leaves, she scooped up Tickle to her chest and carried him across to the next room and flopped down on her bed, a battered old settee, settling down for a snooze. But she had more to say before closing her eyes.

'Had hard lives, me and Barbara. A nice sum of money would set us up for a long while, we deserve it.' Gabby brightened. 'Barbara could do her place up a bit. New curtains, she's always wanted new curtains. I'll get her a wireless and one of them gramophones; see her face then. We could have a bit of music when we get together. We could go on a little holiday. Never had a holiday in my life. Yet them posh bitches live all their lives as one long holiday, living off passed-on money, prancing round doing good deeds and 'specting everyone to be grateful and kiss their bleddy arses.' Angry again. 'Then they've got the bleddy nerve to turn their noses up at people who work and graft and make good money for themselves. You'd like a holiday, wouldn't you, my handsome, my precious boy?' she cuddled Tickle in tighter. 'Blackmail it is then.'

A moment passed. 'And lots of trouble too and lovely red faces.' Gabby drifted off to sleep with a blissful grin on her ugly features.

Fourteen

'Wow, what a sight, all those delicious cakes!' Lily enthused, scanning the tables crammed with every kind of sponge sandwich and variation of iced, fruit, cherry, caraway seed, yeast and saffron cake, in round, square or loaf shapes. There were pyramids of cupcakes, and sandwiches and savouries. In her best red matching hat and coat, shoes polished, and her face scrubbed and shiny, she had arrived between her doting parents holding their hands, but had soon left them for Joe and Richard. 'See the sign? You can buy a whole cake or buy the slice to drink with a cup of tea, or cordial for us. I don't know what I'll choose. Mum and Dad have each given me a sixpence, and I've got a lot of pennies from all my brothers. They're all coming, except Douglas, of course, he's still too 'shamed to show his face anywhere. I've got heaps for the bran tub. I'm going to be first in line.'

As usual Richard was in a grumpy mood. 'We're not interested in what you're doing. Soon as I can get away I'm off.'

'Do what you like,' Lily smirked at him.

Joe raised his eyes to the sparsely decorated, plaster ceiling. The moment his friends met and started their sparring, he was practically forgotten. The tea room had filled up quickly with people, and he sought his mother, anxious to see she was strong enough for this, after all the hard work she had put into the planning stages, and the endless baking. He'd had enough of the smell of cake, and he had tasted many at the mixing stage, so he would choose from the hills of sausage rolls and savouries. Then he saw Christina, with Beth beside her, and his heart was filled with pride. His mother was the most elegant, tastefully dressed woman in the room, and to him the most beautiful. Her understated softly styled clothes and hat, her careful sparing use of jewellery and make-up, made her chic and graceful. People were giving her second and third looks, and approaching her reverentially and leaving her gratified at whatever words she had given them. His mother was the lady of the moment, not the stuffily clad organizer Mrs Opie. His mother was the lady of the house instead of the jittery Miss Howard-Leigh, who was flitting here and there like a demented moth, plainly not knowing where to go or what she should be doing. Kitty was there, as stunning as ever, with her brother and his family. Joe was disappointed to see Kitty had not lessened her thinly veiled hostility towards Mrs Copeland.

Jacob, who had been welcoming the arrivals as they filtered in from outside and along the passage, thought it was about time to go through to the dining room and get Bettany to formally open the event. After her indignation of the morning she had stayed frosty with him until after their quick light lunch, but had then become sharply nervy. She had written her speech days ago and had been confident and happy with it. A few minutes ago she had fluttered the paper in front of his eyes, finding fault with every word, and he had seen in her near panic. Why was she acting like this? Speech making and event opening had always been part of her life, from her venerable grandfather and father, her mother and herself. 'It's perfect, darling,' he had stressed. 'You'll impress everyone, there's nothing to fear.'

'Well, as long as the know-all Mrs Opie approves, I suppose it will do,' Bettany had snapped, and Jacob had felt impatient over her continuing sarcasm.

Jacob gathered Bettany, Christina, the Opies and the other committee members together in front of the crockery table. His staff and some lady volunteers, including Mrs Reseigh, were on the other side, wearing white aprons, and ready to put to use the steaming urn and huge teapots. Pitching his sermon voice, he called for hush. After a few moments and lots of shuffling everyone was facing him. Then Alison Praed and Judy Crewes entered with their respective fiancé and husband. Behind them came Rob, one arm still in a sling, the other proudly bearing a radiant-faced Evie, her gloves off to display her Vage heirloom engagement ring. 'Ah,' Mrs Reseigh sighed in the way women do when seeing something wonderfully poignant. People looked and took notice and a wave of ahhs went round the room. Rob paused in the doorway to show off his bride-to-be. Joe and Richard exchanged

152

looks that this sickened them.

'Magnificent.' Jacob went into full oratory stride. 'Our other cause for celebration has arrived – our two future bridal couples. I'm sure we all wish them our heartfelt congratulations! I'm sure everyone is eager for our first annual Grand Tea Party to be under way, so I shall duly hand over to my own charming bride-to-be, Miss Howard-Leigh.'

'For goodness sake get on with it,' Joe hissed between his teeth.

Applause resounded. Then people were annoyed to be shunted aside by Gabby Magor. Noses wrinkled and hands went up to faces at her mouldy smells, and disdainful looks appeared over her outlandish appearance. She had her usual man's outfit on but had added a discoloured thimble-shaped hat with turned up brim across her hefty brow. People shuffled back to find cleaner air and put space between her and them. She headed for the Copelands, and Louis sank back against his father's legs. 'Got that money you owe me boy?' Gabby rasped.

Louis nodded nervously. He had tried to talk his parents out of them all coming here today and when that had failed he had hoped he could secretly slip the thirty shillings, most of which he had filched from his mother's purse, to the frightening woman. Timidly, he put his hand out, the money held within it.

'What's this about?' Stuart demanded angrily. 'Louis, do you owe this person money?'

'Yes, he does. He can tell you why later.' Louis squawked in fright as Gabby snatched the money out of his hand. He would get a lecture and punishment for his misdemeanours and he would own up to them all, but that was better than the worry of this witch suddenly showing up and threatening him again.

Beth whispered to Christina, 'Why of all people did she have to turn up?'

The astonished faces that were beaded on the Copelands shifted, sparing the family some of their embarrassment, as Gabby went on to her next quarry, the smartly suited Mark. He was near the front of the gathering and had Rowella up in his arms. Mark glared at Gabby then ignored her. Rowella stared at her from curious eyes.

'Ahem,' Jacob reminded the crowd of the proceedings. 'Miss Bettany Howard-Leigh. A patter of clapping started up, and Bettany stepped forward and glanced at her note card. She raised her chin, determined to show her superiority and right to be the foremost lady here. 'A very good afternoon everyone, it's with the greatest pleasure that the Reverend Benedict and I welcome you all here today on this the inaugural occasion of...'

As Bettany continued, Gabby reached for Rowella's tiny hand. 'You're a dear little mite, aren't you?'

Unsure of her, Rowella turned away and snuggled into her father's neck. Sighing crossly, Mark moved to deny the ogress direct access to his daughter. Immediately offended, as Gabby actually wanted to be, she spoke louder than Miss Howard-Leigh, now well into her speech

154

stride. 'I 'tended no harm to the little maid, you know! Have you ever known me hurt a kiddie? You gen'rally bid me good day, Mark Reseigh. Aren't I good enough for you now then? Think you're going up in the world, do you, now you're courting the Miss Hoity Beth Tresaile?'

'Now all that remains for me to do...' Bettany went on, trying to raise her voice over the blatant disrespect. Greatly offended, she was horrified at the appearance of the hag and the beastly smells that had now reached her.

'I don't know what you're talking about,' Mark hissed over his shoulder at Gabby. 'Go away. I'm trying to listen to the speech. Don't be so rude.'

'Don't take on with me,' Gabby bellowed, tapping him hard on the shoulder. 'I'm only telling the bleddy truth, heard her say as much with me own ears, I'm telling 'ee.'

Beth hadn't quite heard the start of Gabby's disruption, only the insult to her name, but her main concern was how Miss Howard-Leigh's discomfiture was changing from irritation into wrath. Mark wasn't in a position to eject Gabby, a scuffle would surely ensue and there would be risk to Rowella. Beth would have to do something herself, plead with Gabby for reason. But she didn't get the time to move an inch.

'Woman, will you please be quiet!' Bettany snapped, her cheeks blood red, her eyes steaming with indignation. 'Or leave at once.'

'Leave!' Gabby screeched. 'I'm not leaving, why should I? I'm not going nowhere. I've lived in this parish all my life, and so did my parents

155

and grandparents and their parents before them. You've only been here a few weeks, you're an outsider, you got no right to order me about. Damned cheek!'

'That's it!' Bettany threw down her speech. 'I've had enough. I can't stand this.' Tossing up her head she made for the door, the bystanders respectfully making the way clear for her. Giving Christina a rueful look, Beth gently pushed her way through after her, hearing the furore of accusations shot at Gabby.

Bettany ran down the passage, reached the stairs, threw aside one of the posts and stormed up to her room. Beth reached her door to hear her ordering her maid to pack their things. 'As quickly as you can, Collins.'

Gingerly, Beth tapped on the door. 'Miss Howard-Leigh, it's Beth Tresaile. May I please come in? I am so sorry that you were barracked by the infamous Gabby Magor, our local misfit. Everyone is mortified on your behalf by her rude disregard. Please don't take it personally. She's like that with everyone, I'm afraid. Please don't leave. I'm sure she's being ejected this very moment. I can assure you she's the only person like that in Portcowl.'

Bettany yanked open the door. 'I do have the perception to realize that,' she uttered curtly, her nostrils still flaring. 'I saw for myself how respectable and pleasant the inhabitants of Portcowl seem to be, although certain people are above themselves. I thank you for your concern, Miss Tresaile, and please pass on to your mother that I appreciated all her kindness to me. What I

156

meant downstairs was that I've had quite enough of this place altogether. I've made a mistake. It's as simple as that. If you have any feelings for me at all you will refrain from any more explanations, and certainly not embark on questioning me. Now, I am asking you a great favour, to telephone for a taxicab. I wish to leave in the hour. You need not trouble informing the vicar,' she ended at last with tears in her eyes. 'He has not followed me up here. I'm sure he would prefer to comfort his flock.'

'Weren't no need for her to run off like some highly strung filly,' Gabby bawled, silencing the hubbub and anger hurled at her.

'Leave my house this moment, Miss Magor,' Jacob ordered furiously, taking advantage of the uneasy hush. He was forced to keep his wrath in check, not wanting to add to the distress. 'How dare you come here and upset my fiancée and the event the village has been looking forward to for weeks. And there are children here. You are guilty of the most insulting behaviour. People have worked very hard to make today a success and you have not offered your services to help. I shall escort you to the door myself, and then I shall have the task of trying to retrieve the afternoon.'

'But I've got something else to say,' Gabby leered, standing her ground.

'This is not the time and place to say whatever it is. No one wants to hear it.' Jacob marched up to her. 'Come with me, now.'

'You sure no one wants to hear, vicar? From the look of some faces here I be'lieve they do.

Everyone loves a bit of scandal, and 'tis scandal I've got to tell. Heard it myself on a nearby beach.' Gabby's bleary eyes fell on Stuart and Connie, who had huddled Louis and Martha to them and had put their hands over the children's ears, as other outraged parents had done to their offspring. Gabby was disappointed Beth Tresaile had hurried away for she would have stared at her too, but the Copelands should get the message that she had overheard something of a scandalous nature on Mor Penty beach about them. Today she'd had the most fun of her life. On leaving here she would fetch Tickle from Craze Wyn then go straight to Barbara and tell her all about it and they could plan what they would have to look forward to. Two hundred pounds would do nicely.

'All right,' sneered Gabby, 'I'm going. Don't want to spoil the day for them here who've got nothing on their conscience.' She barged her way out of the room, people scurrying back out of her way, as if in fear a mere touch from her would taint them with her vile odours.

'What was that all about?' Stuart hissed in Connie's ear. 'Why did she stare at us like that?'

Connie's voice trembled. 'Can't tell you now. Let me go out there and find Beth. I need to talk to her urgently.'

Fifteen

'How are you ever going to face Mark again?' Kitty laughed. In her silk pyjamas, she was lying on her front on Beth's bed, the following morning.

'It's not funny, Kitty,' Beth said, sitting at her dressing table. Her eyes were heavily shadowed from lack of sleep but she wasn't worried about that, or the fact that her bobbed fair hair was sticking out at odd angles and would probably refuse to lay flat and neat all day. 'You couldn't find a more private person than Mark. He must have been horrified to hear that vile woman saying such a thing in public.'

'But you've admitted you said something of the kind to Connie about Mark being your love interest. It's awful that Gabby overheard you, but you wouldn't have said it if it wasn't true.'

'It isn't!' Beth stressed, hating it that she was blushing. She hoped Kitty wouldn't see she had a lot more to hide, and a lot of fear. 'I like Mark, of course I do. He's a good man, but I don't see him in that way.'

Laughing gaily, Kitty persisted. 'Don't be coy, you silly. You can't really tell me that, or Connie wouldn't have got the idea that you and Mark were having a romance, would she?'

'I suppose not,' Beth sighed. This was dreadful. Kitty loved intrigues, she was one of the most curious people on earth and she would dig away until she had stripped a subject bare. Beth had to be extra careful with every word she said to Kitty. She had to keep up the pretence she was presently suffering nothing more than embarrassment. Thank goodness Kitty didn't appear to know that Connie had found her in the vicar's study, making the telephone call for Miss Howard-Leigh's taxicab, and had engaged her in a frantic conversation.

'Go on, no more holding back. We're best friends remember. I know you through and through. Explain,' Kitty ended in mock drama. 'What exactly did you say about Mark to Connie? And before you try any more denials, lady, I've actually seen you giving the handsome gardener more than a second look.'

Beth secretly took a deep breath. She whipped up a similar jaunty look to Kitty's and swung round to her and put on the same joking voice. 'Connie and I were talking on the beach about the garden at Mor Penty, the day we all went there, and I mentioned that Mark looked after it for me. She said he was good looking and I agreed, rather enthusiastically to my own surprise. She speculated on the possibility of me forming a romance with Mark. I merely said he was a very pleasant man and admitted I'd looked closely at Mark once or twice. Gabby Magor obviously overheard and put two and two together, but, and I stress but, Kitty, she got the wrong sum. Mark and I have absolutely nothing in common. No one could say Mark has ever given me any extra attention. It's one of those really silly things, and has now turned into a major embarrassment for Mark and I. He left the tea party the instant Rowella had pulled a prize out of the bran tub.' Beth was glad of an excuse to become serious. 'Now I'm worried he'll stop doing the gardening for Mum and me. That would be awful for Mum. And I've yet to face Mrs Reseigh when she comes here on Monday morning. Oh, I could wring that wretched Magor woman's neck!'

Kitty sat up on the bed and drew her knees in under her chin. 'Yes, I see all that. Mark feeling he couldn't work here again would be unfortunate and give the gossips more room to talk about you both. No, I'm sure he wouldn't do that. Mark is not a coward. He probably won't say anything at all, to anyone.' Kitty arrowed a look of reproach at Beth, 'What I want to know is why you've spoken about Mark to Connie but not said a word to me.'

Tension made Beth's head ache and she rubbed her brow. Kitty's resentment and distrust of Connie was making her jealous of anything that passed between Beth and her sister-in-law. 'Oh, it's just a subject to prevent us both discussing her and Stuart, I suppose. Her marriage is private to them. I certainly don't want to get involved in it. I'll be glad when they've left Mor Penty and have gone home. I can't see that them staying around here any longer would be of any benefit to them and the children.' It was with great relief Beth saw Kitty smile at her with understanding.

'This has all been rather a trial for you,' Kitty

said apologetically. 'I shouldn't have asked you to allow Stuart to use your home. Sorry about that. Actually I don't think Stuart will want to stay on. The family are coming over here later today and I'm fairly sure they will announce they'll soon be catching the train home. Can I borrow your car to run them to the station?'

'Of course.' Kitty's family leaving today would suit Beth even better.

'Actually, I'm rather proud of Louis. Oh, I know he was very naughty, well, dreadfully naughty to steal from his mother's purse, but it's no wonder he'd do something so bad after all he's been put through. I think it was rather clever of him to ask Gabby Magor to get him a puppy. She's the adult, she should never have agreed, and when he explained to her on the beach that he no longer needed a puppy because his parents were going to get him one, she shouldn't have demanded the money off him, scaring him, and again in public too. When I think of her poking her ugly disgusting face into Louis's camp I could cheerfully wring her neck myself!'

'And she drove poor Miss Howard-Leigh away,' Beth added, with equal indignation, taking the subject away from Kitty's family. 'That woman has got a lot to answer for.'

'The Reverend Benedict didn't even know she had gone until the tea party was over. He must be feeling very foolish for having declared it a success at the end.'

'He didn't even go after her to see how badly Gabby Magor had upset her or to try to coax her to return to the event. He's an excellent vicar to his flock but the most inattentive fiancé. He should take a leaf out of Rob and Alfie's book. They weren't at all shy about showing how much they're in love with Evie and Alison.'

'You have a valid point, Beth, but I think Miss Howard-Leigh came across as a spoiled madam. How could she allow Gabby to disconcert her so, and then go on to make a spectacle of herself, running out like a petulant child? She didn't care any more than Gabby did that there were excited little children there and the adults had turned up hoping for a grand happy occasion. The people are used to Gabby's troublemaking. Now they're all saying that Miss Howard-Leigh wouldn't make a suitable vicar's wife at all. She made it quite apparent she didn't care in the slightest for Portcowl and its inhabitants. No, she's drawing room material only, and if she refuses to be reconciled with Mr Benedict, then I say he's had a lucky escape.'

'I suppose so,' Beth mumbled, tweaking at her wayward hair, her own troubles overwhelming the concerns at the vicarage. 'Oh, this stupid hair of mine. Well, never mind. We had better get dressed and go down and get breakfast if we're going to be ready in time for the morning service. The church will be filled with a few nosy parkers hoping to learn more about yesterday's drama, no doubt.' As she had hoped, Kitty left for her own room to get ready.

Sometime today Beth would have to slip away alone – which would raise eyebrows at not inviting anyone to go for a walk with her – and go to Claze Wyn. It was either that or to wait in trepidation for Gabby to pounce on her. Beth had never been to Claze Wyn, likened to worse than a pigsty. It was off the beaten track, and she had only a rough idea where it was. Joe had spied on Gabby Magor many times to ensure she wasn't mistreating any animals, and from his descriptions of the place, Beth knew she was in for a rough muddy trek. From Connie's anxious account of what Gabby had hinted at yesterday, and Gabby's smirking looks at Connie, she had overheard all Beth's and Connie's guilty secrets. Beth could choose to ignore it and when, inevitably, Gabby blurted out the information to all and sundry, Beth could try to bluff that it was Gabby's word against hers. Gabby was a notorious liar. But searching questions would be asked. The truth would be rooted out or revealed one way or another. There was going to be a cost. Gabby would demand money to keep her blabbing mouth shut. Blackmail was an ugly business. It would taint the rest of Beth's life. The alternative, however, would be infinitely worse.

Resting her elbows on the dressing table Beth put her head in her hands and fought back a wave of tears. She felt cold and clammy. And sick with worry. She had been so happy in her new life, the wonderful year she had spent united with her mother, and enjoying her life in Cornwall, with Evie, Joe and her uncle Ken. *Be sure your sins will find you out.* Jacob Benedict had preached the sentence in a sermon, and Beth had shifted uncomfortably in the front pew. 'I'm sorry God, really sorry. Please don't ever let my past sins be revealed. I might deserve all the hurt that would come my way but the others don't,' she whispered. But God might want to force her to face up to her sordid actions and lies.

'Please God,' she wept quietly. 'Kitty and Louis and Martha don't deserve all the heartbreak the truth would give them. And my mother and Joe would be horrified with me for the scandal it would cause in Portcowl. They would lose all respect because of me. Evie and Uncle Ken would understand I'm sure but it would be embarrassing for them. And Mark, I can get round this silly romance thing if I barely take any notice of him, as I'm sure he will me, and it should all be soon forgotten, but I really don't want him to think badly of me, or Mrs Reseigh, or the rest of Portcowl.'

A strange gentle hush fell over Beth, like softly falling flower petals; it was almost a tangible thing ... Her tears stayed wet on her face but a calm entered her whole being. *What was this?* She waited expectantly. Something was coming to help her. No, it was someone. She felt some help. Then came a smell familiar to her, of the most tender and softest and most gentle thing on earth. It was one of the most fragrant evocative smells on earth to a woman, the scent of a baby. Beth knew at once who it was. Her twin brother Philip had been born and had died shortly afterwards in this house.

'Philip? Hello, Philip.'

In the reflection in the dressing table mirror a shadow moved, not of someone so very small, but an adult male equivalent of Beth herself.

While she gazed in wonder and love at the form of her twin brother, Beth listened to him in her heart. 'I understand,' she whispered. She wanted so much to turn round in the hope of getting a clearer view of Philip but knew she would see nothing at all. And she knew his image would be in the mirror for only as long as his purpose for appearing to her lasted.

Her heart cried out in a moment of painful loss when a mist covered the place where Philip's reflection had been. 'Goodbye, Philip,' she whispered.

Philip's purpose was over and after he had left Beth knew exactly what she now had to do. She must call on all her wits and without flinching summon up her courage. She looked again in the glass. The mist had cleared as if nothing strange had happened; perhaps it had not, but there remained the faint gentle smell of a baby.

All through breakfast Beth was quiet and deep in thought. Christina was worried about her, and Beth pleaded a headache and said she would not attend church. She went up to her bedroom, changed into walking clothes and returned downstairs. Christina and Kitty were in the kitchen, washing and drying the dishes, and Joe was grooming Chaplin and Grace. Mrs Reseigh did not work here at the weekends and the women took turns with the domestic duties. 'I'm going for a walk. It will do me good,' she announced, putting on a bright voice to prevent unnecessary concern.

'Are you sure, darling?' Christina dropped the tea towel and went forward to feel Beth's forehead. 'You don't seem to have a high temperature, but is it wise to go out? There's a steady drizzle and from the look of the grey sky it's not going to let up all day.'

'Don't worry. I'll wear my mac and rubber boots and wrap up warmly, and take my brolly. There's plenty of spots to shelter in along the way.' Beth was already heading for the door.

'A walk is better for a headache than lying about, I always think,' said the sporty Kitty. 'I'd go with you but I'll first need to drive Christina to church.'

'I don't mind staying at home,' Christina offered.

'Don't be daft, Mum,' Joe scoffed. 'Beth isn't made of fine china. And you and Kitty are eager to find out what the Reverend Benedict will preach about this morning. Why not take the dogs with you, Beth?'

Beth flashed Joe a brilliant thank you smile. 'I won't actually, thank you. It'll be good to be alone.' She hurried to the hall to don her outdoor clothes.

'Don't go too far,' Christina cautioned her, as she left the house.

A fresh batch of tears stung Beth's eyes. She turned and waved to her mother, watching her and waving from a window. It brought Beth comfort knowing that she would always have her mother's love and support.

Her head down under her umbrella, Beth strode briskly along the lane in the direction leading away from the cove. She soon reached the place

167

where the woods stretched out to the lane and she walked on until she reached a clearing. Beth knew she must cross the lane and then follow a long winding rough public footpath, between two high hedgerows, on the edge of Boswarva Farm. Joe had mentioned he reached Claze Wyn by a faster easier route over the fields but Beth wasn't about to risk getting lost. The way was pitted, stony and deeply muddy in places and it made Beth lurch and skid and her umbrella kept getting snagged on the hedges. Brambles in particular hung out like grasping tentacles. Beth closed her umbrella reluctantly but found she preferred the less claustrophobic feel about her head and accepted the rain dripping off her waterproof hat in the way Kitty would. Kitty was less fussy about weather conditions and loved the wind on her face, and illogically Nature had kindly allowed her to keep her flawless looks. Beth regretted her thoughts about Kitty. She needed to keep Gabby Magor uppermost in mind and the outcome of a meeting with her.

Leaving the relative shelter of the hedgerows Beth reached open ground and she found herself buffeted by the strong winds. The sky was darker now, with growing sweeps of bruised purplish-grey, the colour of a stern dowager's hair. Beth put up her umbrella but had to hold on tightly to the handle to prevent it being snatched away on the wind. The track beneath her mud-splashed boots, the way to Claze Wyn, was marked out from the years of Magors plodding to and from their home, but it was just as pitted and slippery as before. Beth could pick out Gabby's deep boot prints and Tickle's tiny paw prints. Sometimes Gabby used a shaky old bicycle to get around on but such a conveyance if used in these conditions would need to be pushed until reaching firmer ground. All Beth had to do was to keep going and sooner or later the hag's property would come into view. Apparently elder trees grew behind it, from which Gabby harvested the berries to make wine, which with other fruit and vegetable wines she sold to regular customers. Beth was praying Gabby would be at home so she could get this meeting she was hoping for – which Gabby had hinted to Connie, that she herself would be seeking – over with. But meeting Gabby on her own ground was getting more and more daunting. Beth was sure it would be dreadful to be near or actually inside what would be, no doubt, a filthy, stinking hovel, and there was the risk of Gabby's fierce temper and ready fists. She had been to prison years ago for badly beating Davey Vage after he had merely ignored her. She had served another sentence for receiving stolen goods. At the least, Gabby would gloat and swear and threaten Beth if she didn't agree to her demands, which almost certainly were going to amount to blackmail.

Suddenly Beth was falling, slipping on the slimy mud and she went down on her side, her upper arm and hip hitting stones and the breath was thudded out of her. 'Owahh,' she whined miserably. Struggling and slithering to her feet she walked onwards over waterlogged rough ground to retrieve her umbrella, sent flying out of her hand and blown some distance away.

The umbrella was broken. Folding the cloth and fastening it up round the long handle she used it as a walking stick instead. Trudging back on to the track she carried on, choosing her ground a little more carefully. Making headway was painfully slow and it seemed Gabby must live in the middle of nowhere.

Finally Claze Wyn was ahead, partially concealed behind willow bushes and other wild growth. As she closed in on the place Beth saw it was more dilapidated than she had imagined. Partly enclosed by tumbling walls of grey stone, the thatched, four-room cottage and miscellany of outhouses, sheds and abandoned chicken coops were all in advanced states of disrepair, except for a small, stone, padlocked building with a tiled roof which Beth rightly assumed was Gabby's wine keep.

The reek festering in the heaps of rubbish hit Beth full in the face. The smells must be revoltingly intense in hot weather. Narrow muddy paths of sorts skirted the refuse and led to the cottage and outhouses. Spent matches and dog ends lay scattered all about and Beth thought uneasily, in a reversed kind of way, of the folk tale of two lost children dropping bread in the unrealized hope of safely finding their way back home. There was no wicked stepmother in Beth's current predicament but Gabby was easily a witch, even if her place wasn't made of gingerbread.

Glumly, Beth knew at once Gabby wasn't at

170

home or Tickle would have barked at her approach. However, she went all the way to the cottage and rapped on the battered door. No reply, as she expected. Puffing out her cheeks in disappointment Beth considered if it was worth waiting for a while. But she had no way of knowing when Gabby had gone out and when she was coming back. No smoke was coming out of Gabby's chimney, but Gabby was known for not really feeling the cold so she probably didn't light many fires. There were no kitchen smells, mixed with the foul ones, of a breakfast having been cooked, but the chances were she had spent the night at her cousin's home. A sudden thought filled Beth with panic. What if Gabby had been to, or was soon intending to show up at, Owles House demanding to see her? She couldn't risk her talking to Kitty or her mother. She must hurry all the way home but that wouldn't be easy.

'She'll be coming round the mountain when she comes!' sang out a raucous common voice. Beth jumped and her heart banged and raced. It was Gabby on her way home. Thank goodness she was apparently in a good mood.

As soon as Tickle saw Beth he shot off from Gabby and yapping loudly headed straight for Beth. 'Eh?' Gabby stopped singing and peered short-sightedly after Tickle. 'Tickle, what's the bleddy matter?'

Shivering in front of Gabby's doorstep, Beth called out to her. 'Miss Magor! It's me, Beth Tresaile.' Tickle had reached her, and rather than have the tiny dog jumping up and muddying her

Beth crouched down and tried to pet the squirming white and patchy mongrel and got a dirtying anyway. Gabby was roaring with gleeful laughter. Beth groaned inwardly. *I'm in for it now.*

'Tickle, leave the lady 'lone,' Gabby bawled, and Tickle instantly scurried back to her mistress, and Gabby picked him up and held him under one arm. Tickle licked her affectionately on the hand. 'Miss Tresaile, how very kind of you to call on me.' Gabby mocked her with a gurning smile. 'I was over my cousin Barbara's. Good job I come back to get her some parsnip wine to go with the roast she's cooking for us. Got a shilling's worth of brisket today.'

'We both know why I'm here,' Beth said firmly. She had made a decision after seeing Philip's presence and she was going to go through with it. 'I have something I'd like to say to you. Will you hear me out please?'

'Please?' Gabby raised her beetling brows while smirking. 'No one never said please to me before. So, Mrs Copeland got my meaning then, and you too? Yah, you lot think you're better than the likes of me, but you and that woman are deceivers! Got no more morals than a pair of bleddy alley cats, so why shouldn't I profit by it, eh? Eh? S'pose you're going to argue about that. And that vicar's bitch! Think I got no manners, well what manners did she have yes'day, throwing a tantrum and clearing off in a huff? All two-faced hypocrites.'

Beth swallowed hard. 'Actually, I roughly agree with all that, although I don't want to remark on Miss Howard-Leigh.'

172

'What?' In incredulity, Gabby stuck out her upper jaw over her heavy lower jaw making her seem all wobbly chins.

'Please let me explain. I haven't come to argue with you, Miss Magor.' Beth said, finding herself breathless and a little light-headed.

Gabby stared at her suspiciously but not without interest. She noticed Beth was bedraggled. 'Oh, fallen down, have 'ee? Hurt yourself?'

Beth's hand went unbidden to her arm. 'I expect I'll have a bruise or two here. I just feel so cold.' Her voice emerged small and teary and Beth was cross with herself. Gabby would jeer at her and believe she would be very easy to exploit.

'Well, you better come in then, don't expect you to do business out here in the rain.' Gabby put on a posh tone and wiped at her straggly hair as if she was aware for the first time it was raining. 'Come in for a cup of tea. I've got a primus stove, have some ready in a mo. You go first, just push on the door, it's never locked and latch's been broke for years. Do mind the mess. I wasn't expecting visitors, you see.'

Beth surmised Gabby's new pleasantness was a tactic she planned to use to her financial gain. At that moment Beth badly wanted to get inside out of the rain and sit down for a minute. She pushed on the door and pushed on it again until it finally moved inwards on much squeaking and shuddering. She reeled at the rank smells that hit her like a living force of rotting things. She could even smell urine. Just feet ahead were the stairs and it was obvious from all the junk piled up on every step Gabby had not used the top part of the house in years. Beth eyed the filthy floor in case Tickle had messed on it. It seemed clear of dog's faeces but it was impossible to determine what the floor covering was, or if indeed there was any apart from rubbish, old newspapers, rags and broken items, including a bicycle wheel.

'Mind your legs, Miss Beth,' Gabby said, from right up behind her, making Beth shudder in horror. She felt she was entering an unpredictable creature's den. ''Fraid I'm not much of a housekeeper. Sorry about the whiffs, forgot to empty the commode. Go to your left, into the kitchen. Damn me, you're shivering, aren't you? Got a fire laid in the grate. I'll put a match to the kindling and I'll soon have you warm. Oh, just a minute, step aside for me. I need to go first and clear a space for you.'

'Th–thank you,' Beth stuttered. She had never felt so cold in her life, not even when she had ran down Portcowl Hill when abandoned as a child on that stormy winter's night. She knew it was her soul and her spirit, rather than her flesh that was numb and chilled, for by the end of the day her life would be changed forever.

Leaning against the greasy doorway, she watched with a strange fascination as Gabby gathered up the stuff heaped on the table and dumped it into the already overflowing stone sink and on the mouldy wooden draining board. Black dots lay everywhere – dead flies. Gabby rooted about in stuff falling out of a cupboard and grunted in triumph as her huge tanned dirty paw picked up a 'clean' rag. Wetting it at the tap she wiped hard at the creaking table. Then finding a 'clean' folded towel, that had probably been left so for years, she laid it on one of the two high back chairs, the only seats in the room. 'Sit down here, Miss Beth.' Gabby patted the towel. 'I'll just put a match to the fire then put the kettle on, soon have you as warm as a buttered crumpet. Tickle, you go lie on your bed, my handsome.' Wagging his long, thin tail Tickle did so, his bed a heap of crumpled clothing under the table.

Feeling as if her legs didn't belong to her, Beth shuffled to the chair and lowered her frozen limbs until she was sitting down. She looked on longingly as Gabby struck a match and the scrunched up newspaper and kindling wood caught slowly alight. It was a large open fireplace – there was no cooking range – and logs and scavenged wood were piled up at its side. It would not take very long to give forth some much welcome heat.

'Tea next,' Gabby said, glancing often at Beth. Beth could see the grotesque woman was puzzled by her sudden frailty. Good, Beth thought, it might work to my advantage.

When Gabby had the tin kettle on top of the primus stove, set up on the hearth, and tea leaves in a dusty white teapot she had dug out from somewhere, she said, ''Scuse me a minute.' She left the room. Beth heard furniture being shifted and Gabby grunting. Gabby returned, holding something pretty and delicate, with pride. 'From my mother's treasured tea set, never used it

175

myself. Mother used to bring it out just for Christmas Day. We had good Christmases, me, her and Father. Don't expect you to use my horrid old mugs, Miss Beth.'

'That's very kind of you,' Beth said, almost wearing a smile.

'Turn your chair round, get nearer the fire. Flames will be licking up nicely soon. Got a good clean chimney, swept it myself. Father had his own brushes, got a bit of work from 'em at times.'

Beth nodded. She moved her chair to the hearth. Taking off her gloves she held her hands to the burgeoning warmth. Her eye caught a sepia wooden framed photograph on the cluttered sideboard. It was a studio depiction of a thin woman sitting on a chair with a girl on her lap and a stocky man standing at their side. 'Is that you with your parents in the photo?'

Gabby paused from throwing scraps of bread to Tickle. She stared at Beth as if she was seeing something utterly amazing in her kitchen. 'No one asked anything about me before, 'cept occasionally Mark Reseigh. "How are you, Miss Magor?" he'd say. Nice of him, I always thought, though he don't never hang about long for much of an answer. He weren't nice to me yes'day though. Do you really want to know about my parents?'

'Yes, actually I do. Really,' Beth answered truthfully. She was so grateful to be receiving warmth from the fire, for her mind to be clearing as the horrible shivers died away that she felt an unexpected appreciation towards the fire's

176

owner.

As Tickle chewed up the last of the bread, then curled up to sleep, Gabby picked up the photograph and held it in front of Beth. 'That's my mother. Florence Ellen May, was her name. She married my father, Albert George, when she was sixteen years old. She was quite pretty when she was young. I'm about seven, an ugly child, always been ugly, no use denying it. Got teased for years, called names, had stones thrown at me, got deliberately tripped up. If I was down in the cove on the beach I'd get thrown into the sea. So I learned the only way to deal with it was to toughen up. So I did, and I made some of them rotten buggers pay for what they did to me, I can tell you.'

'Have long have you lived alone?' Beth asked, understanding now why Gabby had turned out to be so aggressive and defensive. It could not be mistaken that the girl in the photograph, with a big bow and long ribbons in her curly hair, had been passed by on good looks. Albert Magor was holding his cap and had a thick brush moustache. Florence Magor, in a Victorian blouse and long straight black skirt, had a gaunt look.

'Father passed over years ago, just after Mother, can't remember how long it is now.' Gabby made a cheerless face.

'You must have been very lonely at first.'

'For a while, but I don't begrudge them their eternal rest.' Gabby then gave a smile that could almost be described as cheeky. 'Mother was untidy in the house but I s'pose I've let things go a bit. Least, I've always had Barbara, my cousin.

177

She lives a couple miles from here, got a little house on the roadside. She's a good bit older than me. You wouldn't have seen her. She's never been to Portcowl in her life, shops in Leaford. And I've got my Tickle, he fills my life.' She bellowed with mirth. 'Don't know why; ugly little mutt.'

'He's quite sweet. I'm glad for you.'

'Are you now?' Gabby's suspicions returned and she eyed Beth sharply. She glanced down at the kettle. Steam was beginning to show from the spout.

'Time to get on with things,' Beth said, taking a deep breath to steady herself. 'This will surprise you Miss Magor, but although I'm very anxious, I'm also feeling quite relieved that you've brought my rather lurid past to a head.'

'Oh? What does that mean?' Gabby dragged her chair to the hearth where she could make the tea by just leaning to her side. She put hawklike eyes on Beth. 'Spell it out with no fancy language.'

'That's what I intend to do. I've made some decisions, you see. I'm going to confess to my friend Miss Copeland about my affair with her brother. Stuart and Constance Copeland's marriage is their own affair, and they have kept no secrets from each other. But I have kept another secret from Miss Copeland, which I also intend to admit to her. When Constance Copeland came to stay at the Grand Sea View Hotel she got in touch with me. She knew about my affair with Stuart, but she had forgiven me, knowing herself what it's like to believe you're in love with

178

someone else, someone who turned out to be thoroughly unsuitable. Constance Copeland was afraid that Kitty, who didn't trust her following her desertion, would try to prevent her from making a successful attempt to repair her marriage, and Constance asked me to keep Kitty out of the way. It's been a heavy burden keeping my secrets from Kitty but now I can see she deserves to hear the truth. If I lose her friendship that will be my punishment and I will have to bear it, also the disappointment of my mother and the displeasure of my younger brother.

'I know you are looking to gain a sum of money from me, Miss Magor, in exchange for your keeping what you overheard on the beach to yourself.'

'And now I won't be getting a penny! That what you're saying?' Gabby snarled, her dark expression like that of a sulky child, glaring at Beth, and then the whistling kettle.

'No, I am not.' Beth leaned towards Gabby. 'What I plan to do, I fear, and I am genuinely afraid, Gabby, if I may call you that, will cost me much more than money. The money isn't at all important. But I would like to offer you something in the hope that you will agree to never ever mention a word of my shame, and the Copelands' situation. It goes without saying that I'd hate for my past to be turned into a scandal. It would greatly hurt my mother. I'd hate for people to lose their respect for her over something I had done. I'm not proud of what I did, and believe me I have suffered because of it in many ways. Do you understand all I've said?'

Beth ended on a plea.

'I do that.' Gabby nodded, her ugly face passive for once. 'Just a sec.' She turned off the primus and poured the boiling water into the teapot. 'Right, how much?'

'I would like to give you one hundred pounds as a gift rather than as a bribe. Would you like to think about it?' Beth searched Gabby's wrinkled eyes for signs of discontent or greed. If anything she seemed stunned. 'It's a willing act on my behalf, I swear to you. I can drive to the bank in St Austell tomorrow and get the money for you, and meet you out in the lane on my way back.'

A huge grin spread across Gabby's flabby face. 'I was thinking of two hundred pounds but one hundred is still a bleddy fortune. Be enough to do all the things Barbara would like and enough for us and Tickle to go on a holiday.'

Beth was actually moved to admire her would-be blackmailer, the persistent local trouble-maker, for putting her cousin first. Gabby looked so happy, she was like an excited child. 'What will you buy for yourself?'

'I might get a silk neck scarf. I've always liked the ones you ladies wear. P'raps some new clothes, but I don't know what'd suit me. Don't s'pose I'd look right in a frock. Oh, let me pour the tea. Got no milk though. You take sugar?'

'One spoonful please,' Beth said, looking forward to the hot drink and not caring how horrible it might taste. 'So we have a deal, Gabby? May we shake hands on it? For a one-off gift of one hundred pounds and for the facts behind it never to be mentioned again.'

180

Putting down the packet of sugar, Gabby stuck out her doorstop-sized hand. Her tanned cheeks blushed and again she was like a girl. 'Never shook no one's hand in the proper manner before. I won't spit on it, not right for a lady. It's a deal, Beth, forever, on my life and the memories of my parents. I'll never do the dirty on you. You can sleep at nights on it. We're sort of friends now, eh? Anyone ever hurt or annoy you and you want them sorted out just you come to me. Aw, got a new packet of biscuits in the larder. Bought 'em the other day, so you can rest 'sured they won't be stale or dirty. Me, you and Tickle can have a feast.'

Huddled in the longed-for warmth, less anxious now she had succeeded better than she had hoped for with Gabby, Beth sipped the tea, actually wonderfully refreshing, and munched on chocolate-coated biscuits. Gabby dunked her biscuits in her mug and she and Tickle, begging appealingly at her feet, were soon smeared with chocolate.

'Nice having company here,' Gabby said happily. 'No one been here since the last vicar called here after Father died. The new vicar called and left his card but I was out. Oh, one or two have come to buy my wine, I'm famous for it, you know. Make it over Barbara's, if you're wondering, then I bring the bottles over here. Got a little handcart in the shed. I'll give you a bottle sometime.'

'Thank you very much, Gabby.'

'Don't s'pose ... Can I...?'

'Yes?'

181

'Can I come with you in the car tomorrow? Never been in a car before. Be the biggest treat in the world. No one'll see us and wonder what the hell's going on.' Once again, Gabby had her child's face.

Beth couldn't help smiling. 'Of course. I'll pick you up out in the lane, um, at ten past ten. I've got some things to pick up for my mother, so you'll be able to do some shopping.'

Gabby giggled, a rumbling twittering sound. 'Bleddy hell, I mean crumbs, will be better than Christmas. Then can you drop me off at Barbara's?'

'Ah,' Beth suddenly frowned and set down her teacup and saucer.

'What?' Gabby's voice was steeped in disappointment.

'Your cousin Barbara, I take it you have told her about your, um, plan concerning me?'

'No, I never mention my dealings to her. She's a bit simple-minded, wouldn't understand anyway. She's used to me turning up with stuff. I'll tell her I won some money betting on the horses. I'll carry what's been said here to my grave, cross my heart and hope to die!' Gabby ended dramatically.

'Well, that's all settled then. I really must go.'

'Aw, shame, but I got to get back to Barbara anyhow. I'll bank the fire in. Off home to your mother's?'

'Yes, but then I'll drive straight over to Mor Penty and tell the Copelands they must leave very soon. I'm sure the Copelands will be glad to go. I hope to get back before the others come

182

home from church. When the Copelands are safely home, I shall have the daunting task of telling Kitty the whole sorry truth.'

'Aw, she'll come round in no time; a fine lady like you.'

'No, she won't think kindly of me at all. Kitty is honest and rather innocent, she's trusted me since we met as children. She'll see it as the biggest betrayal of her life. But it's not right to keep my secrets from her any longer.'

Sixteen

It was breakfast time at the Opie's house. Richard was wolfing down scrambled egg on toast, under his mother's disapproving glances. Marjorie was nibbling demurely on toast and thin cut marmalade. Douglas was enjoying his second cup of tea while making notes regarding the day ahead at the hotel. Claire had finished eating and drinking, unaware that she was also under her mother's penetrating gaze.

Claire's mind was entirely on her dream last night. A romantic dream that she had been sorry to wake up from and realize was not real. It was never going to happen, a handsome foreign prince arriving to stay at the hotel and inviting her to swim with him in the cove, and afterwards proposing to her with a triple diamond ring.

They had planned to slip away and marry secretly to avoid her mother making an inevitable fuss over the arrangements. No one was going to promise her the stars and the moon and endlessly glorious days spent in a faraway palace. It had been a lovely dream though.

No, she thought, sighing mournfully, it was life as a spinster for her. At the moment she had the consolation of the stylish Beth Tresaile and the beautiful Kitty Copeland not even walking out with a young man. Neither of them seemed interested in seeking love and marriage, but rich young ladies had more independence than less well off women. Stifled by life under her mother's dominance and nagging, and often irritated by her brother's messy noisy ways, she longed for a home of her own, hopefully like the house her parents had, quite newly built, large with the modern conveniences and a sizeable garden, where she could make her own decisions and have some peace and quiet.

With a sudden scrape of chair legs, leaving crumbs and milk spatters behind him, Richard was up and announcing he was off to school. Douglas and Marjorie said it was time for them to move too, he to drive Richard to Owles House where Richard would share a taxi with Joe to their private school at St Austell, and then on to the hotel, where he would stay until after midnight. Marjorie checked Richard's shoes were polished to a brilliant shine then ordered him to straighten his tie. She did not kiss him goodbye. She loved her son but was fazed by his rough boy ways, his whistling and general untidiness

184

and was always glad when he left the house.

Claire fetched a tray and started to clear the table. She always did this job to help the shy young housemaid, Jean Whitley, a fisherman's daughter. Claire braced herself, her mother had closed the door after seeing her father out with a mere peck on the cheek. Now would come the barrage of what she wanted Claire to do today, how she had wished Claire would dress and style her hair. Marjorie was dismayed at Claire's decision to dress down rather than present herself at her very best. 'How do you expect to find yourself a husband if you insist on looking little better than an ordinary working class girl, indeed?' When the finding fault was over next would be Marjorie's glee over any local gossip, and there was plenty of that to mull over right now. Claire had once enjoyed sharing in gossip about the downfalls of others, it had made her feel better about her own rather sad life.

The theme on her mother's lips for the last few days concerned the vicar suddenly being bereft of his fiancée. 'How could she have embarrassed the poor man like that? She must have always had little regard for his feelings. She showed utter contempt for his hard-working, trusting parishioners that's for sure, showed it in glaring colours! She might come from an exalted background but she's proved she is no more a lady that Gabby Magor. How dare Miss Howard-Leigh throw a tantrum merely because that detestable creature issued a heckling? As for the notion that Mr Reseigh and Miss Tresaile are involved in a secret romance, poppycock! I don't

185

think he's gone to Owles House yet. I'll wager he'll keep a very low profile, most embarrassing for him, and for Miss Tresaile. If the Poor Reverend Benedict has any sense he will break off with that neurotic woman forthwith, but he's an honourable man and doubtless, unfortunately, he will stand by her. What a life he will have as her husband. Apparently he took the Sunday services with his usual aplomb but underneath it people swore they detected a definite trembling in him. It's a terrible shame. You must look sharp, Claire. You would make a perfect dutiful wife. You might get the chance to step in there, and then your father would be more likely to change denominations.' Claire had not liked her name mentioned side by side with the vicar's and implicating her father. She was not a girl to be married off for positional advantage.

Her dream forgotten, she returned to a notion that had been on her mind for a while: to strike out on her own, as a person of rather fortunate means, thinking what she might do to make the lives of those less fortunate more bearable. Perhaps she would buy some wool and call on old Mrs Coad and ask her to kindly teach her how to knit. Claire could make socks, gloves, mufflers and woolly hats for the poor. It would be a simple enough effort to start with, something her mother couldn't interfere with too much.

'Leave that Claire.' Marjorie pounced on her in the kitchen as Claire put down the fully laden tray. 'I want you to run an errand for me. It's teeming with rain so you'll need your umbrella.'

'Of course, Mother,' Claire replied, pleased to

186

be getting out of the house.

'You can pop into Wrights and get an ounce of your father's tobacco, and then I want you to go along to Half Street and call on Mark Reseigh. You should find him there. I can't see that he will be able to do any work in this awful weather.'

'Why do you want me to go there?' Claire frowned, puzzled. 'Father usually arranges our garden work with Mr Reseigh, and as you've said yourself, he won't be able to work today.'

'I know that, silly goose. I want you to take a message to him. I have written a note and on the envelope I've requested that you may wait for his reply. I'm thinking of having a summer house in the back garden. I'd like to consult Mr Reseigh about the various styles and the best position to have one built. You may tell him, if he would care to call later today he may bring his little girl. You're capable of entertaining the child for half an hour.'

'There is hardly any hurry for a summer house. It's nearly November,' Claire protested, thinking her mother was being ridiculous to want Mark Reseigh to call today, but her mother was 'at that time of life' and was being more fussy and hence more difficult than usual. She could easily become heated over the smallest thing and grow as hot and flushed as a beetroot.

'I know that too – don't be facetious Claire. I'd like to take my time with the design and planning. I want it ready by next spring. We have many very pleasant days in spring. Must I remind you of that? Please do as I ask and don't

187

question me. It will bring on one of my head-aches. And do put on a little make-up, you're as pale as new linen.'

'I'll go at once,' Claire said, heading for her bedroom. The last thing she wanted was for her mother to take to her bed, from where she would issue endless orders and complaints. Claire put on some make-up, red lipstick – not too dark – and a dab of pale-blue eye shadow and a hint of rouge. She didn't linger at her mirror. She was blushing, for she knew her errand to see Mark Reseigh was a ruse on her mother's part to place her in Mark's company in the hope he might notice her. If he were at home he would be there alone with Rowella. His mother would have just arrived at Owles House. For the last few days Marjorie had also chattered about Mark's desir-able points. 'He's the steadiest man in Portcowl. With the right opportunity presented to him he could enlarge his little enterprise, digress into other things, and have employees while he runs his own company. I know he adored his late wife, they were childhood sweethearts and he was utterly grief-stricken when she was tragic-ally taken, but the devotion he shows towards his little girl should, with the right encourage-ment, lead to his wanting to provide her with a new mother. With a little persistence from a young lady of high standing and exemplary morals, well, who knows what it might lead to?' Claire's red face was mostly to do with her mother's outrageous assumption and horrendous lack of subtlety. She had no intention of throw-ing herself at Mark. She did like him, however, for many reasons. She put on her prettiest hat.

With the tobacco and a few other purchases, including some white, blue and green wool, various size knitting needles and patterns in her leather shopping bag, Claire fought against the pitiless wind to reach Half Street. Situated above Quayside, its close proximity to the harbour offered small shelter. Three times her umbrella was blown inside out and she had to stop and right it. Thankfully Half Street, as its name suggested, was only a short terrace but she arrived quite breathless outside Thrift Cottage, named after the pretty pink wild flowers that adorned the cliffs in summer. It was half slate-hung, the other half was painted pink. It had a white fence and gate, a slate path, and a porch that in summer was virtually hidden by rambling roses.

Half hoping Mark Reseigh was out, Claire employed the iron door knocker. At once she heard Mark's voice, probably saying something to Rowella, and she wrung her face. What would he think of finding her on his doorstep? Hopefully, he would see nothing unusual in it, he was too wrapped up in Rowella's welfare to care about much else. If her mother had not stipulated she wanted a reply from Mark, Claire would have simply pushed the note through the letterbox and left.

Lowering the umbrella Claire huddled under the porch, then, as she always did when faced with something potentially difficult, she aimed her thoughts at returning home and getting warm and dry and drinking a hot cup of coffee. But with that cosy thought came the prospect of the

189

barrage of questions and, probably, recriminations from her mother. The door opened and
Claire raised the umbrella until she was at
Mark's eye-level. She opened her mouth to explain why she was there, but Mark got in first.
'Miss Opie, please step straight inside out of the
weather. You must be cold.'

She closed her umbrella and put it down. He
ushered her in past him, and she stepped on the
bristle doormat and then the shiny linoleum of a
narrow white-painted passage. 'Thank you, Mr
Reseigh, you are very thoughtful.'

'Daddy, who? Who?' At the end of the passage
Rowella was in the doorway, pointing at Claire.

'It's Miss Opie, precious, you saw her the
other day, remember?' Mark was near Claire's
shoulder. 'Would you like to go through, Miss
Opie? Hope you don't mind being in the kitchen.
It's nice and warm in there and Rowella has her
toys out.'

'Not at all,' Claire said.

Rowella, always a friendly chirpy bundle, in
patterned woollens and black patent shoes tod-
dled up to Claire and reached up a chubby hand.
'Come in, you come me.'

'Ooh, you're gorgeous.' The heartfelt senti-
ment ripped off Claire's tongue. She wanted to
gather up the beautiful black-haired little girl
and cuddle her in her arms. 'I mean,' she glanced
back apologetically at Mark, pinking up. 'Your
little girl is so sweet.'

'There's no doubt about that,' Mark replied
proudly. 'Rowella wants you to take her hand.
She always runs to lead me or her granny into

190

the kitchen when we come in.'

Stooping to hold the little warm hand, Claire laughed as she was escorted into the cosiest haven she had ever experienced. She stalled herself from nearly blurting out, 'What a lovely room!' That would have been an embarrassing faux pas. It was dark owing to the dreary weather but the fire burning in the black cooking range made a rosy glow. The square kitchen table had an embroidered cloth over it and matching chair backs adorned the easy chairs. Claire liked the way the working people had comfortable chairs in their kitchens. It must be so much more relaxing to be in the hub of their homes. Everything was spick and span but a few things lay casually about, toys, a knitting bag, a book, a shawl and Rowella's sleeping blanket. Potted greenery was dotted everywhere, a lot was crammed on to the deep window sill. 'The reason for my call, Mr Reseigh is to bring you a note from my mother, regarding our garden, of course. She asks for your immediate reply.' She handed over the dainty white envelope.

'I see,' Mark said.

While he read the note, Claire kept her attention on his daughter and admired the knitted rag doll Rowella held up for her to see. Claire noted the photographs up on the overmantel and the china dresser of Mark's late wife, Juliet, a beguiling, smiling image of raven-haired supreme femininity. It was no marvel that Mark still grieved over her loss. Claire felt sad that the young woman she had barely known had been denied the upbringing of her delightful child,

191

and very sad also that Rowella had lost her mother.

'That's fine,' Mark said, drawing Claire's eyes to him. 'If it's convenient for Mrs Opie, I could call at four o'clock. My mother will be home by then to take care of Rowella.'

The bewitching eyes of Juliet Reseigh in the nearest photograph caught Claire's eye. There was no way she was going to repeat her mother's invitation that Mark was welcome to bring Rowella with him to the house. Claire would not be party to her mother's wilful attempt at match-making. Mark would be appalled and rightly so. And, Claire thought, she would never make a suitable replacement in Mark's mind for Juliet, perhaps no woman in the world would. If it was Mark's wish to remain a widower all his life that was his business alone. And if Claire remained a spinster until she died it would not be the disgrace her mother often insinuated it would be. It was not a previous century and she would not live her life as if she was in some old romantic novel. She had bought some chocolate drops for Rowella but would not ask if it was all right to give them to her.

'I'll tell my mother. Thank you for your prompt reply. Now if you'll excuse me I really must get on. I have other calls to make.'

'I'll show you to the door,' Mark said.

'No, please don't trouble yourself. I'll see myself out. Goodbye, Rowella, bye-bye,' Claire cooed. With a brief smile at the little girl, she headed smartly for the front door and was outside. Whipping up her umbrella from the porch

192

floor she marched down the path, carefully shut the gate and without looking back set off for Mrs Coad's cottage. Her mother would be anxious for her return home. Well, that was too bad. From now on Claire would concentrate on doing something useful with her life and never again allow her silly, patently transparent mother to treat her as marriage fodder.

Inside Thrift Cottage, Mark hunkered down to Rowella and drew her in for a close cuddle. 'Right precious, it's time for your milk and biscuit.'

'Lady gone,' Rowella piped.

'Yes, she went in a bit of hurry,' Mark said to himself, frowning as he got on with the chore. He made coffee for himself, and then with Rowella up on his lap they drank and ate his mother's home-made butter biscuits.

A short time later Rowella drifted off into her morning nap and Mark settled her down to sleep curled up on his mother's chair. He carefully tucked a knitted blanket around her, which Juliet had made when excitedly looking forward to their baby's birth. As usual, he stroked Rowella's fine silky dark hair, and then gazed at Juliet's photo. 'You should be here,' he whispered, sorrow on him again.

Minutes later he was still aware of Claire's gentle, warm perfume. He wondered again why her departure seemed so abrupt and whether she would be at home at four o'clock this afternoon.

Seventeen

Beth grabbed Evie by the shoulder. 'I've got something to tell you. It's why I asked you to walk with me somewhere completely private.' The sisters were high up on the cliff path, having walked over a mile down the coast under the rays of a generous sun, the wind at their back. There was no sign of dwellings and no livestock in the fields, which were separated by natural hedging and wire fencing from the cliff top. The sea in the bay was deserted, not even the small boat of a lone crabber checking his pots was bobbing on the busy waves way down below. Several hundred yards out from the rocky, sand and shingle shore, inaccessible to man at this spot, reared up a jagged citadel of barnacle-covered granite. It was a dangerous place for unwary boatmen, especially the occasional holidaymaker out in a canoe, for most of the rock lay hidden under the water's surface and its uneven structure caused eddies and minor whirlpools. It was known as Young Man's Folly. Youths had died in the past daring to navigate in a close circle around the rock and leave evidence of their conquest by throwing a neckerchief to snag on an inner pinnacle. Young Man's Folly was a place where cormorants rested and spread and shook out their long black wings to dry. But today no huge bird was in situation. All appeared to be deserted, not even a customary gull was jogging on the foamy water or circling high overhead. The sense of desolation suited Beth's anxious frame of mind, or was it that she was bringing down the atmosphere? Evie was her usual quiet undemanding self, with the added lift of being in love and looking forward to her wedding next spring.

'I gathered that,' Evie said. 'You've been downhearted ever since the Grand Tea Party was ruined, and the Copelands sudden departure. You're not blaming yourself, are you? Over Gabby Magor upsetting the family with her bullish ways? I gathered Kitty was very cross that they decided to shoot off home, but surely that was the right thing to do to mend their marriage properly and get the children settled down to the fresh start. Your mood isn't something to do with Mark, is it? Do you really like him? Has Gabby's big mouth spoiled any chance you were hoping you had with him? I know he was working at Owles House yesterday. Did he ignore you? Were you both embarrassed?'

'It's nothing to do with Mark,' Beth answered so vehemently that she slumped her shoulders. 'I wish it were just that. Yesterday we simply behaved as if nothing had happened. Hopefully, people will soon forget Gabby's silly mischief-making remarks. Mark's an attractive man but we could never have a future together. Anyway, I don't think I'm fated for love and all that goes with it.'

'You can't possibly know that, Beth.'

'But none of that is important, Evie. The thing is, and this may shock you, before I left Wiltshire to come down here for the first time I did a terrible thing, something without thought or honour and I've been found out.' In tense, short, rapid sentences, Beth told Evie everything about her affair with Stuart, how Kitty had comforted her during her miscarriage without knowing the baby's father was Stuart, the alliance she had gladly made with the prodigal Connie to reclaim Stuart, her children and their marriage, and how Gabby had overheard her and Connie talking on the beach.

'I'm not shocked, Beth,' Evie replied, although her eyes had widened considerably. 'Not in the horrified sense but I am amazed. And now Gabby is trying to blackmail you?'

'She was but not any more. I wasn't going to allow that to happen. I knew I couldn't go on with the deception of my dearest friend any longer, so I went to Claze Wyn to confront Gabby, to tell her that I was going to tell Kitty everything, the whole sordid story. I can't tell you how horrible the condition of Gabby's home was, but the peculiar thing is, when Gabby saw how wet, cold and muddy I was from a fall on my way there, she was a little kind to me. She told me a bit about her life, how she was bullied as a child, and as strange as it seems we sort of formed an understanding. I was touched at the way she wanted to spend most of the money she'd intended to demand from me on her cousin.'

When Evie had heard the rest of the tale, she whistled through her teeth, a habit she had picked up from Rob, and one she would not dare perform in her father's presence as he would jump on it as a way to snipe at Rob, something he did every day. 'And you actually took her into St Austell dressed the way she does? Does Kitty know that?'

'Yes, I picked Gabby up as planned but I wasn't going to hide it from Kitty. It would have been impossible anyway. Gabby made the car reek. Kitty insisted on helping me wash and disinfect all the leather work and polish the wood. Then we left the doors open for a few hours. 'I can't believe you did such a favour for that dirty troublemaker,' Kitty said, and she went on about it for hours. I told her I didn't really have a choice as I'd almost knocked Gabby and Tickle down in the lane and I had to do something to make it up to her. It wasn't strictly a lie. Gabby was so excited about riding in the car and having money to spend she jumped right out in front of me. She and Tickle were very lucky they weren't mown down. Gabby made quite a sight in the town and shop managers were none too pleased to have her enter their premises, but she was unusually polite and so childlike she succeeded in getting all that she wanted. On the way back she asked my advice about a lot of things but I won't go into that now.

'Well, as you've probably guessed I went to see Stuart and Connie to tell them I intend to come clean with Kitty. Stuart tried his hardest to talk me out of it but I refused and then I asked them to leave as soon as it could be arranged. Like me, Stuart is afraid that Kitty will never forgive either of us. I promised I'd give the family plenty of time to settle in at home before I talk to Kitty. That was four days ago now and I'm trying to work up the courage to do it. In the meantime I've told Mum – she knew already that I'd had a miscarriage – so she knows what to expect when I make my big confession. I wanted you to know too, Evie, in case Kitty gets so upset she makes it public to shame me, and I wouldn't blame her if she does. I didn't want you to hear about it through inaccurate rumours. Of course, she may simply pack up and leave and wish to never see me again. I know it's going to be awful, the hardest thing I've ever done. And if all hell is let loose I shall lose nearly all of Portcowl's respect and my life here will never be the same again. I don't think there's the risk Gabby will come after me again for money, but in the end I can't go on denying Kitty the truth. She will think I've been playing her for a fool and she doesn't deserve to have it go on.'

Eighteen

Beth was fighting against an immense weight and the cold in her bones was shattering and overwhelmingly cruel. Clawing tentacles of foul salt water were dragging her down to her death. She was in the sea and it was killing her. Reason broke through her anguish and terror. *It's a dream, a terrible mocking nightmare and I deserve to be taunted in this degrading way. I'm contemptible.* Her guilt was punishing her. In her dream state she knew she could force herself awake with a heart-wrenching shudder, gasping to breathe, but she abandoned the fight and allowed the freezing saturation of the sea, the eternal master of humankind to engulf her, to pull her down and down. She accepted her watery grave.

'Are you going to tell me what's troubling you, Beth, or do I have to drag it out of you?' Kitty demanded.

Beth swallowed hard, already near to tears over what she was going to say and the fear of the consequences. Any moment now the salty drops would spear down her frozen cheeks and spatter on the cold hard ground at her feet. She had asked Kitty to take a walk with her, without the dogs. In sight was Young Man's Folly and not far behind them the woods that closed in on Owles House. The cliff graduated down in sweeping stages, until reaching a sheer thirty-foot drop. When the tide was out it would reveal, from here, a thin line of beach.

'Beth, you're frightening me. You've been wan and preoccupied for days, and now you look ill and you've gone ghostly white. What is it? I know you haven't had a serious quarrel with anyone so it's not that. Is something wrong with Christina?'

Beth shook her head wretchedly, barely able to scrape her eyes off the unyielding rock and meet Kitty's anxious expression.

'Is it about yourself? Are you seriously ill? Is that what you're trying to say? Beth, tell me!'

'Oh, Kitty,' Beth grabbed her arm but immediately let it go. 'You are going to hate me.'

'Don't be daft.' Kitty frowned. 'You couldn't possibly do anything to make me hate you.'

'But you will, Kitty.' The huge tears, building up painfully in Beth's heart since her talk to Evie, hit the cold air and washed down her face, staining streaks on her crimson skin. 'I've been deceiving you for over two years.'

'What? I don't understand. How could that happen? There's nothing—'

'But there *is*,' Beth cut in, unable to bear Kitty's bewilderment. 'I'll only have to mention one name and you'll guess what I'm trying to tell you. St–Stuart...'

'Stuart? What about him?' Kitty pondered, compressing her lips. Moment after moment

200

passed each like an aching torturous lifetime to Beth. Then Kitty's drawn brow furrowed deeply and her jaw sagged down and her beautiful eyes leapt into planet size. 'No...' she mouthed. She shook her head. 'You mean ... you're saying ... you and he, you and Stuart!'

'I'm so sorry, Kitty,' Beth sobbed, a trembling hand across her mouth, her look imploring Kitty for forgiveness. Her legs felt like water and she feared she would sink down to her knees.

'It was Stuart who fathered your baby.' Kitty's voice rose in horror and disbelief, shaken to the roots of her soul. 'So that's why Connie left him. He was the first to have an affair, and all this time I've been blaming her for the marriage break-up. Stuart strayed with you. How could you? You betrayed us all. Stuart was a happily married man. You had no right to go after him. You should have walked away the moment you felt attracted to him. Poor Connie, she must have been humiliated. It's no wonder she fell for the first lounge lizard that crossed her path. And what about Louis and Martha? They've been through hell because of you. I can see now why my stupid errant brother so readily took Connie back. It was more than loneliness. He had a guilty conscience. Both of you betrayed the rest of us. You were supposed to be my dearest friend. I can't believe you did this!' She ended with a piercing shriek and it echoed across the wide, open spaces of the air and the churning grey sea. She was shaking from head to foot in shock and fury. 'Sorry? You're sorry? Like hell you are. How dare you do that to all of us. You bitch! You bloody disgusting bitch! Did Stuart know about the baby?'

'Yes,' Beth nodded feebly.

'And I suppose he was relieved when you miscarried. A very neat solution for him.' Kitty issued sarcasm and disgust like darts.

'I'm sorry, so very sorry, please believe me, Kitty,' Beth pleaded. She would go down on her knees if necessary.

'Did you love Stuart? Or was it just wicked fun? You soon fell out of love with him, that's apparent. When he asked to come down here the moment Connie had deserted him you brushed him off. Now I understand your reluctance when he asked if he could bring the children down for a long stay. You must have been appalled that he wanted to stay in your home. I suppose it must have frightened you when Connie suddenly turned up with Stuart and the children at Owles House. My God, but now I think about it you and Connie were thick as thieves. You spoke up for her whenever I mentioned my doubts about her repentance and honesty. You wanted her back with Stuart. Why? Out of guilt?' Kitty's gorgeous looks took on an ugly expression. 'Or was it from a sense of sisterhood of dirty whores? Why should I feel sorry for her? She hurt her own children. You both hurt them. And to think you came down to Cornwall to seek revenge on the mother you thought wrongly had abandoned you. Portcowl couldn't see a bigger hypocrite! You took on the cause of a woman who actually abandoned her own children, and no doubt at one point you would have gone off with Stuart and denied my precious niece and nephew their father.'

'Kitty, please, can't we talk this through?'

'No we damned well cannot! How dare you throw all this on me? It was your burden not mine. I didn't want this truth of yours. I'd rather have stayed ignorant. You're utterly selfish, Beth Tresaile. If I'd have found out all this from Gabby Magor's poisonous tongue I could have coped better with that than this confession of yours.'

'Kitty, please, I couldn't help falling in love with Stuart. I've been sorry about it ever since. We both regretted it and ended it long before I lost the baby.'

Pulling off her thick gloves, Kitty wrung her hands together then held them up claw like, and Beth knew she was aching to scratch her face to ribbons. 'The baby, I stayed with you throughout your pain and heartbreak not knowing it would have been my niece or nephew. Wait! Why are you telling me this now? Something must have happened other than Connie's reappearance. That's it, isn't it? Are you going to own up or do you intend to keep that from me and go on being a vile deceiver?'

With an effort, Beth forced out one slow ragged word at a time for she was finding it hard to breathe over her despair and Kitty's loathing. Her guilt had intensified and she was disgusted with herself. Her confession had shocked caring, kind-hearted Kitty into this dreadful display of hostility and made it all the more appalling. 'Gabby ... Magor ... she ... was ... going ... to ...

blackmail ... me.'

Kitty howled like an animal in dire pain. 'So you were only thinking about yourself! You selfish evil bitch!'

'No! It's not like that at all,' Beth wailed, her desperate plea making her gag and choke, and her laboured breathing making her light-headed. 'Please let me explain.'

Beth reached despairing hands to catch hold of Kitty, but Kitty moved smartly and pushed her away. 'No! Don't you dare touch me! I can't bear to look at you another second. You feared I'd hate you and I do! I hate you with all my heart and strength. I'm going back to pack and I never want to see or hear from you again.'

Beth was brought to stagger forward, her hands still aimed at Kitty as she tried to regain her balance. 'Get away from me!' Kitty scream-ed in utter repulsion and she shoved hard on Beth's chest. 'You make me sick!'

Beth was sent backward and then she was falling from the edge of the cliff path. She grab-bed a bare thorn bush, the spikes ripping through her glove and one foot hit a rock ledge covered with loose scree, which was sent scattering down. With a struggle she managed to catch her other foot on a ledge. She searched up with her free foot for the ledge. Halted in storming off Kitty stared down on her coldly.

Gasping for energy Beth lunged up for the thorn bush and there was a terrible tearing sound as the old bush was pulled up from the roots. The cliff, covered in withered grass and dead heather, sloped away sharply and Beth cried out in pain and fear as she slid and slithered down and down, her front hitting hidden rocks. She tried to use her feet as brakes but could gain nothing solid and her plunge went on and on. 'Kitty, help me!'

She reached the cliff edge and there was an overhang and Beth sought wildly to get a grip on it. Then she was falling into space, hurtling down and down, too numb to scream until she hit the freezing salt water with a bone-jarring splash. Her leg slammed against submerged rock and her flailing hands failed to get a grip on the slippery jagged granite. Her weight took her down. The icy cold took her down to ever more coldness. She lacked the strength for a fight to the surface. She wasn't having a nightmare, this was really happening to her.

She was in the sea and she was drowning. Her last thought was how heartbroken her mother would be to lose another loved one to the sea. Beth had told the truth but the truth was not worth the price Kitty and other innocents would have to pay.

Nineteen

Jacob was in his study, his place of retreat, and even more so since Bettany had fled the vicarage during his first important social event. During the following sleepless nights and often throughout the days, he had paced the square room and berated himself for being an idiot, a hopeless lover and a blind fool to Bettany's needs. He had been thoughtless to plan the tea party to coincide with her first stay at her new home. He had given no heed to his duty to romance, to continue wooing her. He had left her alone too often, taken her for granted. Any woman would hate taking second place in her future husband's life. That sort of thing had been necessary during the Great War, the duty of all men had to be warrior first, to fight for liberty and justice, to provide a safer world for their loved ones, for King, country and Empire. Actually, his first duty was to God, but God would not have expected him to be such a crushing fool in his decisions. The social event should have been held at another time. It was his irresponsibility, his disappointing her, that had led to Bettany getting flaky while delivering her speech. The incident with Gabby Magor had been unfortunate, but Jacob could not blame the unsanitary harridan. He had let

Bettany down badly, and his parish too. It was justice that since then Bettany's answers to his telephone calls had been brief and increasingly offhand and condemnatory.

It was his own fault that his favourite room had taken on the gloom its former incapable incumbent had left it in. Jacob had ordered the shutters to be permanently thrown back, for the last sticks of squat leg furniture to be hidden away up in the attics, the dull glass frontage to be removed from all the bookshelves, and the few sombre pious paintings to be replaced by his own collection of colourful Renaissance style religious dramas. He had a large pottery Celtic cross, which Bettany had admired on her arrival, and he, the inadequate inexperienced swain that he was, along with Bettany's approval of the new bathroom, conservatory and grounds, had taken that for her utter delight in him and the vicarage. How blind and pathetic he had been. The study might as well still be dank and carpetless. He could hardly concentrate on his parish work in here any more.

He had preached the same sermon at both Sunday services, his theme forgiveness, and he had humbly asked his increased (probably just temporary) congregations to forgive him for not ensuring the previous day's event had gone as it should have. He had thanked the attendees and donation givers to the two good causes, announcing that his flock and the Methodist flock, and other contributors, had done themselves proud, that the very satisfying sum of seventy-two pounds, eight shillings, four and a half pence had been raised.

His eyes caught the pile of post idling on his desk, official stuff mostly, where he had dumped it when Mrs Morcombe had brought it in to him. He couldn't keep ignoring his duties. Clearing his throat apologetically to God and his correspondents, perhaps charities asking for help, he summoned up some purpose and strode to the desk, and after a weary sigh, got on with his job. The weight of the letters was satisfying in his hand, it would be a worthy distraction to his pained mind. Answering everyone today and meticulously would see him spend a good deal of time, then it would be time for luncheon, and then he would make a call on someone. He had no planned engagements for this afternoon but he would make at least two calls. He favoured Rob Praed, who was to return to the *Our Lily* to do light work next week. Jacob liked Rob, the rough diamond, now softened and more pliable since the boat incident and his engagement. Rob's flintiness was underlined with a forthright wit, and he was intelligent and keen for warrior-like banter, which Jacob found little opportunity for among the other local men. They were either accepting or stoical with their lot or ambition driven. Rob had not reached a point of forgiveness yet for his cousin Douglas, but it spoke a lot of Rob's worth that he was prepared to work with Douglas again. Douglas's return on the boat had, apparently, caused friction and his father had ordered him off again. Jacob would be interested to learn more about that from Rob.

Jacob thought, if only I'd had Rob's approach

to my chosen future other half, I wouldn't be going through this self-inflicted down in the dumps misery. It was true that while currently laid up Rob had lots of time to concentrate on Miss Vage, who was delightful and sweetly appealing in maidenly new-found love, but Jacob could imagine the tougher, steelier Rob furthering his claim in a constant stream of ways on his bride-to-be. The passion Rob had for Miss Vage, and her obvious intense anticipation of him radiated out of their every pore.

Jacob kicked his shin, a rightful quest for a little unbearable pain. Damned inconsiderate numbskull, he was. He had shown Bettany the importance a teetotaller gave to strong spirits. When with her late at night, when the servants had gone to bed, in the soft mysterious glow of candlelight and fireside, he had harboured passion for her – in his loins, to his disgrace, because his sexual awareness had been the dominating factor. 'Dear God, forgive me,' he whispered. He knew now he had hardly really looked at Bettany, had barely stayed by her side even during their engagement party. If Bettany summed him up she might come to one damning description of him, a terrible let down, or something less flattering.

Remorse swept his hand to the telephone. He must speak to her at once and beg her to forgive him. He would ask the archdeacon for compassionate leave and forsake the parish and go to Bettany and entreat her to believe that he had seen his glaring errors and he would make her a truly attentive husband. The brash motion scattered the pile of letters out like a deck of cards. As if an unseen force had lifted one envelope to stand out for his eyes he recognized Bettany's feminine, curving handwriting.

He snatched it up suddenly afraid, but he knew what he would read and he was not to be mistaken. Bettany's message went straight to the point.

Dear Jacob,

I find no joy in writing this. I am really sorry but after hours of deep thought and anguish I have decided to break off our engagement. It will be painful for both of us for some time, but I am sure after a while you will agree with me that it is for the best. We are not really suited, and I don't think we would have made a very successful marriage. I believe our feelings for one another did not grow into a strong love.

Perhaps we both thought it was the right step for us, but we did not really blend well together. We both want and hope for different things out of life and I could not make a supportive helpmeet for you. While I found Portcowl charming it is not a place where I could live happily, as you seem to do. I beg your understanding. Please do not think too badly of me. It is my hope that if, God willing, we should at some time meet again we may pass a hand of friendship.

I shall be returning your ring and your family's engagement presents.

Therefore this only leaves me to wish you

well for the future and to offer you my sincere hopes that you will go on to find true happiness with the right woman one day.

Jacob did not read her farewell. He got up on legs of lead and went to the window. His whole body let out an involuntary massive sigh and he clutched the latch and pressed his forehead against the cold glass. Guilt roasted high colour up from his throat to his scalp, for his overwhelming feeling was one of relief, of an escape; deliverance, blessed freedom.

Darkness. It was all around her, becoming part of her. She wanted to be consumed by it, to become darkness itself. She was cold, such a bitter bone-eating invasion. She longed to be numb, to lose her whole being, to have her existence cut off. The sound of water was running through her head, in rivers, in thundering cascades, turning her head into a whirlpool.

Kitty drew herself deeper into the hole. An old fox's lair in the heart of the woods, which Joe had showed her last year. Thick damp earth trickled down her neck and back. An itchy wriggling spoke also of grubs and insects. Tree roots, long, invisible tapering fingers dangled down and stung her face, and dirt worked its way relentlessly into her eyes. She choked on the rich cloying earth and spat it out. Her nose was thick with the stuff. She was sitting on hard sharp objects and more were digging into her sides; bones and other dinner stuff left by the foxes. She had fled here after seeing Beth plunge to her

211

death. Not with the intention of concealing herself in here particularly. She had merely fled from the cliff and stumbled wildly and blindly into the woods, crashing through the undergrowth, her trousers ripping, her hat snatched off by a branch, twigs jagging her flesh all over. She had splashed through a fast running stream, getting muddied and bloodied while scrambling in and out of it. She had hared on only in some crazed instinct and had ended up here, desperate to be out of sight. She wasn't hiding away. She wasn't fit to be seen. To be spoken to, to commune with another soul in the world.

She had killed. Pushed Beth then watched her falter, lose her balance and slip away and disappear from her sight while frantically clawing at the savage foliage that refused her grasping efforts to end her plunge. She had listened in a crazed fascination to Beth's screams and then for the splash, the hideous watery sound that would signify Beth's agonizing entry into its depth and her death.

Kitty had waited. Time passed but as if it was almost standing still. How long would it take for a body to finish being slammed against the cruel rock and crash into the jaws of the restless sea? There it was, Beth's final scream. Cut off. Silenced forever. And then the splash, more of a half-hearted splish it had sounded from that far down. It was over. But it wasn't, not yet for Beth. She had to endure the terror of being sucked down, the pain and suffering. Beth had confessed her crimes. Kitty vented hate in return. Enough to send Beth to her death. Kitty's abhorrent crime surpassed Beth's, outweighed it in intent and monstrosity. Less than a minute it had taken her. To kill Beth.

Kitty had stood there screaming and screaming, it was all she had known, the repugnant horror at what she had done, the despair of killing her best friend. Her head felt it would burst, explode and all of her with it. She couldn't stand it. Finally she had abandoned Beth. It was monstrous of her. But she could think of nothing else to do. She was a monster, not fit to be anywhere near anyone else ever again.

Here she was now, her back against her dank shifting prison chamber. Knees drawn up to her chin, arms grasping her knees and her head down. Eyes tightly shut. She swallowed earth. She was choking. Suffocating. She would die from ingesting earth. It was over for Beth. She was already dead from ingesting the sea. Floating and swirling, propelled by the waters' unmatchable will, washed about in the infernal depths, only to reappear days or weeks later on some lonely shore.

Killer, killer, killer, the water started hissing in Kitty's head, booming through her brain. It was her maelstrom of hate that had turned her into a killer and now it had come to taunt her for all eternity. Here, in her hostile tomb.

Claire was dragging her heels towards the vicarage gates. Her mother had sent her to deliver another, no doubt, unnecessary message. Claire didn't know what this one was in regard to, perhaps some silly idea that could be put forward to the social committee. The moment she had arrived home after the embarrassing trek to Mark Reseigh's door, arrived home late to her mother's chagrin, it seemed Marjorie's mind had been striving even more in Claire's absence and she was on tenterhooks to tell Claire her new idea.

'We must watch carefully,' Marjorie had declared, taking hold of Claire's hands, in drama.

Claire had sighed in her depths. Now what scheme?

'I've been thinking.'

'I gathered that. May I go and change?'

'Don't be facetious Claire, and no you may not go yet. Listen. There may be a greater hope, a finer position for you. If Miss Bettany Howard-Leigh finds she cannot reconcile to the Reverend Benedict and calls off their engagement there is hope for you. He would give you all you could dream of, and you he, as an educated local young lady of the highest reputation. He has already witnessed what a willing hand you are to his plans for the parish. You must start attending church. I have not talked your father round yet about changing our place of worship but he cannot stop you from going to a service at St Irwyn's. Your father is reluctant to give up as a lay preacher on the Methodist circuit but once we switched denominations he could become a church warden, serve on the PCC. Mr Benedict will then be able to turn the parish round excellently.'

'Mother, you are taking a lot for granted on Father's and Mr Benedict's behalf.' Claire was appalled at the insensitive display of vanity and arrogance. 'And mine too. Please will you stop this striving to be matchmaker for me? I would love to be married and raise a family but only if a man truly falls in love with me. I will not do the running. It's humiliating. Anyway, at present I have taken on a new commission for myself.'

Marjorie's thin, bow-shaped lips had pursed in offence. 'I'll thank you, young lady, not to speak to me in those tones. What new commission?'

'There's no need to look so shocked, Mother. I am perfectly capable of thinking for myself.'

'What have you there?' Marjorie pointed agitatedly at the packages Claire had brought home, having just noticed them.

'Wool, knitting needles, patterns and trimmings.' Claire raised teasing brows.

'Oh, who for?'

'For me, I'm going to learn to knit to make items for the poor and I'm to learn at the academy of old Mrs Coad. I've asked her and she has said she would be delighted to teach me. I will be having my first lesson tomorrow. Evie Vage happened to be with her and she said she would be happy to teach me to make lace. I'm going to become a hive of industry. Turn over part of my bedroom as a workplace. Father asked me the other day what I would like for my birthday. I'm going to ask for a sewing machine.'

Mrs Opie was clearly outraged by her daughter's flippancy. 'I will not be mocked, Claire. And I will not have you become a seamstress indeed! Charitable works are worthy, be sure

215

everyone knows that is your reason for doing this. Oh, I'm getting one of my headaches. I shall have to lay down for the rest of the day.'

'That won't be possible, Mother. Mr Reseigh is calling this afternoon, just as you had hoped.'

Claire had not stayed in the room during Mark Reseigh's call. Instead she had stayed in her room reading through the simplest of her knitting patterns and practising casting on stitches. Mrs Coad had said the Salvation Army would eagerly take baby's bonnets, blankets and other items, which they would distribute among the less fortunate.

Since then Claire had triumphed in her first goal, a plain but perfect, white baby bonnet. I would rather be showing the vicar my achievement than handing him this pretence note, she thought, vexed with her mother. Hopefully, he would be absent from home. She would return home and rearrange her bedroom furniture, with Jean's help, for the arrival of her sewing machine. Claire's birthday was not for a week but her father had ordered a Singer machine immediately upon her request.

As the vicarage came into view Claire had to jump out of the way as the Reverent Benedict sped towards her in his motor car, the top down.

'Ah, the very person!' He eased up beside her and leaned across and opened the passenger door. 'Please get in, Miss Opie. There may be a crisis at Owles House. I'll explain on the way.'

Claire got in and had to hold on tightly to her hat as the motor car sped along. 'Is someone ill? Has someone had an accident?'

'An accident possibly. I've received a telephone call from Mrs Vyvyan. She's fearful for Miss Tresaile and Miss Copeland who are long overdue from a walk over the cliffs. Unusually, Miss Tresaile requested they didn't take the dogs. Mark Reseigh is at the house today and he's following the route they took down the coast, with the dogs. If there proves to be a problem, I am confident you, Miss Opie, will be very useful with both a comforting voice and practical help.'

'I'm delighted you have confidence in me, Mr Benedict. I'm always very pleased to offer help and support in any way that I can.' Claire's heart was pumping with gratification and purpose. At last she had a proper reason to justify her existence. Heavy raindrops hit the low windscreen and Claire felt icy wet spikes on her face. They would soon be in for a tremendous shower. 'Oh no, I do hope Miss Tresaile and Miss Copeland are safe and well.'

Twenty

A group of hushed women stared out of Christina's sea-facing bedroom window hoping and praying for signs of the search party of Mark, Mr Benedict, and Ken Tresaile, whom Christina had also alerted to bring Beth and Kitty home. Christina was using binoculars to scan the cliffs and she had lent a pair to Evie, who had joined Ken after he had arrived on Evie's doorstep with the worrying news. Claire and Mrs Reseigh were on either side of the pair. The viewing was hampered greatly by the dusky dark sky and the rain battering on the panes, and although a fire was lit in the room all the women found themselves shivering at times.

'What on earth could have happened to them?' Mrs Reseigh whined for the umpteenth time.

'We have no idea, Mrs Reseigh,' Christina said patiently, although she was twisted with worry inside. 'I'm sure the dogs will find them. Mark might have come across them ages ago. It's likely one of the girls has twisted her ankle, something like that. They may be in a rather awkward place and Mark may have chosen to stay with them until more help arrives. He knows the Reverend Benedict would come after him.'

'Someone will come along the cliff soon, I'm sure.' Evie glanced uncertainly at Claire, who returned a sympathetic look, and then Evie strained to scan the land again. As much as she was anxious about Beth and Kitty, Evie was angry with her father. When her uncle Ken had turned up, Davey, at home for his morning crib, had scowled. 'Can't see no point in Evie going up there.' He had made it sound like an order. 'She can't do nothing to help. They're grown women, probably back by now taking a genteel cup of tea.'

'I'm going.' For the first time Evie had, crossly, opposed her father. 'Beth is my sister, my flesh and blood. I need to know she is all right. If she's had an accident she might need me.'

Jerking his head sourly back to the food and drink before him on the table Davey had muttered. 'The likes of her always need cosseting.'

'Good for you,' Ken had said, as they had hurried up from the cove, arms linked. 'About time you stood your ground with Davey. You'll be a married woman soon and he's got to learn he can't run your life any more. I'm sure Beth and her friend is fine, but like you I want to be there, just in case either are hurt. How are the wedding arrangements going? I swear I've never seen a man happier than Rob about his future. I know you'll make a good marriage.'

'Dad's putting obstacles in the way. When anything's mentioned he always says there's plenty of time and that whatever it is can wait. I'm proud to wear my Vage engagement ring but I

219

believe it was a ruse of Dad's so I wouldn't have one from Rob. He sighs with impatience when I go ahead with making my wedding dress and he only made a face when I showed him the pattern and material. I swear he sneers while I'm working on the lace for my veil. Beth offered to buy my bridal shoes but he wouldn't hear of it. Demands to buy everything himself, but when I ask him for the money he comes up with excuses. Rob and I see his suggestion of a spring wedding as a delaying tactic. We're sure he'll try to break us up. He won't succeed though. Whatever happens I will marry Rob and there's nothing he can do to prevent it. I love Dad, he's been a wonderful father, but it would be too selfish of him to deny me my happiness.'

'I'm glad you see that for yourself. You don't owe Davey your whole life's devotion. He should be delighted for you, especially now Rob's more settled in his ways. Be careful, Evie. If you need anything you can always come to me.'

'Well, if Dad gets really narky, who knows, you might end up giving me away, Uncle Ken.' And if that were to happen Evie would resent her father until he had a change of mind. He was ruining what should be a happy time of her life. It was selfish and nasty of him. It would be difficult living next door to him if he remained obstinately against her and Rob.

'Perhaps Miss Tresaile and Miss Copeland got talking and forgot the time and walked further than they had anticipated,' Claire tried, hoping to bring comfort.

220

'But even if they had reached Porthellis they should be back by now. Mark should have met up with them ages ago. And anyway they would have given up long before in this dreadful weather.' Mrs Reseigh twisted her hands round a crumpled handkerchief.

'You're not helping, Mrs Reseigh. I know it seems ages since the other men followed Mark but it's not really,' Christina sighed. She had heard quite enough of the older woman's fears. 'The wetness is why it would have been easier for one or both of the girls to slip. Carrying one or both of them back would be slow progress. Why don't you go down and put the kettle on again? Miss Opie, would you mind helping Mrs Reseigh to bring up a tray. By then we may have seen someone returning.'

'Of course, I'd be glad to.' Claire kept her tone light. 'Come along, Mrs Reseigh. And we could prepare another tray and food for the men. They'll be cold and wet. And towels. We'll need lots of towels. And I'm sure Miss Tresaile and Miss Copeland will welcome the bathrooms being made ready for them.'

Christina silently worded, 'Thank you,' to Claire. Then out loud to Mrs Reseigh she said. 'Yes, keeping busy is the thing to do.'

When the two had left, she and Evie peered through the binoculars again. They saw nothing but a hostile wintry land and seascape, and Christina gripped Evie's hand.

Visibility on all sides was poor and unheeding but more so out over the bay. Jacob walked ahead of Ken, for the path in most places demanded single file, both men using the walking sticks that Christina had handed them for safety's sake. They saw the woods only as a large shadowy shape of indistinct distance, looming behind the slanting sheet of rain. They had also brought with them rope, strung over Ken's shoulder, and a silver flask of brandy. The wash of the sea below sounded hollow and eerie. Jacob's hat was tied on with his scarf, and his skin stung from the freezing water dripping off the wool. His eyes shifted constantly from the muddy slippery ground, down and up and from side to side, as did Ken's, for clues, for signs of the women's whereabouts.

'Beth! Kitty!' The men shouted often, but the names were carried wilfully away by the wind that was buffeting and rocking them.

Every so often the men halted and peered through the hostile gloom and listened hard, but they saw and heard nothing save the booms and lashes of the harsh conditions. At the start Ken had said. 'This just isn't like them. If they had gone on to Porthellis and stayed there they would have phoned the house. Otherwise, they wouldn't have stopped somewhere to wait in shelter but continued home. One of them must have had an accident and the other is staying put. We must look for signs of distress.'

Suddenly Jacob pointed to the ground and yelled, 'Look there! A ladies glove, held fast by a stone.'

'Wait,' Ken grabbed hold of Jacob to prevent him picking up the glove. 'See the way it lays?

The thumb and three fingers are curled under. The forefinger is pointing towards the cliff edge.'

Leaning forward the men stared beyond the path edge and both saw the straight line of crushed foliage on the cliff's descending surface. 'No!' Ken bawled. 'Someone's gone over.' He made to scramble down but Jacob yanked him back.

'Don't be a fool man. We don't want another accident. Look along the path. It's a man's scarf, Mark's. He's laid it flat and pointed the ends, another message. Is there a way down further on?'

'Yes, several yards on there's a place where a climb down can be made to the beach below but it's very tricky, foolhardy in this weather. Mark might be trying to get down to it. There's an old smuggler's cave high up above the shoreline. There's hope. Let's get on.'

Long minutes later they covered those several yards. Jacob called out. 'Yes! Just down there, it's Grace! She's been stationed there. You can see where Mark has climbed down.' From under the inadequate shelter of a wind-vexed scrubby bush the saturated collie-cross barked and bounded and slithered up over the treacherous ground until she reached them.

'Mark! Mark! Chaplin.' Joining Grace's excited barks the men yelled at the tops of their voices. While Grace fussed round their feet, Jacob ordered her to be quiet. The men listened praying they would hear Mark shout back but all they heard was the wash of the waters and the whistling of the tormenting wind.

'Please don't let Mark have fallen, but I doubt if he and even Chaplin could hear us,' Jacob muttered through gritted teeth.

'The tide's turning,' Ken said. 'The beach will be more exposed. That's good.'

'I'm going down, but will use the rope. It will be safer and quicker than the usual climb which turns a lot,' Jacob said. 'You stay here with the dog, Ken. If I see anyone I'll tug twice on the rope. If I tug thrice or you don't see any sign of us in about half an hour hurry back and get more help. We must keep up our prayers.'

'Right vicar, you be damned careful. If I was the younger man it would be me going down there. Beth's my niece.'

Ken secured the rope around an immovable boulder then fed it round his waist. He had helped half a dozen cliff rescues over the years and swiftly tied the other end round Jacob's waist. 'Don't worry,' Jacob said grimly. 'I've done rock climbing before. I'll abseil down where I can.'

Although not a religious man Ken uttered, 'God guide you. Take care, young man.'

First rubbing and beating on his cold limbs Jacob began the climb down and soon he was leaping out and downwards, passing Grace's former place and in quick stages he reached the cliff overhang. He steadied himself and looked keenly below and up and down the slowly growing small stretch of beach. Yes! He could see Chaplin sitting high up on a rock near the cliff face, way back in the direction he and Ken had come from, as he'd been ordered to stay there. Thank God. It seemed Mark had discovered someone, hopefully both women, and needed help and had cleverly marked out the route for help. He looked up to Ken and motioned with one finger then pointed at Grace, indicating he had seen the other dog. Ken nodded and put up a thumb in recognition.

'Chaplin!' Jacob shouted, continuing with the abseil, having to swing in from the overhang to find firm rock with his boots. Part of the overhang of the cliff had been worn naturally away and if he sat on its edge and slid down his feet would soon land on rock, then there was a tricky clamber over more rocks. In a few careful leaps he reached the sand and shingle shore, just yards away. Chaplin had heard and seen him and was barking madly but he obediently stayed put. As fast as his cold aching legs allowed him to, Jacob ran towards Chaplin. He could make out a round blackness near to Chaplin, the old smuggler's cave. Hope surged in Jacob's chest. 'Mark! Mark! Can you hear me? Have you found Beth and Miss Copeland?'

Seconds passed and then he saw a woolly head appear out of the blackness, and then Mark beckoned to him. 'Vicar, up here. Thank God you've come.'

Clambering up Jacob crawled inside the cave entrance and found he could stand up if he kept his head bent down. Mark was there, shivering violently, soaked through, probably to the skin but he seemed strong and well. Jacob looked past him and saw two figures huddled together

225

on the cave floor. 'You've found them both! Praise God. Oh, it's Miss Tresaile and...?'

'Douglas Praed,' Mark said. 'He was sitting wanting to be alone at the cave entrance and saw Miss Tresaile falling into the sea. He dived in and rescued her. She was badly gashed on the leg and nearly drowned and he got dashed into the rocks hauling her out of the water. They're both in a weak state. Douglas managed to tie up her leg tightly. He's been here a lot lately and had brought a blanket down and food and he had a flask of hot tea. That has probably kept them going. I couldn't get them up by myself, all I could do was to stay with them and keep them awake so they didn't succumb to the hypothermia in the wait for help.'

Jacob only got a glimpse of the grey faces, both blinking uncomprehending from the wrapped confines of the blanket. 'I've brought brandy and I came down here by rope. Ken Tresaile's up top. It's going to be difficult but let's get them up and home. Has Miss Tresaile mentioned if Miss Copeland went to get help for her? She still hadn't turned up when Ken and I left Owles House.'

Mark gazed down on the woman, still in Douglas's arms from when he had brought her here and tried to keep her warm. Her blue eyes did not blink or waver. He stooped to lift her up. 'No, she hasn't said a word to Douglas or me. He's past talking now. We need to act fast. As for Miss Copeland, if she's got lost I'm afraid the rain will have washed away all traces of her scent. The dogs certainly weren't on to her.'

226

Twenty-One

Late that night an urgent knocking brought Joe to the back door. Swinging it open, he called eagerly, 'Kitty? Oh!'

'S'only me, Master Joe,' Gabby bleated, as wild looking as the weather. She had Tickle up in her arms, both sheltered under a long waterproof hooded cape. 'Don't shut the door in me face. Saw all the lights on. So it's true that Miss Beth went missing and was found hurt? I'd like to know, you see, Miss Beth was some kind to me the other day.'

'I'm afraid it's true. Come inside, Miss Magor. We're all wide awake, except for my sister. She hasn't stirred since she managed to sip a little soup.'

Entering the back kitchen, Gabby shrugged off the cape and stepped out of her muddy rubber boots. Her stockinged feet smelled rank but Joe couldn't care less about that. 'So she's not too bad then? Going to be all right?'

'Come into the kitchen. My mother is in there making hot cocoa. Join us. You can bring Tickle.'

'Very civil of 'ee.' Gabby sniffed back her sopping nose. 'Always said you were a nice young man, our future squire in a sense. Any news of

Miss Copeland yet?'

'No.' Joe heaved a mighty fretful sigh. 'It's a complete mystery about what's happened to her. People have been asked to check their outhouses and sheds. We're desperate. Do you have any ideas, Miss Magor? Another one for cocoa, Mum. I'll fetch another mug. And put some water and biscuits down for Tickle.'

'Good of you to let me into your fine home, Mrs Vyvyan,' Gabby rasped, glancing round in amazement at the room, her hooded eyes twinkling at each modern appliance, like the refrigerator and the pieces of fine china on the dressers. Chaplin lifted his regal head and sniffed curiously at Tickle. Grace was down flat on all fours whining for her mistress, her great brown eyes clearly saddened the newcomer wasn't her. ''Fraid I got no idea about Miss Copeland but I've been looking out, all round my place and anywhere else I can think of since I heard the news. Bleddy awful. Oh, 'scuse my mouth.'

'Do sit down, Miss Magor.' Christina used the same welcoming tones as she would any other visitor. The woman was a nuisance and long ago she had mocked Christina over her mental breakdown, but Beth had suddenly taken to her, and Gabby was a local who knew the area through and through and Christina did not want to discourage her from continuing with the search for Kitty. 'Help yourself to biscuits. We've spent a lot of time in here. It's cosier somehow. The search has been suspended until daybreak. We're praying that Kitty has found safe refuge somewhere.'

'Yeh, she's a clever woman,' Gabby said, warming her big calloused paws round the mug.

'Yes,' Christina agreed absently. No one wanted to say that now the hue and cry had been sounded up and down the coast that the local shores would be searched during the next few days for a body. Then, with tearful emotion, 'I've informed her brother. Mr Copeland is coming down on the night train. My poor daughter hasn't been able to say a word so far, so I can't offer him an explanation about the accident as of yet. I shall be going up to her again in a moment. Mrs Reseigh is with her now. She is going to stay overnight.'

'So, Douglas Praed's gone from villain to hero? Who'd have thought that?' Gabby said, spitting out crumbs on the whole digestive biscuit she had rammed into her cavernous mouth.

'Thank God he saw Beth's fall or she surely would have been lost. After the doctor had checked him over, Mr Praed, who had brought Douglas dry clothes, took him home. Thank goodness Mark found Douglas and Beth or they might have slipped away into unconsciousness and we might have lost them both that way.'

'Vicar and Ken must have had a job getting 'em up the cliff and carrying 'em here.' Gabby gurned in appreciation at the biscuit, took a gulp of cocoa, burped loudly and snatched up another biscuit. 'Good strong men though. I heard Miss Beth's got a badly cut leg. That going to be all right?'

Joe lifted up scruffy little Tickle who had

wolfed down his food and had come to scrabble up his leg. He tickled the mite under his pointed chin and Tickle licked Joe's hand. 'It's a deep graze, from shin to knee. It will have to be carefully dressed and might leave a scar. Poor Beth was terribly knocked about in the sea. Her recovery will take a few weeks after her ordeal. Some people think she should be in hospital, but Dr Powell believes like my mother, that she will do better being carefully nursed at home. He and the District Nurse will be calling regularly.' For the first time since hearing the shock news Joe allowed tears to edge his eyes. 'If only we knew why Kitty just disappeared. Douglas Praed is convinced only Beth fell into the sea. Gabby, you know the area like the back of your hand, will you help in the search tomorrow?'

'Goes without saying, Master Joe. Rain or no rain I'll track her down.'

A piercing scream from the top floor of the vicarage woke Jacob out of his doze where he was still sitting up in his study. He raced up the two flights of stairs and found Winifred crumpled on the landing floor, below a small window, and the other servants emerging from their rooms in their nightclothes, the cook holding a lighted candle. 'What is it, Winifred? Were you sleepwalking?' He lifted her gently to her feet and kept his hold on her for she was shaking.

'N—no sir. Out there,' she pointed to the window. 'I couldn't sleep. Then I heard these noises, like tapping and scratching. At first I thought a cat might have got inside and was

230

chasing a mouse, so I got up to look. Then I realized it was coming from outside. So I peeped out and I saw it, a ghost! A monster! Like something evil come up out of the grave.'

'Don't be silly girl,' the cook scolded. 'You had cheese for supper, that's all it was. A nightmare. Then you found yourself out here and got scared.'

'Calm yourself, Winifred,' Jacob said kindly, frowning at the scornful cook. 'It was probably only a wild animal. To settle your fright I'll go down and take a look.'

'Oooo, be careful, Reverend. I know I wasn't dreaming and I swear I saw something larger than an animal.'

Jacob lifted up the window and peered through the oppressive darkness. The rain had stopped but the air was murky and heavy with the odour of wet dead leaves and earth. He detected nothing moving. He closed the window and marched off down the stairs, the cluster of servants creeping after him.

Switching on the porch lights and unlocking and pulling open the arched front door Jacob stepped outside. He looked straight ahead. 'Hello, is anyone there?' He groaned inwardly. Why had he used the standard seance question? Ghost? Monster? Poppycock. There was nothing but the gravel drive and lawn and then the trees beyond them.

A scattering sound followed by a low moan made his heart leap against his ribs and every last hair on the nape of his neck stood up stiffly. 'Holy God, protect me.'

231

'Ugh!' Something touched his foot and he leapt backwards.

'Uh, uh, uh...'

What was that ungodly noise? Nervously Jacob looked down. Just in front of him was a strangely lumpy shape.

'What is it, Reverend, an injured animal? Be careful, it might be savage.' It was Mrs Morcombe. The shape lifted up and the housekeeper was sent screaming fit to burst her lungs. 'It's a demon straight from hell. Get inside, lock the door!'

For a second Jacob was petrified to the spot, staring down at what seemed like glazed orbs in a dirt-smeared indefinable contour. Then his senses returned in full. 'Miss Copeland!' And he was reaching down and his outstretched arms bypassed Kitty's imploring arms and he picked her up and had her limp body within his grasp. He nearly knocked over the dithering Mrs Morcombe as he swept Kitty into the house.

He carried her into the drawing room, still lit by the embers in the hearth, and set her down on the sofa. 'Lights, towels, hot water, Dr Powell,' Jacob ordered strongly but softly so as not to alarm Kitty. His mouth went dry when he realized she was staring into nothingness. He could only think some instinct had drawn her here, to a place of safety.

'Oh, our dear Lord,' Mrs Morcombe fussed over his shoulder, after lighting the room. 'She's lagged in earth, she must have fallen down a hole, poor lady. All will be done, Reverend. I'll make the call to the doctor.'

232

'Then call Owles House. Even if Mrs Vyvyan has managed to sleep she will want to be awakened and be informed straight away.'

When alone, Jacob rubbed Kitty's wrists. 'Hold on, Miss Copeland, all will be well. Miss Tresaile – Beth – is alive and well. I hope you can understand me.'

Kitty moved her filthy head on the cushions. Her hair stuck out in muddy tats. Her gritty eyes met his but Jacob could not be certain she recognized him. 'B–Beth...' Her voice was raw and did not sound quite human, but Jacob was relieved she knew her friend's name.

'She's been rescued Kitty.' He soothingly caressed her scratched cheek. 'You have nothing to worry about. The doctor will be here soon to attend you. If you are well enough tomorrow to travel to Owles House you can make your recovery together.'

'No,' Kitty whimpered shaking her head in dire agitation. She grasped Jacob's hand, digging in with her sharp broken nails. 'Never, never! I want to stay here. See no one, not ever. Promise me!'

'Very well, I promise. Now all you need to do is rest. Your brother is on the way down to Cornwall. He will be so relieved you have turned up.'

'No, no, no!' Kitty's frenzy started up again. 'Not him, never see him again. Promise! Promise me or I'll leave, I swear.'

'You have my word as a man of God. No one but myself, the doctor and a maid will see you. Now rest, rest Kitty. All will be well.'

With his vow claimed, she fell into a stupor.

Jacob held her hand firmly, his expression deeply troubled to have witnessed such terrible distress. It was obvious something gravely untoward had happened to, or between, the two friends up on the cliffs. Why had they ventured out denying the usual company of the dogs? Had one of them something critical on her mind and had needed to share it? Jacob was faced with giving sanctuary to Kitty Copeland and he did not mind that at all, but he would be called on to convince her friends and her brother that on no account, at least for now, did she wish to see them.

Twenty-Two

A large canvas bag slung over his shoulder and lugging a heavy sack under his good arm and yet another lighter one with his healing arm, Rob was taking supplies to *Our Lily*. For the last three days he had done a lot of light work on the lugger and it was good to be useful again, out in the fresh air, unbothered, as he had been all his life by the cold, wind and rain. Lofty was refusing to allow him to fish out at sea for another week yet despite his assertions that he was strong and well enough to.

This morning Rob had made his usual plea. 'I won't be a liability, Uncle. You've been struggling with two men down for far too long.'

Douglas's heroism at rescuing Beth Tresaile had gone some way to cancelling out his neglect and lies over Rob's injury and he would return to work for good in time. His prolonged soaking in bitterly cold seawater had led to him suffering mild pneumonia. With Rob happy to win Evie as his bride he had got over the last of his hurts and anger with Douglas. He had reclaimed his old adage that blood was thicker than water.

Lofty had shaken his head, sagely, immovable on the matter. 'Sorry, boy, I'm not taking any risks on you getting hurt again. Don't reckon that arm's quite up to it yet and neither does the doctor. You'll have to be patient a bit longer. Soon be time to load up the herring nets and head for Plymouth waters. I'll see about it then. Here's the money for the rest of the shopping. Don't forget my baccy. Get yourself some fags.'

Once again Rob trotted off dutifully to the chandler and general stores, not minding too much as Evie was accompanying him, as she always did, to get her daily shopping. And Davey hated it, as he did now over the manner in which Rob hailed him cheerfully on the way back from this trip. 'Evie's putting the kettle on, Davey. Are you joining us?'

Davey muttered under a dark expression, 'I'll be in when I'm ready.' That would be only after Rob had left his house.

Rob shrugged. 'If that's the way he wants to be, what can we do? Gives us more time to be alone.' Rob wasn't bothered, but Evie was getting more and more frustrated with her father's hard line.

'It's so unnecessary,' she said. 'He's even refusing to go to chapel with me. It's not fair of him.'

If Davey kept up his growing hostility he would lose Evie's respect and perhaps her love, and Rob would have little to do with his scowling father-in-law after the wedding. Davey could try what he liked but he wouldn't stop Rob making Evie his wife. He would elope with her if things became really bad, once he had walked Alison down the aisle, two days before the start of the herring season.

'Oh look,' Evie said, 'It's Douglas on the quayside. Glad to see he's wrapped up well. Glad we're having a dry day at last.'

'Auntie Posy's got him coddled up like a baby,' Rob laughed. 'Can he join us for crib?'

'Of course,' Evie said. Her father would not like it and his attitude was too bad of him. She had been hurt and horrified that Davey had not uttered a single word when she had got home that awful day and reported that Beth had been found alive, although far from well. If he would have preferred it that Beth had drowned in the sea then it was just as well he was refusing to attend chapel.

'You go on in, boy,' Lofty told his recuperating son. 'Too cold for you to stay out here. Should be home by the fire.'

'I just wanted a look at the boat, Dad,' Douglas murmured. Although bundled up he was a slim sight for he had lost a lot of weight. His rugged face had lost its colour and he had a noticeable beard and moustache, the blackness of his facial

236

hair accentuating his paleness. His appearance was different and so was his demeanour, part of his attempt at a fresh start. His shoulders had lost their droop now his father had told him he was proud of him again. 'Had to get out for a minute. Thanks Rob, Evie, just a quick drink, thanks. I promised Mother I wouldn't stay out long.'

'Take my arm, Douglas,' Evie said, sticking her elbow out to him.

Douglas could only nod. His eyes were wet with emotion to be accepted again wherever he went. He had received many a kind remark during his slow walk here. A sudden coldness washed down his spine and instinct made him look across two of the moored luggers at *Morenwyn*. Davey Vage was glaring at Rob as if he wanted to kill him.

Once Douglas was ensconced in Evie's little armchair near the warmth of her range, he asked, 'How's Miss Tresaile? I hear she's still not too good, nor Miss Copeland. Strange business the way she turned up at the vicarage. She going back to Owles House soon? Mrs Vyvyan kindly sent me all sorts of thank you gifts, and a letter, chocolates, flowers and a book. Everyone would love to know what really happened that day. No one's sure yet, are they? Except 'tis believed when Miss Tresaile fell Miss Copeland went into shock and ran off and must have fell down where it was earthy; had to be in the woods. God knows how or why she ended up at the vicarage, some sort of instinct, I suppose.' Mentioning instinct made Douglas recall the ghastly feeling that had made him look at Davey Vage and witness the man's venomous expression shot at Rob. *Evil, it was evil,* Douglas thought, shivering horribly.

'Here, drink this, it's cocoa, do you more good,' Evie said, giving Douglas a big mug. She handed him a tea plate with a large round of hevva cake on it. 'You've answered most of your own questions. Both Beth and Miss Kitty are still laid up in bed, and both are barely speaking a word to anyone. Miss Kitty is refusing to leave her room, and she refused to see Mrs Vyvyan when she called there to reassure her she was welcome back to Owles House, that there was no need to feel guilty about leaving Beth, if that's the problem. Even Mr Copeland isn't getting anywhere with Miss Kitty. He's staying at the vicarage too but she hasn't spoken to him yet. She'll allow Miss Opie to read to her for a little while each day and the vicar to pop in and say a prayer, but that's all. It's such a worry. Doctor thinks Miss Kitty's had a complete nervous breakdown and might need specialist help. We must pray and hope they will both return to normal soon.'

Evie was not going to divulge all she knew about her sister and Kitty. She had only told Rob the full details. That Beth kept sobbing and crying, 'It's all my fault. Poor Kitty, she doesn't deserve her suffering. Tell her I'm so sorry.' Further to that she could not be drawn. Apart from Mrs Vyvyan's call at the vicarage she had hardly left Beth's bedside, and would only be relieved by Mrs Reseigh or Evie, or Joe for short minutes. The district nurse called every day to

238

give her a blanket bath and Dr Powell called every other day. He declared Beth's distress was emotional and had little to do with physical pain, and that it was understandable she was having the most dreadful nightmares. It might prove necessary for Beth to also need psychiatric help.

'If only we knew what Beth means by the accident being all her fault,' Mrs Vyvyan would lament anxiously. 'It's such a mystery. What could Beth have to be sorry about? She and Kitty have always been the best of friends. It doesn't make sense. And why is Kitty refusing to see her brother? She was devoted to him. He was everything to her. He knows something, I'm sure he does, but he's keeping tight-lipped.' Mrs Vyvyan spoke about a mystery but her eyes would dart away to Evie. Beth had told them both about her love affair with Stuart Copeland, and that her confession to Kitty had gone horribly wrong. A mystery? Not to Evie and Mrs Vyvyan.

Bang, bang! 'Eh! Anyone there?' It was Gabby Logan. She was a regular visitor to Owles House's back door. 'Got news for 'ee.'

Just home from school, Joe let her in. 'It's just me downstairs, and the dogs. There's no change in Beth, I'm afraid, Gabby.' He carried out a little custom that had come into being. Gabby, today in an ancient mouldy trench coat, had Tickle up in her arms and Joe passed her an old towel to wipe Tickle's paws. He filled a small crock with water for Tickle, who greedily, noisily and messily quenched his thirst. 'So you've

239

got news? Go on.'

'He's just had a pee and a poop so your mother's floors won't suffer,' Gabby grinned impishly, but it was rather ogress-like. She put Tickle down and the three dogs began a tussle over the towel. Joe demanded the towel and sent them to lie down, each with a dog biscuit. He was the only other person Tickle obeyed.

'I'm a dab hand at tea making. Would you like some?'

'Ais, proper job! You do have a lovely way of talking, Master Joe. Lots of sugar, if you don't mind. Got any grub? My guts is so empty it's practically festering.'

'Take a seat. Call me Joe. You're Beth's friend and that makes you my friend too.'

'Really? Blimming heck, never had friends before.' Gabby beamed with delight and her fat reddened nose deepened to an even darker shade. While Joe got busy with the domestic things, Gabby plonked down on a chair, after bringing it out sideways to the table. She sniffed, swiped at her runny nose and began her news. 'I've been scouring the woods with Tickle every chance I've got. Think I've found where Miss Kitty ended up. Deep into the trees, the old fox's den down the steep drop, near the crossed-over fallen trees. Know where I mean?'

'Yes, I do,' Joe said, spooning tea leaves into the dark blue teapot. 'I remember showing Kitty that place a long while ago. Can only think she ran there just by some instinct.'

'Well, I believe she was trying to hide away. Tickle went right in and came out with shreds of her clothes and her missing scarf. I s'pose something spooked her 'ventually and she scrambled out, but by then mad as the bled-blimming Hatter and wandered about till, thank God, she stumbled on to the vicarage.'

Joe nodded. It cleared up only a tiny part of the mystery.

'Or...' Gabby said enigmatically, devouring two chocolate cream biscuits together from the biscuit barrel Joe had put on the table.

'Or what?' Joe eyed her. 'Don't muck about.'

'Why the vicarage, I asked myself, even if she were mazed in the head? If she was operating on instinct could've been sanctuary she was after, not cus she was scared, not that sort of sanctuary, but out of guilt that she didn't try to save Miss Beth from falling.' Gabby raised her awry eyebrows, deadly serious now. Beth had obviously told her friend about her secret affair, and probably Gabby's attempt at blackmail and things had got way out of hand, and Gabby felt some responsibility over the whole thing.

'I don't believe that,' Joe answered stridently. 'I've run the facts through my mind again and again. Certainly something very wrong had happened between Beth and Kitty on that cliff walk. My mother knows what it was all about but she refuses to tell me. It brings me back to the common belief. Beth fell and either Kitty froze and couldn't help her or Kitty tried to but failed. Then the horror of believing Beth was dead shut down Kitty's mind. I'd like to see Kitty, but Mum says there's no point in trying.' Joe sighed wearily, sitting down at the table and pouring two mugs of tea. 'It seems it's going to take a long time before Kitty is well enough to face anyone or anything.'

Gabby took the liberty of dropping five sugar lumps into her mug and then feeding several lumps into her jacket pocket. She took a big glug of tea, the scalding liquid apparently not searing her tongue and throat. 'Seems to me that if Miss Kitty's refusing to see grown-ups, and she pro'bly got her reasons, then you're the only one she might care to see. You're a wily boy. Easy enough job for you to slip into see her, don't you think?'

Suddenly Joe's handsome dark face was lit with design. 'I'll take some flowers over to her tomorrow, and make sure that I see her, never fear.'

'Good boy.' Gabby gobbled and slurped, swallowed and burped.

Joe was considering Gabby from eyes narrowed from intent.

Gabby noticed. 'Got something in your eye, boy, or something to say?'

'Beth's always grateful to hear you've asked about her. She'd said before that she really got to know you during the car journey. She cares about you. It's possible that she might be glad to speak to you for a while. You'll be coming from a different direction to the rest of us, as it were. When we've finished this, perhaps I could put the suggestion to Mum. Would you try, Gabby?'

'Course I will! I'd do anything for the lady who was so kind to me.' Gabby gave an odd look but a touch of the maternal could not be mistaken in it. 'Make up a fresh tray, Joe. When your mother comes out of Miss Beth's room, I'll go in. My face might be as ugly as hell but it could be the one to do the trick.'

Twenty-Three

Before his day's work, Mark took Rowella to Posy Praed, and as usual he took off his daughter's warm winter coat, woollen bonnet, scarf and gloves. He always arrived early enough to linger and to make sure, always unnecessary, that Rowella was settled.

'How come you're at the vicarage this morning?' Posy asked, when he headed for the door, his tin crib box tucked in under his arm. 'I thought you were expected at Miss Chegwidden's now and the vicarage later.'

'Oh, I asked the vicar and Miss Chegwidden if I could change over. It's more convenient for me.' Mark pulled on his cap and was out the back door and gone. He was telling himself his change of plans was more to his liking but it didn't really make any difference to his day. Spinster Miss Chegwidden, the last of a centuries' old fishing family, lived down in the cove in a tiny cottage and Mark was to reset the slabs, two were lifting and quite hazardous, in her little back yard. Hearing of Miss Chegwidden's need Mark had offered to do the work free, but proud

Miss Chegwidden was insisting he would take a shilling for his dear little 'cheeil'. His work in either place would take roughly the same time, but someone in particular was due at the vicarage this morning – although Mark was trying to ignore the fact.

He had judged it right. Claire Opie was only inches from Wildflower Cottage's gate. He lifted his cap to her. 'Good morning, Miss Opie,' he called politely. 'Do you happen to be walking up to the vicarage?'

'Yes, actually I am, Mr Reseigh. Why?' Claire asked, surprised to be hailed so heartily by him.

'Me too, can I walk with you?' Mark could hardly believe what he was doing. This had come about over a casual remark of his mother's, that now the highly-strung, unsuitable Miss Howard-Leigh was out of the picture, Claire Opie would make a perfect loyal wife of the vicar, and perfect for Portcowl. It was the place of her birth and she knew every parishioner, and since her change to a humbler heart she was liked and respected by everyone. Mrs Reseigh had pointed out that the local single women were now stamping out a path to the Reverend Benedict's church services and his front door on a variety of matters. Mark had not liked the reference to Claire at all.

For some reason Claire had been roaming into his mind lately and he had been disappointed to see nothing of her since the day she had turned up at his home. She had been unobtrusive and very pleasant, and Rowella had liked her. He found himself annoyed at how it seemed that

244

every time Claire went to the vicarage to attend on Miss Kitty, the vicar happened to be at home. It had hit Mark as a tremendous shock to realize he was becoming jealous of the time Claire was spending at the vicarage, or rather every minute she might be in Jacob Benedict's company. When his beloved Juliet died he'd thought this side of him had died forever.

He had reproached himself, he had vowed to remain faithful to Juliet's memory, but people's remarks had finally broken through to him, even from Juliet's parents, Posy and Lofty, that Juliet would want him to seek love again and provide Rowella with a new mother. He had tried to make himself forget Claire existed, but his mind kept going back to his disappointment at not finding her at home when he'd called on Mrs Opie to discuss the summer house. Mrs Opie had shelved the idea of a summer house, and Mark resented the obvious fact that the woman was pushing Claire in Jacob Benedict's direction.

Right now, although Claire did not seem to mind travelling beside him she did not seem much interested in him either. She did not ask about Rowella but mentioned the weather, that sort of ordinary thing.

'I'm sure you're a comfort to Miss Kitty,' he ventured, but not in the way of gossip. He was complimenting her. 'And my mother tells me you've been busy making little garments and toys for the poor. I admire that.'

'Thank you,' Claire answered, wondering why he was suddenly concerned about her affairs. Had he just given her a warm smile? Could he really be *interested* in her? His hair was neatly barbered and he had shaved closely and smelled of a light aftershave. Now she thought about it, it seemed he had been waiting for her to come by this way. This was all really strange. She glanced at him. He had his cap back so his face was not hidden. She caught her breath. He was looking straight at her.

Your hair is looking very pretty today, Mark was thinking. He saw she was wearing dark pink lipstick and a little eye shadow; for Jacob Benedict's benefit? Was she drawn to the other man? It would be understandable. Benedict was an attractive man and he had a great deal to offer as a husband. If Claire liked him then she shouldn't, Mark thought, rather vexed, she had seen how he had neglected the humiliated Miss Howard-Leigh. But if Benedict was piling on the charm, Mark had better not stand idle. 'Have you been invited to Alison Praed's wedding, Miss Opie?'

Claire raised her softly curving eyebrows. What a strange question from him. 'Um, yes, I have. I've got to know her now I've taken up knitting and I sometimes join her and Mrs Coad, who very kindly taught me to knit. Miss Praed invited me to her wedding only yesterday.'

'Good,' Mark replied, faltering. Was he going out of his mind? He felt safe with his widowerhood and bringing up Rowella, just them and his mother. He liked and he demanded his own space. How could he possibly think he could share his life with another woman? It was a betrayal of Juliet. No, he couldn't hide behind

246

that notion. Juliet had been wholly loving and giving. The last thing she would have wished was for him to deny himself a new start with someone else. But he hadn't really thought it through. What made him think he could love Claire? She had a snobby mother. Marjorie Opie would make an insufferable mother-in-law. *No you wouldn't!* Mark told the haughty image of the woman in his mind. *You'd get short shrift from me ...* but only if Claire returned his interest and things grew serious between them. Mark had never been afraid to meet a challenge, but he didn't think like that about Claire. She was lovely and kind and warm and all the other things a good woman should be.

'Why good?' Claire asked. Her heart had stuttered with a frisson of excitement to swiftly thunder with ... what exactly? Hope? Surely there was no point in hoping this particular man actually *liked* her? If so, she had no idea how she would respond.

'Well, the thing is, I was wondering, you see–' Mark plunged straight in – 'If you would like to sit next to Rowella and me in the chapel?'

In the shelter of delusion, deeper than drifting, Beth clung on as long as she could against any wakefulness. Here, somewhere in her subconscious, she was of no substance, she was weightless, not a being at all, and no one had any call on her. Here there was no darkness or light, no warmth or coldness, no pain, no feeling, and best of all her mind did not exist. So she could not suffer again the heavy wetness, the chilling

247

iciness eating through her flesh and bones, the sound of water forever running in her ears, salt rotting her tongue and throat, dissolving her eyes and making her lungs feel they were about to burst. Staying here, wherever that was, meant she had no understanding of anything. She was nothing, the way she wanted to stay.

Something heavy was shaking her and she was angry. 'No! Leave me!'

But the object tormenting her kept up its torture. 'Beth, wake up, wake up now, I want to talk to you.'

Her ease was being denied her and she awoke fighting. 'Get off me!'

No soothing voice came, of her mother or Joe or someone kind. The owner of the voice was just as angry as she was. She was being man-handled and made to sit up straight. 'Beth, open your eyes right up and look at me. Now.'

She did so but her eyes felt pinched in tight folds. She remembered she had lain down on the day bed in the sitting room, and as she did several times a day, she had sought oblivion. 'St—Stuart?'

'Yes, it's me,' he snarled, his grasp tightly on her. 'Kitty is still refusing to see me but I won't take any nonsense from you. I begged you not to tell her about us. You've ruined everything, damn you.'

Beth was now sharply conscious. She was light-headed and felt nauseous but knew she had no option but to answer him. She could not put this off any longer. Stuart deserved an explanation. 'Let me go. I'll tell you but I can't breathe

248

with you holding me like this.'

Stuart propped her back against the cushions and took his hands off her. Pushing aside the folds of her dressing gown he sat down close to her and leaned over her. 'Out with it.'

Beth licked her stiff lips. Her mouth was so dry and sore. 'I–I thought it was the right thing to do, that she deserved to know, but now I know I've made a terrible mistake.' Her body heaving with sobs she turned her face into the cushion. 'Oh, poor Kitty, she's been through so much. She must have thought I died when I went into the sea. Then she went through another ordeal. Gabby Magor discovered she had hidden in an old fox lair deep in the wood. She went out of her mind and it was all my fault.'

'Yes, it was,' Stuart cried, still seething with anger. 'Kitty's a former shadow of herself. You have caused untold distress to my happy, optimistic sister, and no one knows if or when she'll return to normal. She hates me. You've got no idea what it's been like for me creeping round the vicarage like an intruder, a criminal, an outcast. You've ruined everything. Kitty's life and mine.'

Through her streaming tears, Beth croaked, 'It's typical of you, Stuart, to feel sorry for yourself. You took equal part in our affair. But you still have the children and now you've got Connie back. You have a fresh start. If Kitty won't see you for now, why don't you return to your family and put all your time and energy into giving them a good stable life and wait for Kitty to come round. I'm sure she will in time.'

'I can't,' he growled, then fell down on his knees as if all the energy had seeped from his body. 'You've ruined everything with your stupid action.' He hung his head.

Beth swabbed away her tears. 'What do you mean? What's happened?'

Suddenly Stuart threw back his head and laughed, a single horrible manic laugh. Having heard the commotion Christina and Mrs Reseigh had hurried to the doorway, instinct now telling them to halt and listen. 'Connie pulled a fast one on me, on you, on all of us. As soon as we got home she waited until my first day back at the college, then she packed and took the children to her people in Ireland. She left me a letter saying she won't ever be coming back. She wants full custody of the children, and warned me that if I fought her she would make sure I'd never see Louis or Martha again. If I cooperate with her, and that includes me rigging the usual adultery snap by a private detective of me with a tart, so she can divorce me, then she will allow me to see the children occasionally. So you see, Beth, by admitting to poor dear Kitty what we did means I've lost everything, because Kitty was all I had left.'

While Beth looked down on him, once more stunned and ashamed beyond measure over her actions, he wept quietly into his hands.

Christina crossed the room and placed a hand on his shoulder. 'I'm sorry for you, Mr Copeland. Please get up and take a seat. For obvious reasons no alcohol is kept in the house, but Mrs Reseigh will make some strong, sweet tea. Is it all right with you, Beth, if he stays?'

'Yes, why not?' Beth sighed, bereft of vigour but at last feeling the return of some emotion. She sat up fully on the day bed and put her slippered feet to the floor. 'I'm sorry, Stuart. There's nothing else I can say. I'm only concerned about Kitty, what this whole sorry episode has done to her.'

'Thank you,' Stuart said simply, hefting himself up to sit down on a chair away from Beth. 'I'm sorry for my aggressive behaviour. I'm just so desperate, you see.'

'Of course.'

Stuart looked apologetically at Christina. 'Thank you too, Mrs Vyvyan. Please forgive me for barging into your house like this.'

'May I ask what you will do now, Mr Copeland?' Christina asked sensitively.

'I don't know. I've got more compassionate leave. Actually I might leave the college and the area altogether. I'll be selling the house and giving the proceeds to Connie. I've had a communication from her Irish lawyer, saying it is all she wants from me, to set up a trust fund for the children. I've agreed to that. I shan't be giving Connie any problems. She's promised she'll keep me informed of the children's whereabouts. It's the best I've got for now. I suppose I ought to move out of the vicarage. Kitty will never come out of her room while I'm staying there. I'll book into the Dunn Hotel, it's smaller and more private than the Grand Sea View, wait and see for a few days if Kitty will relent.' Stuart tried to drink his tea but his hands shook too

251

much and he put it down with a clatter of crockery. He was on the verge of tears again. 'Sorry...'

'If you like you can stay at Mor Penty,' Beth said. 'It will be even more private.'

Stuart gazed at her from teary vision. Beth's tone had been bland but sincere. 'Really? I can't thank you enough, Beth. I'll take Grace with me. She must be a lot of responsibility for you, Mrs Vyvyan.'

'Grace is no trouble, but I think that would be a very good idea,' Christina said. 'Jot down a shopping list and I'll get Joe to pop the things along to you. I'm sure you won't want to go down to the cove. They will be so many questions put to you.'

'Oh God, what a mess I've made.' Beth rose, her back straight, her legs steady.

'Where are you going, darling?' Christina asked.

'To run a bath and then get dressed. I've got no right to go on moping about. I've got to try to put things right with Kitty, do anything I can to help her cope. Last night when Gabby came upstairs to me she made a suggestion, that Kitty and I need to talk, that even if Kitty rails against me it might help her. It might be what she needs to get all her anger and suffering out of her system. I know Kitty says she never wants to see me again but I'm going to write and ask her if we could meet, on her terms and I'd let her have as much say as she wants. It doesn't matter how it makes me feel, because otherwise Kitty may stay stuck in limbo.'

Twenty-Four

With Chaplin, and the use of a torch, Joe made his way through the churchyard, heading for the small gate which gave access to the path leading to a side door of the vicarage. He thought it unlikely Kitty would be looking out of her bedroom window over the still, dark, front garden, but Joe feared that if she saw him approach she would get cross and order him to be refused entry. It was not unusual for Joe to walk Chaplin in this way just after school but he had not told his mother about his intention. She would feel it was wrong and invasive and Kitty might be offended. Joe thought it was worth a chance. Kitty had formed a close bond with him long before he had done so with Beth. Because of his youth Kitty was unlikely to see him as a threat.

'Hello, who's there?'

It was the Reverend Benedict's voice, disembodied for a moment until the vicar's tall frame appeared in his high lantern light. 'Oh, it's you, young Joe. I'm on my way to the church. You're a bit off track, aren't you?'

'Just taking Chaplin for a walk,' Joe replied, guarded. 'We like it in the quiet darkness. We get to see a lot of wildlife.'

'I'm sure you do,' Jacob said. 'I've seen all

sorts myself in the churchyard, foxes, badgers, owls. But this way heads straight into my garden.'

'I was going to stop at the gate.'

'Sure you weren't up to a bit of trespassing? I don't mean that as an accusation. I know you rarely do anything without a reason, and you do happen to have a small bunch of chrysanthemums in your hand. Are you hoping to see Miss Copeland?'

'OK, I'll come clean. I think I may be able to make a breakthrough with her. Kitty won't be holding any hurts against me. I was going to leave Chaplin on your pathway and sneak into her. I'm good at that sort of thing. I hope that doesn't anger you. Punish me if you like, but would you please not tell my mother. I hate her getting upset and Beth's past sins have put my mother under a lot of strain. I just want to help put things right.'

Jacob was struck at how precise and adult sounding Joe was. 'Fair enough. I think you might have a good idea there. I wouldn't normally allow someone of your age to attempt such a thing, of course. Nothing that anyone, including the doctor, has tried has made any impact on Miss Copeland. I'll take you inside but will stay outside the bedroom door. If she gets upset in any way at all, I shall come in and haul you out. Chaplin can stay in the hall.'

Moments later Joe was inside and on the landing, his outdoor things left downstairs. He smoothed his untidy hair while the vicar checked with the maid assigned to Kitty to see if entry

254

might be allowed into the sickroom.

'You can go in,' Jacob said. 'Miss Copeland is dozing. Just a few minutes now, Joe, unless you're successful in getting her to talk. You had best say—'

'Excuse me vicar, I know Kitty very well indeed and I'm sure I'll know what I should and shouldn't say to her.'

'Well–' Jacob took a deep breath – 'off you go then.' When Joe had gone quietly into the room and shut the door, Jacob leaned his back against the wall, hoping he wasn't going to regret giving his permission for this.

Kitty was lying flat in the single bed of what had been the former incumbent's daughter's room. She had her eyes closed but she was not asleep. The bedside lamp gave a low glow and a gentle fire was burning in the grate. The maid had told her 'the master' had ordered the fire be lit rather than have the central heating on in this room to give her more comfort and a more pleasant atmosphere. Kitty was grateful to have been taken in at this dwelling but she wasn't interested in the surroundings.

She heard someone slip into the room and assumed it was Verity bringing in fresh water or something.

A light step came right up to the bed. Kitty knew she was being spied on.

'I've no idea how I got here, Joe.' Kitty was sitting up in bed, clutching Joe's big tough hand.

He was perched on the bedcovers, listening in

255

an understanding manner that eased and calmed her. When she had opened her eyes she had cried out as if with enormous release and reached up and clung to his neck and sobbed like a child for several moments, repeating over and over how pleased she was to see him.

'I don't remember anything after the horror of seeing Beth disappearing over the cliff edge.'

Joe told her about Gabby Magor's discovery. 'Is that any comfort to you, Kitty?'

'I suppose it is, that I somehow went somewhere that you had showed me. There are few people I can trust now and you're one of them, Joe. I'm so relieved that Beth didn't die. I hated her when she told me about her and Stuart but I didn't plan to harm her, really I didn't. I pushed her. I wanted her to get away from me but I didn't mean to make her fall. She screamed and I screamed. I can still hear the screaming inside my head. I thought I had killed her. I would have done if Douglas Praed hadn't saved her...' Kitty's grasp on Joe's hand tightened and she was gulping in air.

'It's all right, Kitty,' Joe said soothing away her panic. 'Beth did not die and she doesn't blame you for her plunge into the sea. All that she's concerned about is you, how she's hurt you and how you've suffered since.'

'She's made many people suffer! Poor Christina, she doesn't deserve such a daughter. To think of all those years Beth despised her but Beth had done even worse things herself. Beth took me in. She's a conniving liar, a fake. Her disgusting affair with my weak brother led to his wife betraying and deserting him, shredding the lives of my innocent little niece and nephew. Just because the family is now reunited doesn't excuse what she did, or what he did. They are both repulsive to me and I never want to see them again. And do you know what else, Joe?' Kitty's tear-stained eyes, usually so beautiful and gentle were now beset with despair. 'Beth's made me hate myself. She had made me believe I was a murderer and even worse than her. And even now I know she's alive and will fully recover, she's made me hard and soiled because I can't forgive her for what she's done to me and what she's made me. Don't turn against me for it, Joe, I beg you.'

'I could never turn against you, Kitty.' Joe held her shuddering body against him. 'You're my friend for life. Whatever happens I want us to always remain friends. I feel sorry for you and Beth. And I feel sad. It seems to me that so many adults mess up their lives, all part of being human, I suppose. Natural in a strange way, and natural too that when someone finds their trust and peace destroyed they can't forgive. Perhaps you will forgive Beth one day. I hope you do, for your own sake as much as Beth's.'

Kitty stayed silently in his soft strong embrace. 'Why are you so wise? I can't see you ever devastating someone's life.'

'You can't take a bet on that, Kitty. I'm not infallible. There are times when I've been a right horrid little sod. And who knows what I'll do in the future?'

'But you'd never dream of betraying Richard

or little Lily, would you?'

'No, I'd rather cut off my arm, but it's easy to say that now. No one can tell what the future will bring. My father used to say that a lot, and in the time since, I think he was trying to tell me that he had done things he wasn't proud of.'

'Oh Joe, you make me doubt myself.'

'I hope I do, Kitty, and I'll tell you why. I'd hate to see you eaten up by hate and resentment. It might be exactly that which made Beth shallow and embark on an affair with your brother, but on the other hand she had suffered, her grandmother, my grandmother too, who never knew I existed, and I'm glad of that, deliberately made Beth's suffering worse. The old woman did that because she hated my mother, her own daughter. Beth must have been looking for acceptance and love elsewhere, but unfortunately she found it in the wrong place, and it's had terrible consequences.'

Kitty sighed, but it was not a weary or a despondent sigh. 'You've given me a lot to think about, Joe.' She gently pulled away from him and tugged on his tousled hair. 'The Reverend Benedict has been telling me all sorts of stuff about God, about him sending the right help at the right time. I suppose that meant you coming to me, Joe. Whatever the reason I'm so grateful you did.'

'Suppose the same could be said about Douglas Praed being down on the beach when Beth fell,' Joe said thoughtfully. 'Kitty, I take it you've been told that Stuart has left the vicarage?'

'Yes, I have, and that he's staying at Mor Penty because he's still hoping I will relent and allow him to speak to me.'

'How do you feel about that?'

Kitty shrugged. 'I don't know why he just doesn't go back home to his family. They need him.'

'Ah, you haven't been told everything then.'

'What do you mean? Has something happened?'

Joe noticed a small flicker of Kitty's old all-encompassing concern. 'This is rather shocking.' He relayed the story of Connie's deceit.

'The rotten bitch, but I can't say Stuart didn't deserve it. So Connie behaved no better than him. You're right about grown-ups making a mess of their lives. The awful thing is that it's the children who will suffer more. How will it all affect Louis and Martha? They've been pulled in so many directions. What mistakes will they make in later life because of it all.' Feeling weak again, but not with the same debilitating lack of emotion, she said wistfully, 'I've spent nearly all my life looking through a rose-tinted glow. I feel such a fool.'

'That's the last thing you are, Kitty.'

There was a firm tap on the bedroom door. 'Miss Copeland, may I come in?'

'Yes, do, Mr Benedict.'

Thinking that Joe had been given time enough to be with his heartbroken guest, Jacob entered the room and homed in on the pair. He was struck by the soft atmosphere, the bond between the pair, and the first hint of a return to energy in the once feeble woman resting in the bed. 'Well, I can see my prayers have been answered and this meeting has been a success.'

Twenty-Five

With great care, Beth got ready for Alison Praed's wedding. She wanted to look her best for Evie, and Beth was going to love seeing Evie in her bridesmaid dress. Also, it was rumoured that Kitty, who was still staying at the vicarage, was going to attend. If so, it was going to be the first day out for both Beth and Kitty since the cliff-top incident. Beth was hoping madly that Kitty would be at the wedding, that she might get the chance of a few words with her, or at least to aim a small smile at her, to show how sorry she was and that she longed to regain some of their former friendship.

It gave Beth hope that now Kitty was more or less fit and well again she had not chosen to leave the area and she was always happy to see Joe. Joe had conveyed that Kitty felt she did not really have anywhere else to go. She did not want to go back to her home, it would be too lonely, and she did not feel like staying with any of her distant aunts, uncles or cousins, and she had no interest yet in taking up the reins of her crafts business.

It did not matter to Beth that the whole of

Portcowl knew every detail of the sordid affair, the gossip suspected of being spread via tradesmen by vicarage staff. Apparently Kitty had rambled in her speech a lot during her early days and nights there. It would have been quite easy for people to sum up the situation. Nor did Beth care that she and Stuart had both received malicious letters, one almost every day and each one in the same handwriting, calling them wicked adulterers and the like and claiming their presence was tainting Portcowl. Beth had written to the Reverend Benedict and Douglas Opie, as the main Methodist circuit lay-preacher, to be read out from the pulpits, expressing her remorse and concern not for herself but for those she had hurt. It had been a wise move for some cove dwellers had condemned the malicious letter writer, declaring that she – it was universally thought the culprit to be a woman, as it usually was in these cases – was a despicable coward and worse.

Beth intended to sit at the back of the chapel, with Christina, her uncle Ken and Mrs Reseigh, and Beth would leave instantly if trouble occurred, not wishing to spoil Alison's big day. Mrs Reseigh had proudly put it about that Mark would be there with, 'Miss Claire Opie on his arm, so you won't be the only one being gawped at, Miss Beth. You've said sorry and that should be an end to it. Stick your chin up and damn the wagging tongues.' The wedding was going to be a large affair, the Praed family alone would fill the bride's side of the grey chapel, and Beth wasn't looking forward to that part of it. Evie

261

had said that Rob and Douglas would be looking out for her, and although that was a comfort, Beth had stressed she did not want to be the cause of any bother.

Beth and her entourage stepped on to the concrete court frontage of the chapel, situated at the end of Crescent Street. She was in understated elegant royal blue and grey and was wearing a new hat, the brim turned up to show she was prepared to display her face. It was hard to be a 'fallen woman', something that would stay with her all her life, and she kept swallowing in nervousness, but she met the eye of everyone who passed by her, even the one or two that made a point of ignoring her and those making snide remarks. At least everyone greeted her mother civilly.

The party took their seats in a back pew on the bride's side. Beth lowered her head to pray, aware of heads swivelling round to stare at her and a rush of obvious whispers, which threatened to drown out the organ's praise music. Beth searched the steadily growing congregation for Kitty but she was nowhere to be seen. More whispering, people knew exactly what she was doing. Then Beth got a sense of some of the onlookers holding their breath, hoping Miss Copeland would make an appearance and a drama of some sort would ensue. Shortly afterwards, a smartly suited Mark, carrying Rowella, who was gorgeous in a red outfit, escorted Claire quietly, but with a determined air, to sit in front of his mother. Another round of speculative whispering started up. Claire was in a fur-collared coat of chic lines, more like her former style, with a marcasite brooch, fashioned as a flamingo, sparkling near her shoulder. A little dark net on her bell-shaped hat coyly hid one eye, and accompanied by matching gloves and shoes she was a lovely sight. After offering their customary bowed prayers Mark handed Claire a hymnal from the ledge in front of them. She thanked him. Then they both looked up the number of the first hymn marked up on the hymn boards. They seemed at ease with each other. It seemed natural they should be together. The couple's presence here like this was tantamount to an announcement of an engagement, an occurrence not conceived in anyone's imagination, other than, at one time, Claire's mother's.

While continuing to seek Kitty, Beth wondered how Mrs Opie felt about her daughter's escort. Mrs Opie was self-importantly flitting about and fussing with the floral arrangements and ribbons, her own handiwork. She was usually called upon to perform these skills on formal occasions and liked to flaunt her talents. She tapped in her gleaming black high heels to the back of the chapel. It was getting time for the bridal party to start arriving. She paused ceremoniously at Claire's pew. 'You look stunning, my dear, stunning, like a bride yourself!' This made it plain she was expecting her daughter to get married quite soon and that she found the prospective bridegroom acceptable. Beth knew that gossip had it Mrs Opie had tried to steer Claire in the Reverend Benedict's direction, but once Miss Copeland had been given sanctuary there, and Claire's constant presence at the ailing young lady's side had apparently borne no fruit, Mrs Opie had gladly fallen back on the freelance gardener. Eligible husbands of fairly high standing were in short supply in Portcowl.

When the bridal march was sounded Beth was disappointed to find the conjecture that Kitty might arrive to witness the wedding was just that, conjecture.

Knowing the cove would be practically deserted, with little staff in most premises, Stuart had taken the opportunity to fetch some supplies. His hat down and his muffler up over his chin, he crept about like a criminal. After shopping at the first grocery store he came to, where he had received frosty glares from the stout, florid man on the other side of the counter, he made his way to a bookshop, hungry for something gritty to read to take his mind off his returned, unopened letters from Kitty. Jacob Benedict had re-delivered each one to him personally, and had urged him not to give up hope. 'You have nothing to lose by persistence. I have the feeling that Miss Copeland is merely giving herself time to recover her physical strength before she undertakes the emotional side of things.'

'I hope you're proved to be right, Jacob,' Stuart had answered, unable to shift his crushing misery and the weariness at lack of sleep. 'Kitty has always been utterly forgiving, brilliant about others' shortcomings, but what I, and Beth, did to her is a totally different thing. Kitty wouldn't have imagined such a thing in a thousand life-

264

times. It's no wonder she feels so trampled on. The whole business must have upended her in a way nothing else could. She must take as much time as she likes to come round, if she ever does,' he had sighed. 'I'm just glad Beth had the goodwill to invite me to stay here, and I'm very grateful to Joe Vyvyan for helping Kitty to feel better in herself. With Kitty staying put for now, it gives me hope.'

'I know it's a platitude but it's one that is very true: time is a great healer. Hopefully, soon, Miss Copeland will see things in a better light. I know it to be true that she is a woman of kind and sympathetic character. She shines above most women in honour and integrity.'

'That's the irony. Kitty's innocence and charitable nature is exactly why she was so thunderously brought down.' Stuart had poured them both a small brandy. He always did this to warm Jacob on his way home, and it made Stuart feel good for a moment to follow a routine. He had examined Jacob's bold face. 'You sound as if you're rather enjoying Kitty staying with you, Jacob.'

'Well, I must say that having your good sister under my roof has made me see that Miss Howard-Leigh was certainly not the right woman for me.' Jacob had showed a dash of awkwardness. 'But of course Miss Copeland has too much on her mind to give me any thought except as her host and spiritual mentor, and you may rest assured, Stuart, I would not do a single thing to compromise that.'

Stuart trusted the vicar. He was ashamed that

he was not a man to be trusted himself, and he slunk almost guiltily into the dark, cavernous bookshop. To try to gain some acceptance of sorts he bought half a dozen books on various topics. If the frumpy, youngish, bespectacled woman assistant recognized him from the harsh gossip she made no show of it. In fact she chatted with avid interest on the subjects he had chosen and Stuart had taken his time and left after much thanks and feeling a little uplifted. It gave him the courage to amble down to the quayside and take in the sight of the moored fishing boats. He wished he had brought his camera with him.

It was an evocative sight, the working boats lined up and well maintained, although roughed and scuffed from their tough employment. Oil, tar and fish were strong smells. Gulls flaunted their presence on decks and masts. At this time of year Stuart expected to feel a harsh wind on his flesh but it was calm and pleasant, a good day for a wedding, and he envied the closeness of the fishing community and the enjoyment they now had in the chapel and to come during the reception, when Lofty Praed's cottage would be joyfully bursting at the seams. Stuart had heard the Praed men had cleared out the garden sheds for the overflow of men. He would have liked to have been a part of the male bantering, the cheering and teasing and games playing. But none of the fishermen would want to spit on him let alone consort with him. The locals all had great respect for Kitty.

His thoughts turned to Beth, now thought of as

a scarlet woman. She had made it clear that Portcowl was her home and she wanted to live nowhere else, and hoped one day soon to regain her old life in the community. Her misdemeanour would pass into the background when the next big news item came to the fore, but she would never totally be allowed live down her shame. 'Poor Beth,' he whispered aloud. 'Braving the chapel and hoping to feel she belongs again.'

'Have you heard from your family,' Jacob had asked during his last call at Mor Penty.

'Connie has kindly kept in touch. She says I may go over to Ireland to see Louis and Martha before they start their new school. After that I shall have to decide what to do with the rest of my life. I hope at least by then Kitty will have stomached the idea of communicating with me.'

While he had a chance of regaining at least some of Kitty's time, Beth probably had none. As usual where love affairs were concerned it was the woman involved who was reviled the most. 'Bloody unfair,' Stuart told an uncaring gull.

After viewing all the luggers he walked round to the other side of the quay. The end cottage but one had a large white ribbon on the door knocker denoting from which home the bride had not long left. The cottage would receive a new bride next spring when Beth's sister Evie married Rob Praed, Stuart reflected. He heard shuffling noises and then a thud coming from the back of the cottages and thought it quite odd. Surely all the locals would be at the chapel. He could hear a hymn being sung two streets above him. Then he remembered Evie had several cats. The noises were probably them. Nevertheless, and not really knowing why, he thought he would take a look and satisfy his curiosity. He stole round the end of the terrace.

A short man in an old worn cap, his coat sleeves pushed up, was in the Praed backyard. The weather-beaten man was bent over and appeared to be doing something to the ground. Stuart frowned. It seemed out of place. People often prettified or jokingly sabotaged the place where a pair of newly-weds were to spend their wedding night but this could not be the case here. The couple had their first night booked at the Grand Sea View Hotel, an extravagant gift from Rob Praed to his sister. Ducking back round to the side of the cottage, Stuart silently put his packages down.

He peeped back round. It was just as he thought. The man was up to no good for he was glancing stealthily all about him. Stuart nipped back out of sight. It was really none of his business, but the man had worn a look of utter malice. Stuart was sure the man was Davey Vage, from the description he had heard of him, and there was bad blood between him and Rob Praed. Beth had mentioned once that she feared the old man would do something to prevent Evie marrying Praed.

Picking up his things, Stuart rounded the corner and sauntered towards the Praed's back gate. 'Good afternoon.' He took a good look at what Davey Vage was doing. He had a crow bar in his hands and he seemed about to lift up the edge of a slate slab. 'Doing a bit of maintenance work?' Vage was unlikely to assume Stuart knew who owned which cottage. He was definitely up to something dodgy.

'I've finished now, only got to brush up,' Davey Vage retorted curtly, startled, his irritation at being interrupted plain to see. Then recognizing his conversant, he scowled. 'You! Don't you dare speak to me, the likes of you isn't wanted round here. Clear off and get back to your lust-driven types and I mean well away from Port-cowl.'

'There's no need to take that tone with me. We're all sinners, aren't we?' Stuart stared at the hostile little man and saw anger boiling up in him. Here was one hard-hearted individual, and the description dangerous flashed through Stuart's mind. Vage had been caught red-handed about some devious business but rather than be worried or embarrassed about it he was emanating pure hatred. Stuart repressed a shudder. Meeting such unmitigated enmity Stuart was unsettled but filled with hope. Kitty would never keep hating him or Beth. She had too much goodness in her and in time, when her hurt and confusion died away, she would come round. Kitty was incapable of unforgivingness while this man fed on it and every emotion like it.

Stuart strode away, puzzling over Davey Vage's reason for the crow bar. At some time after dark tonight Rob Praed would return home and enter at the back of the property, it was the locals' way. He would be alone, having escorted

Evie home some time earlier, and he would be almost certainly filled with drink, unsteady on his feet, prime to trip over an obstacle, like an uneven slab. Had Vage's intention been to cause a serious accident, one that would take Praed once and for all out of his daughter's life? But such an accident might not prove to be fatal. Stuart shuddered and was shot through with dread. Had Vage intended to stay awake, ready to creep next door and use that crow bar cunningly about Praed's head? The more Stuart thought about it the more the notion did not seem crazy. Vage's actions had been witnessed and as a shrewd schemer he would abandon his plan, but he wished Praed harm and he was in a hurry to accomplish it. Praed must be warned and before the day was over.

Twenty-Six

'Aw, Verity, you should have seen the wedding. The bride was beautiful and it was a sight to behold when she walked up the aisle on her brother's arm. That Rob Praed is a really handsome man, I can tell you. And Evie Vage, his intended, she looked really lovely. There'll be another lovely wedding next year to take a look at; can't wait. I wouldn't mind going down to this Lofty Praed's house right now and join in the reception. From what I've heard they'll be having a whole lot of fun.'

Kitty was listening in on the conversation between the upstairs maid and Winifred the parlour maid filtering in through the open doorway of the vicarage drawing room. Resting on a sofa, a soft blanket over her legs, Kitty found the cheery interchange more interesting than the woman's magazine she had been trying to read.

'Was Miss Tresaile there?' Verity asked.

Kitty caught her breath. She knew this would be a burning question in Jacob Benedict's household today.

'She was, and she and her mother made a stunning sight, although Miss Beth was as pale as hoar frost and nervous as a kitten,' Winifred replied eagerly. 'She got a bit of stick from some people. I felt quite sorry for her. I've always liked her. She's always had the good grace to ask after all us servants each time she's come here. I mean, what did she do that was so wrong? She fell in love. I know it shouldn't have been with a married man but she didn't kill anyone. And she did walk away from Mr C. Came all the way down to Cornwall and stayed here, she didn't keep chasing after him. It's what some women do. It's just an awful pity he ever came down here. Everybody was so happy before, and Miss Beth, like her mother, has done a lot for Portcowl.'

'That's true, and when you look at it she hasn't looked at a man since she got here, and she's at the age when most of us are lamenting about not catching a husband,' Verity said in a sorrowful

271

way. 'It's a sad case for all. Pity they couldn't put it all behind them or the heartbreak will just go on and on.'

It was a peaceful place. Kitty had stood here before, with Beth, at the little graveside of Beth's twin, Philip Tresaile. Kitty did not know why she had come here. Perhaps she was looking for answers... 'What would you have thought of all that's happened, baby Philip?' she whispered, feeling strange and remote from ordinary life. Her words seemed to actually seep down, down into the grave.

'You would want me to forgive your sister and become her friend again, wouldn't you? Once Beth knew of your existence she often remarked how close she felt to you. Have you been watching her? Did you watch her at the wedding?'

A heavy silence fell over Kitty and she felt compelled to speak again. 'Did you see her fall into the sea? Did you see her struggling in the water? Was she very scared? Oh, Beth! Did you see me push her, Philip? Did you believe I tried to kill her? I didn't mean to. Please believe me, I didn't mean to.'

Kitty suddenly felt helpless. All traces of reality escaped her and she felt she was sinking into something dark and cloying she could never escape from. She knew it would be much worse than it had been for Beth nearly drowning in the sea. Gasping for breath, panic spreading through every nerve of her body she turned and fled.

She slammed into something hard and immovable and she fought against it, her terrified

272

screams emerging silently and terrifying her all the more.

'It's all right, Miss Copeland, it's me Jacob.' He was forced to clamp her arms to her sides. 'Kitty, Kitty, listen to me. You're safe, nothing can hurt you.'

Kitty felt she was dying and the vile sensations she was suffering would stay with her and imprison her forever. Suddenly the last of her resources went, her knees sagged and she slumped against the strong thing obstructing her.

The next thing she was aware of was an acrid smell and she shifted her head away from it. She heard Winifred's anxious voice. 'The smelling salts are working, Reverend, she's coming round. I'm so sorry, I didn't realize Miss Copeland had slipped out. I'd just brought in her morning tea and realized she was no longer here. Thank goodness she had the good sense to put on her furs. Oh, poor lady. Will she be all right? Shall I ring for Doctor Powell?' Winifred sounded almost in tears.

'I'm sure Miss Copeland was just a little overcome,' Jacob said. Kitty found comfort in his strong firm voice. 'Run and fetch another cup. I'll stay with Miss Copeland. If I think she needs the doctor I will ring for him to be summoned.'

Minutes passed, and Kitty was sitting with her feet curled up on the sofa, drinking a second cup of well-sugared tea and almost stuffing down butterscotch biscuits. For some reason she felt a ravenous thirst and hunger. She had her fur coat round her shoulders and the blanket was over her legs.

'Are you warm enough?' Jacob asked, from a nearby armchair.

'I am, thank you. I feel rather foolish now.'

'You have no need to at all. You were clearly distressed. Miss Copeland, may I ask why you were beside Philip Tresaile's grave? I take it you had a significant reason.'

'I don't know what made me go out there really. I overheard Winifred talking about the Praed wedding, about how Beth looked awfully nervous in the chapel. They talked about the goodness in Beth. I felt guilty about hating her so much.' Kitty put her head in her hands and her voice fell low. 'I haven't told you this. I should have, you're a priest and you have the right to know while I'm sheltering under your roof. After Beth told me about her and Stuart I went into a rage. I pushed on her and that's when she fell. I didn't intend her harm but I'm responsible for the fact that she so very nearly died. I thought I had killed her. It's what drove me mad. Hearing about her today I was overcome with guilt at not forgiving her, when it was me that should beg for even more forgiveness from her. I suppose I went out to Philip's grave, a favourite place of Beth's for reflection, to try to gain something from the peace that is always to be found there, from his innocence. It came to me that Beth had lost her twin brother, that she had never known him. It made me feel an utter wretch.

'And then I felt completely vulnerable and panicked.' She gazed up at Jacob in anguish. 'Everything is such a mess. I'm such a mess.

Beth's life is a mess and so is Stuart's. They betrayed me. It hurt me more than anything I'd ever known. If I hadn't given way to fury, hated Beth at that moment and just railed against her instead, if I'd walked back to Owles House and left for Wiltshire and given myself a chance to come to terms with the confession the consequences wouldn't have happened, nothing would have become public. The whole thing wouldn't have become so sordid. I've hurt and frightened people who didn't deserve it, people who have always been kind to me, Mrs Vyvyan, Joe and Mrs Reseigh. I'm a terrible person and I hate myself.'

'No, you mustn't hate yourself,' Jacob said firmly, in the manner of an order. Then he became soft and soothing and took a careful hold of Kitty's hands. 'Miss Copeland, Kitty, listen to me as a priest and as your friend. You are allowed to be human. You were taken by surprise by Miss Tresaile's confession. Of course you didn't mean to hurt her, and your reactions were entirely natural. It's because you are good and honest that your mind could not cope with the horror of everything.' He saw her desperate tear-filled eyes, and moved by more than pity and the desire to help her, he gently placed his hands either side of her face. 'Listen to me, Kitty. You did nothing wrong.'

'Not at first perhaps, but you would advise me to forgive Beth and Stuart, wouldn't you? Or I won't receive forgiveness from God.'

'It's part of my job but it's also the best way, Kitty, to bring yourself peace. You can forgive

275

Miss Tresaile and your brother but it doesn't mean you have to be as close to them as you were before. You might find that hard or impossible for a long time or for always. As I said before, you are allowed to be human, and none of us are perfect. My advice to you is to do what you are able to comfortably do each day.' Jacob was reluctant to retreat from her but he had already compromised propriety and he retook his seat.

Kitty too sat back then gave a wan smile. 'Beth found peace and so much more once she had forgiven Mrs Vyvyan.'

Winifred entered the room. 'Excuse me Reverend Benedict, Mr Copeland is here asking to speak to you on a matter of some importance. He says to apologize for coming here but to stress it's a matter that really can't wait.'

'Oh,' Jacob said, disappointed his time with Kitty had been cut off. 'You had better show him into the study, Winifred. Excuse me please, Miss Copeland.'

Kitty waited a couple of minutes then she was up and heading for the study to listen at the door. *Was Stuart planning to leave Portcowl right now?* She could not allow that without speaking to him. He was her brother. He had always been good to her. She had always looked up to him. They had always loved and needed each other.

She overheard Stuart say, 'It concerns the safety of someone living in Portcowl.'

Kitty's heart dropped with a sickening thud. Had someone threatened Beth at the wedding, threatened her very safety over the scandal? If so, it was partly Kitty's fault. Without a thought she barged into the study. 'Was it Beth you were talking about? Is she in danger? I'm sorry, but I have to know.'

'Kitty!' Stuart leapt up from his chair opposite the desk and headed for her. 'How wonderful to see you. How are you?'

Jacob was astonished at Kitty's interruption but pleased about her obvious concern for Beth.

'I'm not concerned about myself,' Kitty replied, her eyes darting over Stuart's face. 'You're so pale and thin. You need a shave. Um, yes, were you talking about Beth, Stuart?'

'No, not Beth but, indirectly, her sister Evie.' Stuart's eyes followed the flicking path of Kitty's. 'Can't tell you how much it means to have you talking to me. I'm so sorry I hurt you. I'll do anything you want if you'll forgive me. You're a bit pale and thin too, Kitty, but just as beautiful. Will you...?' He tentatively reached out a hand towards her.

Kitty bypassed his hand and stepped up to him leaning against his chest for a hug. 'Of course I forgive you. I could never turn against you altogether. I just lost my way.'

'Thank God, thank God,' Stuart murmured, holding her tighter and tighter.

Jacob allowed them time to unite and pass through the first crucial emotions. Then he said, 'Why don't you both take a seat so Stuart can tell us why he's here. And afterwards you can both talk in the comfort of the drawing room alone.'

Twenty-Seven

Down on the little beach below Owles House Beth was half-heartedly tossing sticks for Chaplin. The dog soon tired of her poor efforts and raced off to explore the rocks and pools, leaving Beth to gaze sullenly out at sea. The wind had turned to the east and it was bitingly cold but she welcomed the chill eating through her flesh and into her bones. She took anything that punished her as a just fate.

She had left the wedding as soon as she and Christina were able to squeeze past the noisy joyful clamouring crowd on the chapel forecourt, pausing only to tell Evie how beautiful she looked. Thankfully, once Alison and Rob Praed had made their spectacular entrance, the happy young couple and the service had claimed the attention of her antagonists. As Beth's ears had taken in the soaring harmonious Celtic voices of the hymns, she had envied Alison Praed, an ordinary woman marrying her decent, hard-working man and looking forward to a steady contented life, carrying on decades of tradition.

Once home Beth had changed out of her finery and then, to please Christina, joined her and Joe to eat a meal of Scotch broth and hot rolls. 'You did marvellously well, darling.' Christina had patted her hand as they had eaten. 'You were very brave to turn up on such a big occasion; people will appreciate that. Things will get better, you'll see.'

Beth had smiled for Christina's sake. Things would get better but not everything. She did not care about the gossips, only that what she had believed was the right thing to do was a huge, foolish mistake.

Joe had stayed quiet throughout the meal, and Beth knew he was still concerned about Kitty. Beth had told Joe more than once how sorry she was about the offence and anxiety she had caused to him, their mother and so many others. Joe had shrugged, a typical gesture of his, but Beth had seen how disconcerted he was at the whole episode, and he had mumbled, 'It's what grown-ups do, mess up. I'll be one quite soon. Hope I don't make the same mistakes.'

When Christina had gone upstairs to rest, and Joe was doing some school homework, Beth had changed again and called the eager Chaplin outside for exercise.

There was not much point, Beth decided on the inhospitable shore, in passing all the distasteful stuff through her mind again. If she made herself ill and depressed, it would be unfair to her mum and Joe. She must make the effort never to be selfish and foolish again, make it her reason for living. She would wait for Chaplin to run himself ragged then she'd return to the house, make a hot drink and prepare the food for tonight's dinner. She must make the effort to keep busy.

Suddenly Chaplin started a riotous barking and was racing for the wooden steps. Beth looked up and her whole being lurched with apprehension. She was frozen to the spot. Kitty was coming very slowly down the top steps and Chaplin was excited to see her. Beth bit her bottom lip and gazed down at the sand, sure that Kitty needed to rail against her again. Beth assumed Jacob Benedict had driven her here. He would then probably take her on to the railway station and she would leave for Wiltshire.

She heard Kitty call to Chaplin, with delight, 'Hello, old boy. How are you then?' From the edge of her eye Beth saw Chaplin had reached Kitty and the pair went through a friendly re-union. A stifling heaviness weighed down on Beth. She felt horribly alone and like a traitor. The only lightness of spirit she felt was the gladness that Kitty was well enough to make the journey to have another go at her.

'Hey, Beth? We're both here!'

Beth looked up again and there on top of the cliff was Stuart. She closed her eyes and gave way to the sudden overwhelming relief of knowing the sister and brother were reconciled. At least she didn't have to bear the guilt over their broken relationship any longer. So Stuart had brought Kitty here.

'Beth! Come up!' Stuart shouted. 'Kitty can't manage all the steps down to you.'

Down to me, Beth thought, her body giving a jerk. She must climb the steps. She couldn't expect Kitty to come down to her. Hardly daring to raise her eyes Beth began the trudge across the sand. She felt such trepidation yet she was pleased to be able to see Kitty to say sorry again, even if Kitty had harsh things and recriminations for her.

Stuart was now helping Kitty to ascend to the top. Chaplin was one step behind them. 'Come on Beth, there's nothing to worry about,' he shouted down to her.

Nothing to worry about? Beth hastened her steps. Surely this did not mean Kitty had forgiven her too? She hurried so Kitty wouldn't have to stay longer than necessary in the exposed coldness, but she couldn't bring herself to look up at the Copelands, fearing the apparent sociability on Kitty's part would change once they were eye to eye.

She reached the top and was on the cliff path and, still keeping her head down, found it necessary to clear her throat before saying, 'Hello, Kitty.' Finally she faced her old friend, feeling like a criminal, penitent and deserving of any punishment coming her way. It was the most uncomfortable feeling of her life.

'Hello, Beth. Mr Benedict kindly lent us his motor car to get here,' Kitty said, and she explained that she wanted to talk things through, to tell Beth she no longer hated her, that she understood her failings. 'I also want to ask your forgiveness for pushing you which nearly led to your death.'

Briskly but brightly, Stuart said, 'It's too cold to stay talking here. Mrs Vyvyan is expecting us and will have hot drinks ready. Let's all hurry to the house.'

281

Beth could only nod. She had listened to Kitty with ever increasing amazement and joy as her misery had been dispelled. Then she and Kitty were hugging and wiping away tears of emotion.

The group set off for the house.

A short time later the walkers were refreshed and warm beside Christina's roaring log fire. 'Well, I suppose you girls have a lot to say to each other,' Christina said. 'I'm sure Mr Copeland won't mind withdrawing with me to the kitchen.'

Before Stuart closed the door, he said, 'I don't suppose either of you really know where to start. I know you're both very sorry and all that, as I am. Why not make things less awkward and painful and decide to take your points as read and go on from there. You were once as close as sisters. Why worry if one of you has more to be sorry about than the other. Neither of you meant to harm the other. Concentrate on building up a new relationship.'

'I think Stuart made some very good points, don't you?' Kitty said, adding a small smile, 'It's the college principal in him.'

'I agree,' Beth replied. 'I can still hardly believe you're here. I've missed you so much, Kitty.'

'This must be worse for you, Beth. Don't let it be. I feel differently about everything now. The visits from Joe, and Mr Benedict's counsel after I'd stood at baby Philip's grave, and finally when I thought Stuart was about to leave Portcowl – he'd turned up at the vicarage on a village matter, I'll tell you about that in a

282

moment – made me see everything clearly. I am sorry for screaming at you that day and for pushing you. I'll always feel bad about that. If you had died I don't know ... if I could have coped with it. My trouble was I'd always seen things in a rosy picture.'

'Not trouble, Kitty. There's nothing of trouble about you. You weren't naive, just wonderfully honest and giving. I'm sorry about my deceptions and how long I kept them up. I was selfish concerning Louis, Martha and Connie, and you, and I shall always feel bad about that. I swear there are no more secrets. I'm sorry for Stuart now that he's lost everything, but glad he's got you. He has, hasn't he?'

'Stuart and I are fine.'

'And us? I don't expect you to want to put our friendship back on the same footing. Will you leave and never come back again?'

'We'll be fine too. I want the past left there and for us to go on as before. I mean I could never forsake dear Joe and Christina. I love to be mothered by Mrs Reseigh, and to hear Richard and Lily squabbling. I love the cove. I want to see if Mark and Claire Opie will actually marry. And then there's Evie. I want to go to her wedding. And it's Evie who is connected to the reason Stuart came suddenly and urgently to the vicarage.'

Kitty relayed the incident Stuart had witnessed in the Praed backyard. 'Mr Benedict thinks Davey Vage was certainly there intent on mischief, maybe to cause Rob injury to prevent him supporting Evie as his wife. Mr Benedict thought

283

it unwise that he or Stuart should inform Rob what had happened. Rob would inevitably confront Vage in a hostile manner and the result that might work in Vage's favour. Evie is devoted to her father. Mr Benedict thought it would be wise if you were to mention the incident to Evie and leave it to her to question her father.'

'I agree. I won't get the opportunity today. I'll see her in the morning. Thanks for telling me, Kitty. It's not right Evie has to put up with this.' Why couldn't the wretched man let Evie live her life how she wanted? She wasn't doing anything in the slightest wrong wanting to marry the man she loved, and Rob wasn't a bad lot any more. Davey Vage certainly was though, and rotten and, Beth felt, somehow dangerous. Beth was sure of one thing: she would not allow Vage, whatever the cost to herself, to ruin Evie's chance of a happy future.

'Are you going to continue to stay at the vicarage?' Beth asked, enjoying a normal conversation with Kitty.

'For two or three more days, then Stuart and I will travel home, to my house, that is. Stuart will stay with me for the foreseeable future. He's already put his property on the market. He will be giving the proceeds to Connie for the children. She's said he can go over to Ireland and have Louis and Martha for the weekend before Christmas. He's booked hotel rooms.'

'And then you and he will spend Christmas together? If ... if you care to, you will still be very welcome, both of you, to spend Christmas here with of us. Joe would love that,' Beth added quickly. 'I don't mean that as emotional pressure, please don't think that.'

'Thanks for the invitation. We haven't made a decision about that yet. We both need to catch our breath, so to speak. But we'll keep in touch.'

'That's more than I could have hoped for just a little while ago,' Beth said, shivering, more with the continuing release of all the stress and strain than anything else.

Kitty jumped up in the manner of her old former energy. 'I'm going to put more logs on the fire and then ask Christina for some more tea.' She smiled at Beth and put a gentle hand on her shoulder. 'Can't have you catching a cold, old girl.'

Twenty-Eight

'Why on earth did you set out to hurt Rob like that?' Evie railed against her father for the first time in her life, having just called him inside from the boat. Her fists were clenched rigidly at her sides and her eyes were burning with anger. 'I couldn't believe my ears when Beth told me what Kitty's brother saw you up to yesterday. What has Rob ever done for you to behave in such a way? When you hurt him you hurt me, don't you care about that? Don't you care about me? Don't my feelings matter to you? You must have seen how much I love Rob, or don't you

285

take any notice of me ever?'

'Oh, so you know.' Davey pushed back his cap and rubbed his chin. 'I knew you would in time. I admit I've been working up the courage to tell you myself.'

'Is that all you can say?' she threw at him, hurt seeping out of her. 'How were you going to explain your dirty actions to me? I've looked at Rob's yard for myself and it's obvious by the scraping and scratching a slab had been disturbed. The instant Rob notices it he'll be round here. He'll know it was you. You're the only one who could wish him that kind of ill, and you had the perfect opportunity with practically all the cove at the wedding. At the least you planned an almighty row. Go on tell me what you'll say to him? You won't tear us apart if that's what you're up to. I've had enough of your jibes towards Rob, and now this. It's rotten and spiteful, and I can't take any more of it.'

Silence fell in the little cottage like a taut covering. Tension bristled like electrical crackles. Evie met her father's unwavering stare. He pushed out his lower lip and breathed in through his nose. 'Of course you can't and why should you? I've been a self-centred, frightened old man. Being caught out by that Copeland bloke kept me awake all night thinking and thinking and made me see sense at last. Sit down, my handsome, and let me explain.' Davey shifted to his chair by the hearth.

Evie stayed motionless, wondering if her ears had heard right. Her father's change of attitude was the last thing she had expected. At the very least she had thought he would argue that Rob wasn't good enough for her and would end up breaking her heart. Her brow creased in suspicion but she did hold a little hope about her father's motives. 'What do you mean, Dad?'

'It's like this, Evie. You know your mother and I never had a marriage in the usual sense. I was a very lonely man living here on my own. Iris needed help and I was pleased to offer her a home and security. We couldn't have got on better, not a cross word ever passed between us. You know how we both doted on you. I was devastated at Iris's untimely death. I'd thought I'd die years before her and leave the both of you comfortably off. I know I've kept you all too often to myself, and discouraged you from any social life, even from knowing your own sister. For years I haven't been able to bear the thought of you getting married and me having to live on my own again, and I'm too set in my ways to live elsewhere or welcome someone else under my roof. Like any father, I was worried about Rob Praed being your choice, but he's changed a lot and it's time I acknowledged it, and there's a lot worse than he out there. What I did yesterday was out of desperation. Last night, as I expected, he rolled home late after the wedding drunk as a lord. I was going to move the slab in the hope he'd take a fall and hurt himself. I wanted you to think badly of him. I was going to point out that you could end up waiting for him night after night when the shine wears off your marriage. But even if that turns out to be the case I got no right to stand in your way. After all, if your

287

marriage proved to be a mistake I'd only be next door to look out for you. So I'm sorry, Evie. I'll tell Rob this too.'

'Do you really mean all that, Dad?' Evie moved warily up to him.

'I do, and what's more I don't think you and Rob should wait till next year to get married. Bring it forward to any time you like. Get a special licence if that's what you want. Come next Monday night the fleet will be shooting our herring nets round the Eddystone and berthing at Plymouth until Saturday. You and Rob got a few days to make a decision. And Evie, I swear on your mother's memory I won't stand in your way. In fact, I'll help you all I can. I've got money in the house. I'll get it right away if you want to go shopping.'

Feeling her feet had been swept out from under her Evie had to sit down. 'Rob and I wouldn't want our wedding scaled down. A Christmas wedding would be nice though.'

'A Christmas wedding it is then. Go to Rob now and then you could both go to see the minister.'

'Say something, Rob.' His long silence was making Evie pent up. She had gone immediately next door to him. He was too used to drink to be suffering a hangover, and had been about to go out to *Our Lily*.

'I'm sorry, darling, but I just don't trust Davey.' Rob threw up his hands in exasperation. 'I could bust his guts for what he was up to. If Stuart Copeland hadn't caught him at it I might

288

well be nursing broken bones. Surely, you don't believe a word he's just said? He spent a long time thinking all night, yes, but he's come up with another sly strategy. He'd rather see me in my grave than married to you.'

'Don't say that,' Evie cried. 'It's too horrible to think about.'

'But you must admit Davey readily agreed with what you want for us but goes on to do all he can to stand in our way. There won't be a Christmas wedding, he'll somehow see to that. He's too smart-witted. Well, there's one thing for it. We're going to outwit him.'

The ups and downs of hopes and anger Evie had gone through in the last few minutes made her gulp with disappointment and bewilderment. She exhaled through her lips to disperse all the frustration. 'It isn't right. Things shouldn't be like this.'

Rob pulled her into his arms and she held on to his body. 'No, they shouldn't, but what other choice have we got?'

'What do you think we should do?' she said, her face snuggled against his neck.

'Elope, today, as soon as the boats have gone out.'

Twenty-Nine

Nearly two weeks had past since Evie and Rob's elopement and today they were due home. Beth was at their back door, the first time she had been in the cove since her accident. She had driven down and parked in Half Street, the closest she could bring the car, for she was bringing bags and boxes of gifts and bunches of chrysanthemums, and she was excited to be joining Rob's sisters to get everything ready for the honeymooners' return. For now she was putting aside her worries about what Davey Vage would say and do when the fleet sailed back from Plymouth waters tomorrow.

Alison Keane opened the door to her, and Beth was caressed with the cosy warmth of the fires lit in the cottage to air it through. 'Come in, let me help you. You've got good timing, Miss Beth, Judy's just put the kettle on.'

'Oh, call me simply Beth. I can see you've both been busy.' Beth smiled, as she stepped inside. 'I've got more stuff in the car. The wedding presents Kitty sent down, and others from Mrs Reseigh and Mark, Claire and Mr Benedict. And lots of food for the party at your Aunt Posy's tomorrow night.'

'We'll help you fetch the things in,' Alison

said.

'It smells wonderfully of lavender polish. I hope you've left some work for me to do.'

'Sorry,' Judy laughed. 'We couldn't stop ourselves getting up early and making a start. Marrying Evie is the best thing that could ever happen to Rob. We thought we'd leave the few things Evie had brought round to unpack herself, including her wedding dress. When it's finished she and Rob will dress up for a photographer. At least she had her bridesmaid dress to wear for her quick wedding. We've put in the new bed linen Mrs Vyvyan bought as a wedding present and laid out the beautiful ivory negligee you got for Evie.'

Alison grinned wickedly. 'Bet Evie's never even seen something so luxurious and sheer before. Rob will certainly like it.'

Judy went on. 'We've brought fresh bread, milk, butter and veg. You best arrange the flowers, Beth, we wouldn't do a such a good job.'

'I'll fetch all the vases,' Alison said. 'While you pour the tea. We don't usually eat boughten cake but for a change we popped into the baker's on the way and bought some chocolate eclairs. Must say they look delicious.'

When the women were eating and drinking round the kitchen table, Beth said, 'I received another postcard from Evie this morning. She wrote she's having an amazing time in London, after moving on from Torquay, seeing all the sights and even going to the theatre. Happy memories for her.'

'Bet Rob is spoiling her,' Alison said dreamily,

291

licking cream and chocolate off her lips. Then her mood changed. 'They'll be very happy together as long as they don't take any trouble from that nasty little bugbear next door. Old man Vage has kept tight-lipped about their elopement except for repeating to everyone, "They had no need to go off like that. I told her I'd thought better of wanting to hurt Rob." Why the heck would he want to do such a rotten thing in the first place? He's malicious and evil. He must be madder than a devil about Evie and Rob getting married but it was he who drove them away, not that he'd ever admit it. Evie wanted to keep the old man's action under wraps but that was impossible once all our family knew. Mr Benedict got nowhere with Davey when he tried to help, Davey told him to mind his own business. Well, I bet for all of Davey's resentment he's glad he doesn't have to fork out for a wedding. Uncle Lofty phoned down with the news that he'd spoken to Davey and Davey agreed to come to the party, but I bet he won't. I hope he doesn't! He'd only cause trouble, bound to.'

'Evie must be worrying about the reception she'll receive from Davey, and that's a great pity. This should be the happiest time of her life.' Beth aimed hostile looks at the wall that divided Evie's new home from her old one, imagining the cold, bitter little man who would soon be back inside No. 1 Quayside. 'If he's lonely from now on it will be no more than he deserves. But he had better be very careful how he treats Evie, or he'll have the might of us at Owles House, Uncle Ken and the whole Praed family against him.'

'The whole of Portcowl too, come to that,' Judy contributed crossly. 'Miserable so-and-so! Evie gave twenty-seven years of her life devoted to him yet he wanted every second of hers until he dies. Our father and mother always said he was devious and hard-hearted. Evie must be warned that if he acts all sweetness and light towards her she had better watch out for him. He might be set on some sort of revenge. Actually, the more I think about it the more I'm getting worried. Douglas mentioned that not long ago he saw Davey glaring at Rob like he wanted to kill him. Strong words, and I didn't think much about it at the time, but now...'

'And after what Vage tried to do to Rob the loathing will be mutual. Rob won't easily forgive and forget that,' said Alison.

'So Evie could find herself stuck in the middle of a nasty feud. Right,' Beth said firmly, 'Davey Vage needs to be watched carefully in case he tries once again to separate Evie from Rob. Whether he goes to the party or not, I think Davey should be told in no uncertain terms that we're on to him.'

'Breakfast, Mrs Praed.' Rob tenderly kissed Evie to wake her. Before that he had taken a moment to caress her warm, sleep-flushed face. He loved the way she was in the morning, so young and lovely, and all his. They had arrived late last night to a fragrant, cosy home, thanks to their respective sisters' work, and Rob had proudly carried her over the threshold. Tired from the

293

long train journey and then bouncing along the twisting lanes in a taxicab, they had gone straight to bed, but not too tired to make love.

Evie smiled happily and stretched out her bare arms for her husband. 'Mmm, you needn't have bothered to do that.'

'I won't get many chances of a morning to treat you like a princess, darling.' He took her hands and kissed them both. 'So I want to make the most of it. I've made tea, toast, butter and marmalade. It's still quite early. I want you all to myself for as long as I can. Sit up, I'll bring over the tray and get in beside you.'

Covering their nakedness they rested against the pillows, laughing and giggling while feeding each other bites of toast. 'I wish every morning could be like this,' Evie cooed.

'We'll make sure we do this as often as we can.' Rob kissed a dash of marmalade off her chin. 'I love you.'

'I love you.'

'I love, love, love you.'

'Me too.'

And they fell into a fit of happy laughter.

Rob finished his breakfast and began to glide his hand all over Evie's back. He kissed her shoulder. Lifted her hair away from her neck and kissed her there. She shivered in delight and he loved it when she did so. 'My beautiful love. Finished with the tray?' His voice was low and husky with desire.

Evie looked into his eyes, gone smoky with intense want, and her femininity leapt into exquisite life and her skin glowed radiant. She nodded. He lifted the tray down off the bed. Then took her fingers and licked the traces of breakfast off them. Evie gripped his face and with her open lips demanded his. When their need turned immediate they shifted and writhed and Rob was on her and inside her. Their act of love was in perfect union, Evie once again learning and giving back his honed skills. When they were finally sated the morning was well into its stride and the cove was coming to life. They stayed in each other's arms for long minutes.

'Rob, darling, I think we should open the curtains,' Evie whispered, looking shyly at the window.

'Why?' he murmured, using his fingertips to feather circles on her arm.

'People will know we're still in bed.'

Rob laughed loudly.

'Shush!'

'Oh, my darling little sea pearl, no wonder I love you so much. People will be passing by smiling with knowing looks and be pleased for us, and most will be envious.'

'Yes, you're right.' She glanced around her new bedroom, lying in the double bed where Rob had been conceived. While on honeymoon Rob had said she could choose new wallpaper and paint. She would eventually but it wasn't important for now. Then her eyes trailed to the wardrobe where last night she had hung up the gorgeous negligee, Beth's gift. She was still shy about making love with Rob. When she got bolder she would wear the sensuous satin creation. 'We ought to get up quite soon though,

295

don't you think? We're sure to have a stream of visitors.'

Rob squeezed her gently. 'They can wait, but OK, let's get up.' He playfully rubbed his stomach. 'I could do with another breakfast, Mrs Praed. Then we can walk out together to get the newspaper and some ale and stuff for the party tonight. I want to show you off.'

The morning was nearly past by the time they returned home. They had gloried in a barrage of good wishes and many a curious question, and little kind gifts. Rob invited everyone they saw to Wildflower Cottage that evening for the celebration.

When they got back they found visitors they had missed had left parcels in the yard and pushed cards through the front letterbox. While they were eating a lunch of sandwiches and fruitcake, the first meal Eve had shared at her new housewife's table, she said, 'After this I'm going to slip next door, to my father's.' It was odd for the next cottage to no longer be her home.

Rob looked up from the sports pages of the paper. 'He wouldn't like that, would he?'

'I don't know, but I've got to collect the rest of my things.' Evie was edgy over this. Would she find Davey had packed up all her things ready to be cleared out of his house? Pointing to him shunning her forever. She prayed he really had meant it when he had told Lofty Praed he would attend tonight's party. 'I want to see how he's managed, and to get the house aired and ready for him, like Beth and the girls did for us. I don't want him to feel I don't love him any more.'

Rob made a wry face. 'I'll come with you, darling, carry your stuff round. I'm sorry for you Evie, that Davey's like he is.'

'No, you stay here in case we get more visitors. I'll tell you when I'm ready.'

Taking a suitcase and some bags to next door, Evie had her former back door key with her, but feeling under a particular large pebble she found the key her father always left there. It was a huge relief to know her father had not tried to lock her out. The key made a hefty clank when she turned it in the lock – she had never noticed that before. She went inside cautiously. It was nearly as dark as night for Davey had drawn the curtains at the back and front windows. Evie drew back the short curtains over the sink to let in some light.

All was neat and in its usual place, not even a washed dish was left on the draining board, but it seemed terribly empty and cold and sad. Evie hoped Davey might have left her a note, he would have been sure she'd come in if she arrived back before him, but it wasn't his way. What he had to say he always said to someone's face. She did not bring provisions, knowing Davey would prefer to get his own. Already she felt like a stranger to him, that her life here from birth meant nothing. The sadness she felt here was hers. The coldness, she hoped, was not to prove to be Davey's feelings towards her, but at least he must have been hurt by her elopement, which had shouted out to him that she did not trust him. What had he thought of the letter she had left for him, begging his understanding?

She lit the fire that Davey had left ready laid in, in the range. Hopefully, he would appreciate the warmth and her thoughtfulness. There was nothing else she could do downstairs so she climbed the stairs, taking the empty luggage, and went into her old room. She had taken most of her stuff next door and it was unbearably empty and almost hard to recognize, with its twin beds, as the room she had shared with her mother, then alone until her runaway wedding. She packed the rest of her clothes and the things her mother's nimble fingers had made, toys, cushions, scented coat hangers, framed cross-stitch pictures and furniture runners. Then there was nothing else to do but leave, which she did with one backward sorrowful look, knowing it was unlikely she would ever see inside it again.

Before going downstairs she stopped outside her father's closed bedroom door. She had only entered it once a week to clean and change his bedding. Now, putting down her things, she went inside to feel a little closer to him, the man who had willingly adopted her and provided all her needs, including affection. Evie knew pangs of guilt. Davey had never smacked her or even raised his voice at her. His only failing was that he had deviously tried to keep her to himself, away from Rob and Beth and her uncle. Selfish yes, but he was not a cruel man. She should have told him she was going off to marry Rob. He could have done nothing to stop her. Yet everyone in the cove, and she herself deep in her heart, knew that she had done the right thing. Davey did not have a valid reason to try to prevent her marrying Rob.

His room was just as it always was, functional and bare. Evie was heartened to see two photographs of her on the tallboy, one as an infant and one taken on the quayside three years ago. Her greatest fear was that he had disowned her; apparently not, but she was anxious about his reaction when he next saw her. Davey had always stressed she put his ironed clothes on the bed and he would put them away. Evie had thought he was kindly saving her a job but now she wondered about it. Had he been keeping secrets? It was quite likely for he was such a secretive man. That aside, she was curious to learn anything she could to give her a clue to his withdrawn and possessive attitude. Feeling bad about it she opened his single mahogany wardrobe. It creaked and she blinked in remorse for she was intruding. There was just Davey's few clothes and pairs of highly polished shoes; no boxes or containers to hold anything of a personal nature. To delve inside his four-drawer chest would disturb his clothes and be obvious, so she opened the small cupboard at his bedside. She hated what she was doing. If she saw nothing unusual she would leave the room. Once downstairs she would take the writing paper out of the dresser drawer and leave her father a friendly note, stating that while she did not regret her elopement, she was sorry to have slipped away secretly, and that she would come round to see him as soon as he got home and imploring him to let her talk to him.

In the cupboard she saw a large rectangular tin

box, one that had once held biscuits. She stared at it. *Don't touch it, shut the cupboard and leave,* a voice in her head warned. But Evie could not help herself and going down on her knees she pulled out the tin and put it on the planked floor. Her heart thudding, she levered off the lid. On the top were her birth certificate and then her parents' marriage certificate. She laid them carefully face down so she could put them and the rest of the stuff back in as it should lie.

Next was a faded photograph of two young smiling fishermen, in the familiar caps, smocks and over-the-knee sea boots with their arms resting on each other's shoulders. One was Davey. Evie turned the photo over finding as she had hoped an inscription – Cyrus and Me. Evie knew whom the man Cyrus had been, his name was on the war memorial, Able Seaman C. L. Mitchell. Evie leafed on, taking out documents, Davey's will and insurance papers, and things connected to his parents and a late brother, lost in childhood. Then came more photographs of him and Cyrus, all smiling, some larking about. There was a local newspaper cutting announcing Cyrus's death, among others, and the black-edged card from his memorial service. Evie felt sad for her father, he had lost a very close friend, one reason perhaps why he had closed himself off so much from others. Perhaps he felt guilty that he had stayed at home in a safer, but vital, occupation while his friend had fought and died on a torpedoed ship.

Then came a batch of letters, all written by the same angular hand, Armed services letters that had to have been sent from Cyrus; sad and poignant memories for Davey. Evie noticed a spelling mistake on an envelope. My had been written instead of Mr D. Vage. She smiled, but saw that more were titled that way; strange. Pulling in her lips she gingerly opened one of the envelopes and began to read the single page of paper. Then laying it aside carefully she opened two more. Sentences jumped out at her. I miss you so much my old dear ... remembering all the times we shared keeps me going ... I can't wait until I'm next on leave and we can go to our secret place ... think of your smile ... what a wonderful time we had that day ... All could be sentiments from a mate but equally, Evie thought, disguised messages from a lover. It had not been many years ago she had learned about same gender love, coming across it in a Bible passage. Such a thing was condemned in the scriptures and was against the law, and Evie had not wanted to think about it again. She might be wrong, but she was sure she was not, her father had been in love with another man and it was vital his secret was never discovered. She had the answer to his guarded way of life, why he had never slept with her mother, although it did not excuse him trying to deny Evie of the man she loved. He knew the pain and grief of losing his lover. Sad for him but horrified, trembling, she quickly put the letters back together and replaced everything as it had been in the tin and put the tin back in the cupboard.

'Evie darling, are you ready yet?' It was Rob and he was on his way up the stairs.

She ran out of the room and slammed the door.

'Oh sweetheart, I can see this has upset you.' Rob held her close but she soon pushed him away. 'Let's get out of here.'

Then with her husband she left her father's house without leaving him a note, but dropping her back door key on the table.

Thirty

'You are happy?' Beth asked Evie at the wedding party, when she was finally able to drag Evie outside for a quiet moment. It was so hot in the overcrowded cottage, packed with adults and children, and they were both glad of some fresh air. They hurried past the few others outside taking a breather or having a smoke. 'I mean, everything is all right between you and Rob? You seem blissfully happy but I can't help feeling something is wrong. I know you must be disappointed that your father hasn't showed his face here, that you and he haven't even spoken yet, but I sense there is something more.'

'You're right, it is about Dad.' Evie walked Beth down to the end of the back garden and whispered. 'I've found out something about him. I can't tell Rob about it, it would be too awful and the source of a lot more trouble. I can't tell you here. Rob is joining the *Young Maid* on

Monday and I'll call on you then. I heard that Kitty and Stuart have left, are you still at your mother's or have you gone home to Mor Penty?'

'I'll be at Owles House for a few more days. Evie, you will take care, won't you?'

'Why do you say that?'

'Well, Davey did set out to cause Rob harm. I'm worried he might try something similar again.'

'But Dad knows we're on to him now, and he would never do anything to hurt me,' Evie protested mildly.

'No, I don't suppose he would ever dream of it, but if he does go after Rob again you may find yourself involved, and hurting your husband would hurt you unbearably. Why don't you spend the night at Owles House? Mum would be glad to have you both.'

'But Beth—'

'Please don't argue, Evie, humour me. I've got a bad feeling about this. I couldn't bear any more pain after all that's happened recently. Talk to Davey tomorrow, you and Rob together and demand to know what's on his mind.'

'But I could never convince Rob not to stay in his own house tonight. He'd never let Dad hound us out. If I insisted on your idea Rob would demand to know the whole story and I just can't tell him that, not ever. I owe Dad that much loyalty, without him my mother and I could have ended up in the workhouse. You'll understand why when I tell you all the facts. Rob will certainly agree to us facing Dad first thing tomorrow.'

'Well, if you're sure,' Beth said, still unconvinced.

They began strolling back to the house, and Evie said, 'Now, tell me how you are? You must be missing Kitty.'

'Very much so, but we keep in regular touch over the phone. It's nice to be able to speak naturally to her, and to Stuart too. He's sold his house already. The nearest neighbours were eager to get it for their daughter, about to return with her family from years in Kenya. He'll live with Kitty for the foreseeable future, but he's also considering he might move to Ireland to be near the children. He's resigned from the college, thinking of doing something different entirely. So it's a complete fresh start for him. Sadly, I get the impression Kitty is still feeling rather lost. I've told her she's welcome to come back to Owles House at a moment's notice. There's someone else who is very keen to see Kitty again, Mr Benedict. He called three times for news of her when you were on honeymoon.'

'It will be interesting to watch if anything comes out of that when Kitty comes down again, possibly another wedding. Oh, and surely even another one, Mark's got Claire with him tonight. No one would have guessed those two would get together,' Evie said, a dreamy bride again. 'But what about you, Beth? Do you want to find romance and a lasting love?'

'I'm sure I'll get round to it eventually now all the old issues in my life have been resolved,' Beth replied thoughtfully. 'After all, who knows what's just round the corner. You and Rob, and

Mark and Claire didn't. I'd just like things to settle down for a long while.'

For long hours Davey had been sitting in the dark. He had allowed the fire that Evie had banked in to go out and the cottage had long lost its warmth. Ages ago he had heard Evie and her husband return quietly home, not even pausing outside Davey's gate. It was not like Evie to be so distant. As he had expected, she had come round at some point to air the home he now lived in alone and to collect the rest of her things. But she had left no other little touches of care. She had not laid out the things on the table for when he made a meal, or filled the kettle with fresh water or left the teapot standing by with tea leaves in it. She had not left him a note. That omission spoke of her hurt and the loss of affection for him. He had pushed her too far. But it was not like Evie to give up on Davey even after all he had done to prevent her marriage. Of course, she was now under the influence of that wretch, her new husband. Praed had worked on her gentle mind until she had willingly run away with him, and he would go on poisoning Evie's mind until she hated him. Praed would also soon seek revenge on Davey for messing with his property with evil intent. Praed had a vindictive side, as Davey acknowledged he had himself. They both used dirty tactics to get what they wanted. To ensure Evie stayed estranged from Davey, Praed would, even though he had sworn not to, reveal Davey's secret.

My secret, my love for Cyrus. The pain of

losing Cyrus, even from the day he had told him he had enlisted in the Navy, was as raw as the first moment. It was love as ardent and wonderful as any other, and Davey had sworn to always protect what he and Cyrus had had, and to protect his memory so people would always read his name on the war memorial with pride. It was why it had been so easy for Davey to set in motion and act out his plan to annihilate Francis Vyvyan. Vyvyan had gleaned the true nature of Davey and Cyrus's relationship, when as a parish councillor Vyvyan had looked through old local photographs the former vicar had taken on various parish outings and events.

The highly respected, almost saintly, Vyvyan had confronted Davey one day when he was tending his allotment. 'Seems you and a certain young fisherman-cum-sailor were very, very close.' Vyvyan, a powerfully built, exceedingly handsome brute, had displayed a fist full of the old photographs. 'Bet you've never seen these. The vicar let me look through them. I'm sure he didn't see that extra little connection you had with Cyrus Mitchell. I would never have guessed we had a pansy living in our midst. I wonder what the rest of the crew on *Morenwyn* would think, eh? They'd keep a careful watch on you, that's for sure. Men like you make me sick. Mitchell wouldn't be thought quite the war hero if people knew he'd liked holding hands with men.'

The hurt caused by Francis Vyvyan's jibes went past the unbearable, there was no way Davey was going to allow Cyrus's name to be reviled. His love for Cyrus had been, and still was, as deep as between conventional couples. He had waited his chance, and when Vyvyan had gone out alone in his boat Davey had followed on in his personal punt, knowing where Vyvyan would stop to do some line fishing. Davey had not listened to Vyvyan's fresh round of jibes. He had got close enough and cracked the intimidator across the head with a ship's block and pushed his body into the sea. Then he had rigged Firefly to drift and make it look like the death was a tragic accident.

Suddenly afraid, Davey leapt up in the darkness. Finding matches he lit a candle and hurried upstairs to his room. His heart racing like drum beats, he opened the bedside cupboard and studied the old biscuit tin, which held his treasure trove. He was always careful to put it back in the exact middle of the cupboard, having marked out two straight lines with a dart's tip as a guide. The tin was now slightly off centre. Evie! When she had come for her stuff she must have come in here to look through his things. She knew! She knew about him and Cyrus and now she loathed him. It was why she had left without a note and tossed down her key.

His first thought, once again, was to protect Cyrus's memory. He had promised Cyrus he would always love him first and the years had not changed that. He would not let anyone take precedence over Cyrus, not even the quiet, caring woman he had brought up as his own daughter, a daughter to be proud of. Davey would gladly deal out the same fate to Praed as he had to Francis Vyvyan. The problem was that even if Praed were dead it would be unlikely that Evie would move back in with Davey. She would own Rob's cottage and she would turn to her posh sister. Davey came to the conclusion, without emotion, that it was necessary for Praed and Evie to go together, and that way Cyrus's sanctity would stay safe.

In the candlelight, sitting with his back against the bed, Davey looked and looked at every photograph of Cyrus, remembering every place they had gone together and every word of love and laughter they had spoken. He read every one of Cyrus's loving letters, and was able to recall every word of his replies.

Years of tears flooded down over his face and dripped off his chin and wetted the photos and letters. It was some time before the shaking of his body stopped and he wiped his eyes on the bedspread.

Then while sobbing intermittently he replaced all the other documents and mementoes in the tin and pushed the tin into the cupboard and closed the little door. Weak from crying and the throes again of his first grief, he gripped the bedspread to get him to his feet. 'Time to say goodbye to all this, Cyrus,' he got out in a hoarse whisper.

Downstairs, he raked out the ashes in the little range and kindled a fresh fire. Numbed all through yet nearly broken with sorrow he burned the keepsakes of Cyrus one by one, making sure all was consumed in the flames. 'You're safe now, my darling. Those old photos the old vicar took are either packed up in his nursing home or been thrown away. Now it's time for me to leave and to come to you. I've had enough. My own crew mates can't stand me for trying to stop the girl's wedding. That was silly of me. I should have seen long before that it's better to put an end to the bitter loneliness of this existence without you. She can keep her man and her new life. She's welcome to inherit this cottage and my little bit of money. She'll get all the things that belonged to her mother. She'll be happy with me out of the way. God bless her for that. Don't know how I could have thought I'd ever have hurt her, not Evie. I'll drop her a line of goodwill and push it in under her back door. Then I'll go for a walk; be getting light soon. Remember our special place on the cliff, way past the hotels. I'll meet you there in the sea.'

Davey hugged himself with ecstasy. 'Why didn't I think of this before? As soon as Evie reached twenty-one she would have been capable of looking after herself. I don't care, Cyrus, what people think, whether I fell or whether I jumped. No one would have cared about us if they had known about our love.'

He dashed off the note. *Dear Evie, Just to say I wish you all the best for your future. Be happy and follow your dreams. God bless you. Your loving Father, Davey Vage.*

'Well Cyrus, that should prevent her from blaming herself for anything. She wouldn't deserve that.'

He put on his cap and coat and left his home, shutting the back door silently and not locking it. It would show Evie how welcome she was to the place. He crept next door and put his hand on the gate but then was halted by a tall figure looming at him.

'Oh, no you don't. What wickedness are you up to this time Davey Vage?' Douglas Praed spat, low and furiously at him. 'I knew you'd do something, and I've been spying on you all night.

Before Davey could catch his breath he was bundled round, his arms pinned with Douglas's hand across his mouth. Davey did not struggle but allowed his weight to go limp as Douglas dragged him round the end of the terrace where they could not be seen. Douglas dropped his hand then pushed Davey hard against the wall. 'Speak up before I wake Rob and then you'll have to deal with both of us.'

'I was only going to leave a note for Evie. Read it, you'll see I wish her no harm.'

Striking a match, Douglas scanned the message of the note. 'Seems harmless but I don't trust you. Why do this in the early hours? What were you going to do next?'

'I couldn't sleep. It's not easy when everyone's against you. You know how that feels. I decided to let Evie know I care then I was going for a walk.'

'Put this under Rob's door,' Douglas growled. 'Then I'll walk with you, make sure you aren't up to any mischief.'

Fragments of light stealing in on the horizon turned the men from shapeless black lumps to threatening grey forms. 'I intend to walk a long way,' Davey rasped. 'I don't intend to come back, ever. I'm sure you'll be very glad about that. Go home Douglas Praed. People will be stirring soon. Make sure you're seen, if you don't want to be implicated in something you wouldn't want to be.'

'You mean...?'

'You know what it's like to want to die because you're an outcast, don't you? I bet you even tried to work up the courage to end it all while languishing in that cave. You and everyone else will think it's my own fault I'm despised. I accept that. But there's nothing left for me now. Let me walk away from you. You and your wretched cousin will never see me again.'

Douglas stood back, mouth hanging down in horror. 'You're crazy.'

'Maybe, but that's my business. Leave me and let me get on with it. I don't expect you'll lose any sleep over it.'

'Certainly bloody won't. The cove will be a safer place without you in it. I won't say good-bye, you're not worth it. You're the nastiest piece of work I've ever had the misfortune to know. I hope Evie doesn't cry over you for long.'

'Me too.'

Davey waited five minutes after Douglas had gone then he slipped through the alleys until he was up on the cliff path. Then striding along, his mind entirely on Cyrus, he took his last long walk.

Thirty-One

For some time Beth had been looking out of the terrace windows, and over the lawn to the cliff and the sea. The waters were grey-green and choppy but not in a restless way. It was Christmas Eve and the day was dry and sunny, a disappointment for those wishing for a white Christmas. Beth was disappointed for a different reason. It was going to be a very quiet festive season without Kitty, who had left her presents behind when she had journeyed home with Stuart. People had said they would call in tomorrow, but the Christmas dinner and tea table would see only her mother, Joe and herself.

The invitation to Kitty to spend Christmas at Owles House had been eagerly repeated, and to include Stuart, who Beth found she enjoyed talking to regularly over the telephone, but last week Kitty had travelled with Stuart to Ireland to spend a few days with Louis and Martha, staying at a hotel close to Connie's parents' property. Kitty had said she did not know when they would be back and that they might stay over in London, taking in a Christmas show. Beth could not help feeling a little rejected, but accepted it was too early yet for things to return to how they had once been.

Mrs Reseigh had been here today. After helping Beth and Christina to prepare for tomorrow's fare she had sipped sherry and eaten mince pies with them, and then Beth had driven her down to the cove so she could get on with her own arrangements. Mrs Reseigh, Mark and Rowella were to spend Christmas Day at the Opies. Beth did not envy them that, although Mrs Reseigh and Mark were not at all fazed by Marjorie Opie's pompous ways, they refused to allow her to make them feel inferior. On New Year's Day a small engagement party was to be held at the Grand Sea View Hotel. Marjorie, while annoyingly creating her usual fuss, was proud that her daughter was getting married, and Mrs Reseigh had no concerns that she would make Mark a nightmarish mother-in-law.

Ken would drop in tomorrow but he would be too busy at the pub to stay long. Jacob Benedict would be seen late tonight when Beth, Christina and Joe arrived for Midnight Mass, a tradition nearly the whole cove looked forward to since Mr Benedict's arrival, when people of different denominations and none attended, and chatted excitedly afterwards when they walked home in torch and lantern light very early on Christmas morning. Mr Benedict would ply Beth and Christina with questions about Kitty. He wrote to her often and it was glaringly apparent he waited eagerly for her replies, but he was always avid for more snippets of news about her. His frustration at her not coming to Portcowl for Christmas was as clear as mountain spring water.

Then, of course there was Evie. She and Rob were expected here just after breakfast tomorrow to exchange presents, after they had placed a wreath on Davey's grave. The coroner had recorded his verdict as accidental death, but almost everyone, including a distraught Evie, believed he had deliberately jumped off the cliff. His body had been snagged on rocks and not washed out to sea, and a holidaying walker had made the dreadful discovery. Most thought he had committed suicide out of bitterness at losing Evie to Rob, and although none had said so to Evie's face, that she was well rid of him. Now she could get on with her life with Rob, whose love and devotion to her included allowing her to have as much freedom as she liked. They would have a successful marriage, and in time, no doubt, raise a happy family. Beth envied Evie that. Beth had made a total hash of her love life and had not even known true romance. Evie and Rob would spend the rest of Christmas Day at Wildflower Cottage for the usual delightful squash of Praeds celebrating.

Beth could not rid herself of an invasion of loneliness but she faced the fact full on that it was all her own fault. Shaking her shoulders she affected a, hopefully, cheerful smile for Christina's sake. Humming a carol she made for the drawing room to suggest to her mother and Joe, and Richard and Lily who were there, a game of charades.

Chaplin started barking and Christina and Joe were shouting to Beth. Her breath fixed in her lungs and she felt sick. No! Not a disaster at

Christmas. All sorts of terrible things ran through her mind from a log falling out of the grate and setting the rug alight to someone taking a bad fall. Then Beth realized the commotion was excited and elated. She flew to the drawing room but everyone was out in the hall and Joe was opening the door. 'What's happening?' She heard a car horn tooting.

'It's Kitty and Stuart!' Christina pointed enthusiastically down the drive. 'Go on, go out to them. Now your Christmas will be made, darling.'

Beth flew after Joe and Chaplin down the steps. The others followed and all waved madly to the newcomers, who were hanging out of the windows waving back. Stuart was driving his own motor car and Beth was thrilled to see it was packed to capacity with luggage. He pulled up and reached back to open the door to let Grace out. The dogs raced off in a flurry of greeting and play fighting.

Running to Kitty, Beth found herself caught in a tight affectionate embrace. 'Hope you don't mind the surprise,' Kitty squealed, in the old girlish way that was hers. 'I know we're very naughty but as soon as we stepped off the ferry, and we had a lovely time with the children, we knew right away the only place where we could possibly spend Christmas was here. Furthermore, we're staying for good, somewhere in the area.'

'Oh Kitty, I can't tell you how pleased we all are to have you here. It just wouldn't have been the same.' Beth squeezed and kissed her.

315

'Hello, Christina,' Kitty said, 'I promise we won't be any bother. If we can stay we'll see to our rooms.'

'Of course you will stay!' Christina laughed. 'Mrs Reseigh and I have made sure rooms are ready for you both just in case.'

A short time later Beth was helping Kitty and Stuart put their presents under the Christmas tree. 'Mr Benedict will be over the moon when he sees you at Midnight Mass.' Beth winked at Kitty.

'I know. Actually we'll be seeing a lot of each from now on.' Kitty winked back.

'Kitty! That's wonderful.'

Later again, Beth was touched on the arm by Stuart. 'Do you think we could have a moment alone?'

'Of course,' she replied at once. 'Let's slip away to the terrace windows. Now it's dark you'll see the marvellous spectacle of the cove's festive lights.'

After Stuart had admired the multicoloured twinkling lights, Beth sensed his mood turn serious and, as in the old days, he became become a little shy and bumbling, something she had found captivating. She said, 'What is it?'

He gazed earnestly into her eyes. 'I just wanted to ask you if you mind me turning up with Kitty. It's an imposition.'

'No it isn't.' She smiled at him.

'Thank goodness–' he pressed a hand to his chest – 'Kitty so wanted to be here and I couldn't bear the thought of spending Christmas alone.'

'I wouldn't have wanted you to, Stuart. You

are as welcome here as Kitty is.'

'And you don't mind the prospect of me living around here? Not long ago you would have been horrified. I'm really sorry I brought a lot of complications into your life.'

'Those days are past. And I'm glad it all happened and is done with. I'm sorry that Louis and Martha are so far away.'

'It's not as bad as it seems. Connie is keen for the children to see as much of me as possible and they will be spending a lot of the school holidays with me. Louis and Martha are happy I'll be settling in Cornwall. They're both looking forward to seeing Portcowl and other local places in the summer. They're happier with Connie. I was struggling quite a bit. So it's all turned out for the best really.'

'Let's go and prepare the mulled wine before we get ready for Midnight Mass and then we'll take a drink to that. Happy Christmas, Stuart.'

'Happy Christmas, Beth.'

'And let's drink to a happy future.'

'Great.' Stuart offered Beth his arm and she laughed as she slipped hers through his. 'To the kitchen it is then.'